DISOWNED ROYAL

CLUB ROYAL, BOOK FOUR

ELOUISE EAST

CONTENTS

To Tina,
For providing the most perfect covers for this series.

SUTCLIFFE ROYAL FAMILY

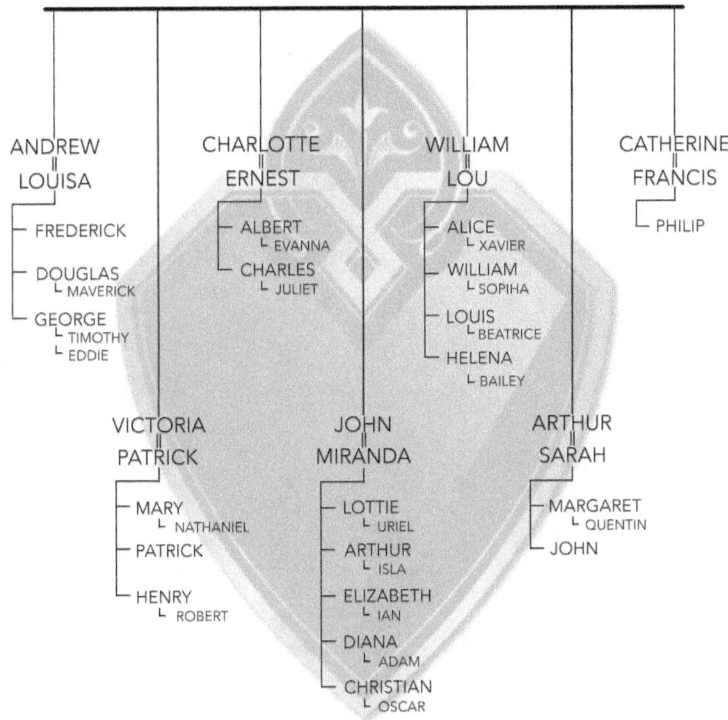

LIST OF CHARACTERS

(ALPHABETICAL ORDER)

Andrew, King of England, Christian's uncle

Brian, Oscar's ex-Daddy

Brett, Christian's bodyguard

Charles, cousin, Charlotte and Ernest's child

Charlotte, Christian's aunt

Christian, ex-Army

Clarice, Club Royal's receptionist

Damon, Frederick's best friend

Daniel, second in command, Army, Christian's friend

Douglas, Christian's cousin, Mav's boyfriend

Eddie, barista, George and Timothy's boyfriend

Felix, Oscar's bodyguard

Frederick, Christian's cousin, heir to the throne

Gemma, Oscar's cousin

George, Christian's cousin, Timothy and Eddie's boyfriend

Gia, Army IT expert, Christian's friend

Henry, Christian's cousin, Robert's boyfriend

Hilary, assistant manager of Book Drunk,
Oscar's friend
Jim, Oscar's father
John, Christian's father
Louisa, Queen Consort, Christian's late aunt
Maverick, social media manager, Douglas's
boyfriend
Miranda, Christian's mother
Oliver, Club Royal bartender
Oscar, owner of Book Drunk
Patrick, Christian's cousin
Portia, Queen Louisa's ex-assistant
Randall, King Andrew's assistant
Robert, florist, Henry's boyfriend
Rodriguez, staff member at Christian's parent's
house
Sally, Oscar's mother
Stephen, Oscar's cousin
Timothy, teacher/therapist, George and Eddie's
boyfriend
Tina, Oscar's cousin
Wally, nanny, Oscar's best friend
William, Christian's uncle

DISOWNED ROYAL

CHRISTIAN

Christian Sutcliffe stared at his father's desk, barely concealing his anger at the man's words. He stood at ease, but his hands fisted behind his back.

"Those sick, perverted people should be thrown from the royal line and be done with it. They provide nothing to the gene pool except diluting it from the purity it should be. There were no such people in previous generations. Everyone now is just wanting to pretend to be one because it's all the 'rage.'"

Prince John paced from window to door in his large office while Christian stood listening to the twisted thoughts of what he could only describe as an evil entity. There was no way the man before him was human, but then to be in cahoots with the people he was, it was no surprise.

"As much as I hate you spending time with them, your information has been vital in finding out what their plans are. It has enabled us to stop them from carrying out certain tasks, which has been beneficial to our cause. This will be over soon. I promise you. And when it is, you'll be much closer to the top of the royal line." John smiled at him, but Christian remained silent as they had taught him.

"Does your commanding officer require your presence today?"

Christian nodded and cleared his throat. "Yes, sir. I will be there for the next four days, maybe five, depending on how long it takes."

John sighed. "Okay. I'll let your mother know when she gets home." He nodded and sat behind his desk. "Keep in touch."

"Yes, sir."

He waited, knowing he couldn't leave until his father had dismissed him. Sometimes, he stood there for half an hour or more because his father loved having control over him. Today, he was lucky.

"Dismissed."

Christian saluted, turned and marched from the room, closing the door quietly behind him. The moment he did, his shoulders lowered, and he stopped to rest his head against the wall. One of these days, he would be free. One of these days, he would see them rot in hell.

Pushing away from the wall, he jogged up the stairs to his room and gathered his belongings. He was already in his Army fatigues—another thing his father insisted upon—and he packed a bag with civilian clothes, toiletries and some books, then left the house with no fanfare. As he was thirteenth in line to the throne, there was no need for him to have a bodyguard, and besides, the Army had heavily trained him. The family provided him with a bodyguard for certain functions and events, but for the most part, he could go about his day without someone looking over his shoulder.

He climbed into his car. It was his pride and joy. A

Bentley Mulliner Continental GT Number 9 Limited Edition. It had cost him an arm and a leg because he had paid for it himself rather than asking his parents for the money—he didn't want to be beholden to them any more than he needed to be. He had other money he could've used, but he refused to use that blood money. Ever.

Despite having a car that could break every speed limit if he wanted to, he always kept to the limit, not wanting to bring undue attention to himself. When he was amongst the public, he received the occasional double glance, but few people approached him. Not like they did his cousins.

As he pulled up outside the house his cousin George now lived in, his shoulders relaxed some more. Once the security guards let him through the gate, he parked up and switched off the engine. He leaned his head against the headrest and closed his eyes. He'd lied to his father, as he had done many times before. He wasn't due to be at the barracks until the following day, but he knew his commanding officer would cover for him should his father call or visit. It wasn't unheard of. But he needed to recuperate with his cousins. Having the occasional evening with them was not enough, but he had work to do. Once it was over, he'd have more time and could spend it with them.

A knock on his window made him flinch inwardly, but he showed no outward response. He lifted his head and smiled at George.

"You coming in or what?"

Christian smiled at his choice of words. George was trying to get rid of his posh-sounding voice, but it was hard for him to keep up for any length of time. Except when it came to his narrating. Not that Christian was supposed to know about that. George didn't know he knew, and he wasn't about to enlighten him or anyone else.

"No. I'm staying here for the foreseeable future," he deadpanned as he climbed out of the car.

"Your loss, then."

George wrapped his arms around Christian's shoulders and squeezed, making Christian feel instantly at home. Why couldn't George be his brother instead of the family he had? In fact, why couldn't anyone except the family he'd received? He brushed the thoughts aside, knowing they would only send his mood plummeting.

"Are you ready for some fun?" George grinned.

"As long as I can walk tomorrow, I'm up for anything." Christian groaned. "That was a terrible choice of words," he grumbled when George pumped his hands in the air and ran into the house.

George had recently moved in with his boyfriends: Timothy, the one who owned the house, and Eddie, who owned his own house, but no longer stayed there. They had vastly improved the security at Timothy's house, and it gave them some peace from living at Windsor, which George had done before they'd started a relationship. There was nothing wrong with Windsor; it was just…big and busy.

He followed George into the house, closing the door behind him, and strode for the living room, where he could hear some of his cousins talking.

"—is nothing wrong with lattes," Douglas said.

"I never said there was, but when you go to the cafe five times in two hours…" Mav raised his eyebrows at him.

Douglas spread his hands. "I'm giving him business!"

"It sounds more like you're stalking him." Damon snorted.

"Look. I had never heard of this place before. It's been open for FIVE years, Mav. How can a place like that have been open that long and I didn't know about it?"

"Fair enough, but stop stalking him. One visit a day is enough," Freddie said.

"I'm not!"

Christian sank into an armchair. "Who are we talking about?"

Douglas sprang forward in his seat. "You'll know. You love books. That place on Thames Street. Is it Drinking Books or something?"

Mav sighed. "How do you not know its name after visiting so many times?"

"It's called Book Drunk," Eddie said. "I saw adverts for barista positions when it opened."

Christian shook his head. "I've never heard of it. It's on Thames Street, you say?" He pulled out his phone and searched for it, bringing up photos of the place and reviews. It had a high rating, and the pictures made it look like a place Christian could lose himself in for hours.

"Oscar has recently—well, two years ago—started offering a library-style service, too," Eddie continued.

"Library-style?" Christian asked, his gaze on the photos of the place.

"Yeah. It serves drinks and sells books, but you can now sit in with a drink and borrow a book to read while you're there. You can't take them home. It's not an actual library, but it's nice that you don't have to buy a book to read it. You just have to buy something from the cafe, then you can sit there and read."

It sounded like heaven to Christian. "How did I not know about this?"

"You have been busy lately," Freddie said. "I wasn't sure we'd see you tonight."

Christian put his phone away. "Sorry. Father has me running errands when I'm not at the barracks."

Freddie nodded towards him. "Do you want to get more comfortable?"

Christian glanced down at himself and snorted. "Yes." He stood. "I'll be back."

He strode towards the bathroom, grabbing the bag he'd dropped by the front door as he passed it. By the time he returned in joggers and a T-shirt, the conversation had moved on to birthdays.

"We're setting something up for Kean towards the end of the month, and then it's Robert's next month, too," Henry said, smiling at his boyfriend.

Robert rolled his eyes. "You don't have to do anything for my birthday."

Henry frowned. "We've been over this many times. We *must* celebrate your birthday. It's the first one we've spent together."

Robert sighed. "Fine, but nothing extravagant."

"Extravagant? Us?" George said, waving his hands and miming a waltz behind the sofas. "I don't know what you mean."

Laughter sounded, and Christian smiled as he reclaimed his seat. "Don't forget, in August, there are three of you," he said, nodding towards Freddie, Patrick and George.

George stopped. "Ooh, are we going big?"

Freddie groaned. "No, we're not. We don't need a big party, George."

"But you're going to be forty, Freddie! And most of our

partners haven't seen a big splash for us yet! We can't let that pass us by."

"Hey, Damon!" Freddie called, interrupting Damon's conversation with Timothy.

"What?"

"What's it like being forty?"

"Fuck you." Damon held up his middle finger and turned back to Timothy.

Freddie grinned. "It's obviously the same as being thirty-nine. He's not changed. He's just older than me!" Freddie raised his voice for the last part, making Damon put his finger up again.

Christian grinned and scuffed his nails against his shirt. "Well, I don't know what it feels like to be thirty, so..." He laughed when several cushions came hurtling towards him.

"Shut up!" several voices said.

Christian held up his hands. "Hold up. Why am I the only one getting beaten? Eddie's not thirty yet either."

George wrapped his arms around Eddie. "Because he didn't tease us about it."

"God, you guys make me feel young," Christian complained.

He didn't mind one bit. He was glad they had even given him the time of day, considering who his parents were. But then he only needed to see how they were treating Albert, their cousin from Aunt Charlotte, who had defected from her family and been brought into their fold, to know they wouldn't let him suffer unless he was on the wrong side. Aunt Charlotte and her husband, Ernest, along with their son Charles and Christian's parents, John and Miranda, were all on the family's shit list after everything that had happened.

Aunt Charlotte had a deep hatred of the LGBTQ+

community and wanted them eradicated from the face of the earth. She had been working on removing people who had come out as gay, bisexual, and of any other orientation that didn't fit into the mould she expected. It made Christian sick to think of how much those people suffered.

How did Christian know this? Because he was his father's spy.

Or so his father thought.

Truth was, Christian *was* a spy, but he wasn't spying for his father. At least, not properly. John had pulled him into the "business" when Christian had hinted he knew something about what they were doing. It had been after he'd found out they were behind the blackmailing and threatening of Henry. It had sickened him when John had sat him down and explained what they were doing, then the man had made it worse by telling Christian he had to spy on his cousins and find out their plans as often as possible because they needed ideas of how to get rid of them.

Christian considered himself lucky because if he hadn't been as close to his cousins as he was, they could've easily swayed him into believing his father's opinions, and that would've ended badly for them all. But Christian had a plan, and he also had backup.

"There's a few of us close to or surpassing forty now." Mav grinned. "You're only a couple of years away, sweetheart."

Douglas narrowed his eyes. "You'll pay for that later."

Mav's cheeks heated, and he sniffed. Christian withheld his smile.

"So, Chris. George mentioned you're up for anything tonight?" Patrick's mouth curled up at the corners, and Christian didn't like the twinkle in his eye.

"Within reason. I have to go back to the barracks tomorrow." He knew he was going to have a headache tomorrow when Patrick held up the tequila. "At least tell me you have salt and lime, too?"

George whooped. "Yes! I made sure after you complained last time."

"Good for me," Christian said, the sarcasm lost at the sudden onset of conversation as they discussed drinks and how to make them. He caught Freddie's eye.

"Are you okay?" Freddie mouthed.

Christian nodded once. Freddie's mouth twisted, and he knew the man didn't believe him. He hated lying to them all, but he couldn't tell them the truth yet. There was too much at stake. Their lives being a collective one.

When Christian went into the Army at eighteen, it was initially as an escape from the suffocating atmosphere at home. He'd been eager to show what he was capable of, and they had promoted him several times in the almost eight years he'd been enlisted. Just before his twenty-sixth birthday, he left the Army.

After the devastating news that his parents were beyond evil, he'd decided to officially re-enlist, but with an unofficial difference. Since then, he'd been working tirelessly to balance "spying" on his cousins, spying on his parents and family, and looking for anything and everything he could to prove what they were doing. It wasn't as easy as he had hoped it would be when he'd first come up with the plan.

"Okay, everyone. Let's take the first shot together." George grinned.

George went around the room, passing out shot glasses, Eddie followed with the bottle of tequila, and Robert finished the line, holding a tray with a shaker of salt and a bowl full of lime slices. Christian held out his shot glass for Eddie to fill, then licked his hand, and Robert sprinkled the salt on it. He grabbed a lime slice and sighed.

"This is not going to end well," he murmured.

When everyone was ready, they licked the salt, downed the tequila and sucked the lime. Christian glanced around the room as he sucked the tart flavour of the fruit and saw a myriad of expressions from his friends. The alcohol burned going down, but it was a welcome feeling when he barely felt anything anymore. As bad of an idea as this was, it was much needed.

Two hours later, he wasn't so sure of his assessment. He had a pleasant buzz going—mainly because he'd shifted to alternating alcohol with water—but most of his companions were worse for wear. Bad singing, loud laughter and idiotic behaviour just about summed up the night, and he loved every minute.

He clapped his hands on his thighs. "Right, I'm going to bed." He stood, holding onto the side of the chair to keep his balance. "Night, everyone."

Freddie stood, one of the few who hadn't been drinking, and followed him into the hallway. His hand found Christian's shoulder and squeezed until they reached the base of the staircase.

"How are you?"

Christian rubbed a hand over his face and pasted a smile on his face. "Drunk." Freddie raised his eyebrows and stared at him. Christian sighed. "I'm okay. Work is keeping me busy and away from the house a lot."

"I still can't believe you re-enlisted. We could've found something else for you to do to get away from them without you having to go back into the Army, Chris."

"It's not so bad, especially now I'm climbing the ranks. I'm still young, but I'm getting there quicker than some."

Freddie smiled. "I knew you'd do well, whatever you chose to do." He placed his curled finger under Christian's chin and lifted it. "Chin up, cuz. You need it more than anyone."

Christian returned the affectionate act they'd created for their group and climbed the stairs to the bedroom he often used when he wasn't at home or at work. When the door closed behind him, he rested back against it and sighed again. He wished he could tell them the truth about his role, but it was too early. There were too many chances of it being leaked if he told anyone, then his parents could find out, and it would ruin everything.

After a quick shower, he climbed between the covers and folded the pillow in half before stuffing it under his head. He stared at the red numbers of the clock and wished his life was different. It was a wish that couldn't come true because he was a member of the royal family, and because of that, he was under a lot of scrutiny. Not as much as Freddie, Douglas or George, but the media documented his actions for all to see should anything untoward happen. As much as he wished he could end this all right now by using the skills he had, he knew it would cause more harm than good.

He needed to bide his time, as his commanding officer had told him. When the time was right, his parents and their collaborators were going down. And if Christian had his way, it would be amidst a shower of fireworks for all to see.

2

OSCAR

Oscar Hall stood in the centre of his coffee book shop and surveyed his surroundings. He still found it unbelievable to think it belonged to him. Well, the bank as well, but mostly him. He'd been lucky when he'd found the place because it was perfect for tourists and locals alike. Opposite Windsor Castle and near the railway station, he couldn't have found a better location. The first year had been worrisome, but he'd pulled through, and the second year had made it worth it. After five years of hard work, Book Drunk was doing well, and he couldn't be happier.

He inhaled deeply, then let it out slowly before wandering to the door to unlock it and twist the sign to open. He was the only person working for the first half an hour because he liked the quiet, and it was never very busy when it first opened. Come eight-thirty, it would get busier, but then Hilary would be in to help, and Jonas would be in the kitchen, and when ten o'clock came, Sam would be in to help with the rest of the day. He didn't have lots of employees, but he had enough to make it work. It was something he had to start contemplating, though, because business was increasing every month.

He drifted back behind the counter and tied his apron around his waist. Sitting on a stool, he pulled the paperwork he'd left towards him. It needed doing, and he usually could get some done before the place got too busy. Before he'd even picked up his pen, the bell above the front door tinkled, and he glanced up with a smile, which froze on his face when he saw who it was.

Prince Christian.

There weren't many people who made Oscar star-struck, but there was always something untouchable about some members of the royal family. Princes Douglas and George appeared the most laid back of what he'd seen, but Prince Frederick would be damn near impossible to talk to because he was so poised, whereas Oscar was not. But as for the man who'd just walked through his door…he had always been someone who'd seemed so out of reach, so…The prince caught his eye and gave a small smile…so pained.

Oscar tore his gaze away and frowned at his paperwork, wondering where that thought had come from. He cleared his throat, inhaled and said, "Good morning. Welcome to Book Drunk. Can I help you with anything, Your Highness?"

Prince Christian winced and stepped further into the store, and Oscar noticed his Army fatigues. "Good morning. Please don't worry about the titles. Christian, please. I've just heard about your store, and I can't believe I didn't know about it sooner, especially with how close it is."

Oscar smiled. "Are you a fan of coffee or reading?"

Christian smiled, his face lighting up. "Both."

Oscar chuckled. "I've hit the jackpot with you, then." He winced. "Sorry, that didn't come out right."

Christian laughed, a low chuckle that vibrated through the air. "I know what you mean."

"Would you like something to drink?"

"Black coffee would be amazing, please."

"Coming right up."

Oscar whirled to the coffee machine and closed his eyes for a brief second before focusing on making the drink. He was aware of the prince wandering around the place, even without the mirror above the counter, where Oscar could see everything happening with his back turned. It was amazing how much he caught when people didn't think he could see them. The mirror also hid security cameras, which recorded everything.

He placed the mug of coffee on a small tray and added a plate with a couple of homemade shortbread biscuits and packets of sugar in case Christian needed them. As he carried it from behind the counter, he tried to focus on his steps and not spilling the drink instead of the man who'd settled into a chair away from the window. He held a couple of books while reading the back of one.

"Here you go. Can I get you anything else?" He placed the coffee, plate and sachets on the table and tucked the tray under his arm.

Christian smiled at him. "I'm good, thanks." He held up the books. "Am I okay to look through these as I drink?"

"Of course." He used his arm to show Prince Christian the shelves. "These are the books people can read while they're sitting, and if you like any of them, the books are available to buy as well."

"Perfect, thanks."

"Enjoy, Prince...Christian." He lowered his eyes and pivoted away, returning behind the counter just as another customer entered. "Good morning, Bridget! How are you today?"

"I'm good. How's business, Oscar?"

Bridget was a regular who came in every morning before she opened her tourist shop down the road. He'd lost count of how many times she came in for a drink every day. She probably single-handedly paid for his lease on this place.

"Business is great, thanks. How about you? Have you recovered from the Bank Holiday weekend?" He chuckled, remembering her complaints about how busy it was, but he knew she was just having fun.

She waved her hand. "It takes longer than a few days to get over it, young man. I'm not as young as I once was. I need my beauty sleep."

Oscar held out the takeaway cup. "You're looking perfect to me, Bridget. Whatever you're doing seems to be working." He smiled.

"Charmer." She turned to leave before noticing the man in the corner. She raised her eyebrows and glanced back at Oscar, who shrugged. "Going up in the world." She winked and waved over her head as she left.

Oscar chuckled and focused on his paperwork. He'd managed a bit more before the bell tinkled again. When he saw Hilary, he grinned.

"Oh, my god. You actually made it!" he said, mouth gaping in mock surprise.

"Shut up. Late nights do not mean I can't get up in the morning, boy."

She slunk through the door to the back of the store, and Oscar glanced over to Prince...Christian; that would take some getting used to. The man appeared engrossed in a book, though Oscar couldn't see which one while holding his mug of coffee on his knee. He watched him lift it to his mouth, sip and lower it again before using his pinky finger to turn the page of the book.

The back door opened again, and Christian lifted his eyes, meeting Oscar's gaze with piercing electric blue eyes. The shock of awareness slid through him, and he dropped his head, fumbling with his pen.

"So, Oz, what's new?" She leaned an arm next to him, resting her head on her fist until she noticed the customer. Her eyes widened, and her face flushed. "Is that...?" she whispered.

"Uh-huh. Shove those sparkling eyes back into your head, missy." Oscar stood, blocking her view.

"But—"

Oscar shook his head. "You know better."

Hilary sighed and pursed her lips. "Fine. It's just that we don't see him often. I know nothing about him."

Oscar raised his eyebrows. "You don't need to know anything about him. It's not your right to know his life without his consent, no matter what the media says. Leave him in peace. I've told you this before."

Hilary's eyes widened at something over his shoulder, and Oscar glanced around, his cheeks heating when he saw Christian standing there with a look in his eyes that Oscar couldn't translate.

"Thank you for that. Few people think the same way you do." He pulled out his wallet. "How much do I owe?"

Oscar waved him away. "First visit is free."

Christian shook his head. "I insist."

Oscar sighed. "Three ninety-five."

Christian handed over a five-pound note. "Keep the change. I think I've found my new favourite bookstore." He winked and left, the bell tinkling long after he went out of view of the windows.

Oscar stood, looking down at the note and memorising the rounded jawline with a slight layer of scruff surrounding a full bottom lip that Oscar could see himself biting on. The thought jerked him out of his daze, and he put the money into the till. He returned to his stool and tried to focus on his paperwork, but the silence emanating from his employee and friend was too distracting.

"For god's sake, what?" He faced her.

She held up her hand, intently focused on cleaning the counter, though he could see a curve to her mouth.

"What?" he asked again.

"It's nice to see you taking an interest." She shrugged.

"I'm not interested in him."

"Okay."

The ease at which she agreed to his words wasn't a good omen. She was like a reader with a gift card for their favourite book shop—she wouldn't leave it alone. He ignored her as more customers entered and the rush began. When Sam arrived promptly, Oscar was ready for his first break of the day, more to get away from Hilary's knowing looks than anything else. He grabbed a black coffee, a bagel and his paperwork and trudged back to his office. He didn't spend a lot of time in his office because he had to work alongside his employees as much as they did, but occasionally, he needed to get some work done on his computer that he couldn't do out front. He had an hour, then he'd be back out there helping for the lunch rush.

Settling into his comfortable chair, he leaned back and closed his eyes for a few seconds. Christian had never been far from his thoughts, but it was because the man was a mystery, not for the reasons Hilary seemed to hint at. As she'd said, Christian wasn't someone who spent a lot of time in the media, and there wasn't a huge amount known about him. If Christian returned, Oscar would like to get to know him from *him*, not by searching for him on the internet.

He shook his head and leaned forward, opening his laptop and logging on. While he waited, he checked his phone, expecting to see a message from his best friend, but there was nothing.

OSCAR: Morning. It's Friday, remember. You need to be here by one-thirty. Let me know if you're not going to make it.

Wally was his childhood best friend and neighbour. They had lived next to each other for years, and while Oscar had moved out into an apartment last year, Wally was still living with his mother, or rather, staying there on his days off. He was a live-in nanny who looked after two young children while their dad worked long hours. It wasn't a job he'd planned on having when they were at school, but he'd fallen into it as a favour to a friend, then realised he really enjoyed it, and a career was born. He'd been with this family for two years already.

To get him and the kids out of the house for a bit, Oscar had started a kids' story time in the cafe twice a week, and Wally was the one who read the stories because he had the perfect tone for it, complete with voices.

Oscar smiled and focused on his accounts, pushing every-thing else aside while he concentrated on making sure his figures were correct. This was one part of paperwork he didn't mind. Anything else could take a running jump, but numbers were something he enjoyed, however nuts that made him sound.

When his alarm sounded, he closed everything down and locked his office before heading back to the front. Every time he stepped back into the front of the store, his heart swelled with pride. He'd done what he'd always dreamed of, and he loved it.

"Hilary, I'm heading out!" he said a few hours later. He grabbed his coat, wallet, keys and phone and aimed for the entrance. "Don't burn the place down before I get back!"

"What if I want a bonfire?" she called back.

"Wait for bonfire night!"

He grinned as he closed the door and took off down the street at a jog. He had never been late to pick up his cousins, even if he'd come close a few times. By the time he reached the primary school, he was out of breath but on time. He shoved his hands in his pockets and waited with the other adults collecting their children. He rarely spoke to any of them, and more than once, he was sure he'd been the subject of behind-hand conversations, but he didn't care.

"Oscar!"

His name drew his attention, and he held out his arms as Tina came running towards him. He scooped her up into a hug, then set her back on her feet.

"Hey, princess. How was your day?" he asked as they wandered through the crowds to Gemma's classroom.

"It was fantastic! Mrs Stuart brought in her pet rabbit for us to see. It's called Honey. Its fur is so white, Oscar! It was so beautiful."

"I bet it was." He waved at Gemma when she came within

sight, and she shouldered her backpack and stalked across to him. "Hi, Gemma. How was your day?"

"Fine."

Oscar sighed. Gemma was nine years old, but she was already exhibiting teenage behaviour and attitudes, something they were all hoping she'd grow out of, eventually. Tina, on the other hand, was seven and just like all the other seven-year-olds around. She had plenty of friends, enjoyed playing with toys rather than spending hours on a computer, tablet or phone, whereas Gemma had few friends—that she mentioned anyway—and lived for her tablet.

His cousins, Stephen, who was fifteen, Gemma and Tina, had come to live with them seven years ago. Tina was just three months old when their parents died in a car accident, so she had no memories of them. Gemma could only remember a little as she'd been two, and Stephen had been eight. The moment Oscar's parents had found out, they'd taken the kids in without an issue, making sure everyone had somewhere to sleep. Oscar, twenty-three at the time, had reduced his uni hours to part-time and spent the rest of his time looking after his cousins while his parents were at work. It was a good job Oscar loved kids.

"Do you have everything you need?" he asked them, setting off down the street when they both nodded. Tina's hand slipped into his, and he smiled down at her.

It took them twenty minutes to get back to the cafe, and Oscar set them up on the stools at the end of the counter with tablets, colouring and anything else he thought might keep their attention for the next two hours until his mother picked them up. This routine was so ingrained in his life now that he barely thought anything of it unless someone mentioned something, which was rare. Stephen, as he was older, often went straight home to start his homework.

"Here you go, girls," Hilary said, placing plates with chocolate cake and glasses filled with coke in front of them.

"That's one way to hype them up for Mum. Thanks." Oscar rolled his eyes but didn't stop her. He winked at Tina, who giggled while sucking her coke through a straw.

"It's not like I do it every day," Hilary said.

"Oh, no. Of course not."

He chuckled and made his way from behind the counter with a tray full of drinks for the group at the window. They were lively and flushed, and he wondered if they'd had a bit to drink. Not that it mattered, as long as they were considerate of his other customers. So far, they'd been fine.

"Here you go." He placed the tray down and handed out the drinks to the correct people. "Enjoy."

"Oh, do you know if any of the royal family is at Windsor today?" one woman asked.

Oscar tucked the tray under his arm and linked his fingers in front of him. "Well, the king chose this as his primary home, so they spend a lot of time here. I don't know for definite when they're here. We only know that the king is in residence when the Royal Standard flag is flying. As for the other family members, we have no clue."

"All right, thanks."

"No problem. Enjoy."

The rest of the afternoon sped by, and Oscar said goodbye to his cousins and mother when she arrived to take them home. He grabbed another break—he always called them breaks, but they were just time away from the front of the store—before the end of the day so he could finish some more paperwork. He had stock to replenish and orders to check before he could go home that night.

He set his phone to shuffle the songs and got to work. Hilary knocked on his door sometime later, pulling his gaze from the spreadsheets.

"We're all locked up and heading home. Do you need any of us to stay?"

Oscar shook his head. "I'm good. I only have a few more bits to do, then I'll be going home myself." Hilary raised her eyebrows. "I will!"

"Okay. I'll believe that when I see it. Don't work too hard. There are more hours in the day tomorrow you can use."

Oscar smiled. "I know. Thank you."

"Night."

"Night, Hilary."

She left the doorway, then reappeared, leaning on the doorframe. "Remember, we're going out this weekend."

"I don't think it's a good idea." His cheeks heated.

She crossed her arms. "You're never going to find the person you want if you don't try looking. It'll be fine. I'll be there, and so will Wally and Sam. You'll be fine."

"Okay, boss." He closed his eyes, his stomach churning at the thought of braving a club to find what he had so far been unable to find. Why couldn't these things be easier than throwing himself out there for anyone to mock and harass?

"We won't leave you. I promise."

He swallowed hard and nodded. He trusted them. It was other people he didn't.

3

CHRISTIAN

Christian settled opposite his commanding officer and sighed. "Nothing." He barely held back from screaming in frustration. "How can they have covered their tracks so well for nothing to show up pointing to them? Nobody can do that."

Neil tilted his head. "No one that we know about, but isn't that the key? If someone was so good at covering their tracks, no one *would* know about it."

Christian couldn't argue with that, but... "They can't be that good. Henry found out about them. There are random musings in diaries from years past that show it was happening before my family got involved. There has to be something." He rose and gripped his hair in his hands as he strode to the window.

"We're closer than we were before, Christian."

"Not close enough. I don't want to lose any more family because *they* decide they shouldn't be allowed to live. Who will it be next?"

Neil came to stand beside him. "We'll find something. I

know we will. I wish I could help more than I already am, but if I bring too many people into this…"

"I know. I don't want anyone else getting hurt. It's fine."

"Look, you've been here four days going through it all. Why not have a break? Aren't you supposed to be at the club tonight?"

Christian nodded, knowing his commanding officer wouldn't tell a soul about what Christian had told him about his family and their business. Other than his cousins, he didn't trust anyone more than Neil. If his family found out he'd told him, though, Christian would be in trouble.

"Get back home. Go to the club. Rest up. Let off some steam, for god's sake." Neil clapped him on the back.

Christian bid goodbye and went to the room he slept in when he was at the barracks. As tidy as always, he grabbed the few things that weren't in his bag and threw them in. He left the room again and headed for his car. Neil was right. He needed to let off some steam, but it wasn't what Neil was thinking. He didn't need to lose himself to sexual release. He needed his cousins.

He knocked off a text to George and aimed the car towards his destination, thoughts of his one and only act of sexual intercourse flitting through his mind.

His first night at Club Royal when he'd reached eighteen hadn't been as eye-opening as his family probably expected it to be, but he'd enjoyed being there. There was nothing like being surrounded by the people he could trust. That first night had been amazing, celebrating coming of age with his cousins, but it was the following night that was seared into his brain. Somehow, his father had found out he was a virgin, and he'd gone ballistic. For once, John had not laid a hand on him but instead had called someone to visit. To begin with,

Christian hadn't understood what was happening until his father had pointed at the woman and told him in no uncertain terms that he was to fuck her. Right there in front of his father.

"What? No way!" Christian said, moving towards the door.

His father grabbed his arm, turning him back. "You will do this. Do you know why?" Christian didn't answer, and John leaned closer. "Because if you don't, you won't like what I'll do to her while you watch."

Hatred, vicious and red hot, flowed through Christian at the man's words, and there and then, he vowed to pay him back for everything he'd ever experienced at his hands. He'd bide his time, but eventually, his father would pay. He knew what his father was capable of, but he refused to allow someone else to be on the receiving end.

Christian clenched his jaw and turned to the woman. She was pretty, and under other circumstances, Christian would've been attracted to her, but not now. Not like this. Unfortunately, he couldn't see a way out of refusing without her getting hurt. She had no idea what she'd stumbled into.

For once, he stood up to his father about one thing. "You are welcome to watch, but not from the beginning. You will wait in the hallway, and you can enter after fifteen minutes." He could see his father's anger rising, ready to decline, but he pushed on a button he knew his father would agree to. "She deserves to be treated like you'd treat Mother. This is not about her. It's about me, isn't it?"

John glared at him, but Christian knew he'd agree. His father loved his mother more than anything or anyone else in the world. "Agreed. Fifteen minutes and no longer." He left, closing the door.

Christian turned to the woman. "Hi..." He realised he didn't know her name.

"Gail."

"Hi, Gail. I'm assuming you know why you're here." Gail nodded, a small smile on her face.

"Your father wanted the best for you."

Christian swallowed the words that wanted to leave his mouth and smiled, holding out his hand. "Shall we?"

As Gail slid her hand into his, he was glad, once more, that he was bisexual and not gay. If he'd been gay, this would've been ten times harder than it was. Not that his parents knew he was bisexual. That was not something he planned on telling them any time soon. Pushing all thoughts aside except for what he had to do, he pulled Gail closer, sliding his hands into her hair and holding her still as he took her mouth.

Christian shook the images from his head. He'd rather not remember what his father would've seen, but he'd not had intercourse with another person since that night. He felt dirty, and no amount of showering could get rid of the feeling. He played with other people at the club, giving them and him a release, but that was mechanical, empty. It kept him safe from anyone who they could use against him should his parents find out.

He pulled up to George's house and climbed out, grabbing his bag. Knocking on the door, it swung open within seconds, and someone pulled him into the house.

"Come on!" George said, dragging him down the hallway.

"What?"

"Just come on. You're going to miss it."

Christian chuckled and just went with it. George wouldn't explain until he was good and ready, so he let George drag him wherever he wanted him to. They ended up in the conservatory they had built on the back of the house. Sitting around a large table were Freddie, Damon, Douglas, Mav, Patrick and Henry playing cards. With it being Tuesday, he assumed the other partners—Robert, Timothy and Eddie —were working.

"What's all this?"

"Shh. Let Henry concentrate," George whispered.

Christian frowned and studied everyone and the table. It was then he realised Henry was about to whip the others' asses. Something that rarely happened because Henry didn't like playing cards and hardly ever won when he did. Had Robert been teaching him?

Both he and George stayed frozen in place until the game ended, and George screamed at the top of his lungs.

"Woooo! Go Henry!"

George ran over and threw his arms around Henry, almost knocking him over.

"Jesus, George," Freddie said and rolled his eyes, although he had a smile on his face. "Damn good job, Henry."

Henry grinned. "Not too shabby, if I do say so myself."

Everyone laughed.

"Nice work, Henry. Have you been practising?" Christian asked, coming to shake his hand.

Henry tilted his head from side to side. "A little. Robert enjoys playing."

"I wasn't expecting to see you today, Chris," Douglas said, throwing his arm around Mav's shoulders, then sipping his drink.

"My commanding officer was sick of the sight of me," he joked truthfully. "And I'm supposed to be at the club tonight."

"Ah, okay." Douglas looked around the table. "Up for a club night?"

George shook his head. "I don't think Eddie and Timothy

would be up for it because they have work tomorrow, but I'll ask." He pulled out his phone, his fingers speeding across the screen.

"I'll check with Robert," Henry said, copying George.

Patrick nodded. "I'm there, although I might not stay all night."

"Damon?" Freddie asked.

Damon shrugged. "Why not?"

Freddie smiled and nodded. "We'll be there."

Christian sighed. "You do realise you don't have to keep an eye on me, you know?"

Freddie rose and stopped in front of him, holding his chin. "We know. We want to. We look after our own."

Christian kept his focus on Freddie, although he wanted to close his eyes and weep. Freddie seemed to understand Christian more than Christian wanted him to and tightened his hold on his chin until it became more of a pinch. The gentle pain centred Christian, allowing him to stay in the present, and he had never been more grateful for it.

"Thank you," he said after making sure he could keep his voice steady.

Freddie let go with a slight uptick of his finger, lifting Christian's chin slightly before stepping back. "Looks like we are club bound." He turned back to Christian. "What time do you start?"

"Eight o'clock."

"Good. We have time for a few more games. You in?" Freddie glanced at him as he returned to his seat next to Damon.

"Sure."

Christian sat beside Freddie and focused on the cards being dealt. He wished he could explain everything to them, but it was for their safety that he couldn't. Soon, hopefully.

♦

"Prince Christian," Clarice said with a smile. "It's nice to see you."

"Good evening, Clarice. How is everything tonight?"

Clarice checked the computer, then refocused on him. "Everything seems to be going well. There was a minor incident with a lock on one door to a private room, and the occupants had to wait inside for half an hour before maintenance resolved it, but apart from that, everything has been good."

Christian frowned. "Was the lock broken, or had it malfunctioned?"

"It malfunctioned. I got a notification when they tried to open it with their thumbprint, and the sensor didn't recognise them. I called maintenance, and they set to work on it immediately. I checked their prints afterwards, and they worked fine on everything else, just not that one door."

"Who were the occupants?"

Clarice winced. "Princess Helena and her partner."

Christian's jaw tightened. Was it a coincidence, or were *they* bringing the "fight" closer to home now? His younger cousin was a lesbian, and it had come at the price of Helena being ignored by Christian's parents and Aunt Charlotte's family. "Have we put the room off-limits for now?"

"Yes, Your Highness." She handed him a club phone.

"Thank you, Clarice."

Christian entered the monitor's changing rooms, which was separate from the rest of the changing rooms, and was met by the conversation of his cousins.

"Here he is!" Douglas announced. "Thought you weren't going to make it, after all."

Christian grinned. "I always keep my promises." He pulled out his personal phone and sent a message to Neil, telling him of the incident, then placed the phone in the locker. He pulled his T-shirt off and hung it up, grabbing the mesh shirt and pulling it on. He didn't like the feel of leather against his skin, so he stuck to black jeans and different types of shirts. Sometimes, he could wear leather straps over the top, but it often made him too warm.

Clipping the club phone to his waistband, he faced his cousins. "Ready?"

"Always," Freddie said.

They exited the changing rooms and headed for the doors, set behind where Clarice sat at her reception desk in the middle of the foyer. He placed his thumb on the sensor and opened the door. Each of his companions pressed their thumbs to the sensor as they followed him. It was how the club knew how many people were in attendance and *who* was there. The club being as exclusive as it was, there was no shortage of people trying to get inside to see what the fuss was all about. Especially media types, who wanted the scoop on who owned the place. Not that Club *Royal* was exactly trying to hide—whoever thought of that name needed firing.

Christian headed straight for the bar and collected a bottle of water that Oliver, the bartender, held out for him. "Thanks."

No one who drank alcohol could play in the club. They were strict on this rule because too many people could get hurt. Whenever someone ordered alcohol, Oliver would put them on the "no play" list that all Monitors could check at any time throughout the night.

"Right," he said. "I'll see you in there." He clapped Freddie on the shoulder.

"I'm coming now," Freddie said, grabbing the water Oliver handed him.

"Me, too." Damon followed.

"We'll be in soon," Douglas said.

Despite his words to the contrary earlier that day, Christian felt less stressed when he had the backup of his cousins. The club was open to every member of the royal family. Some didn't use it, but he knew most did for their various kinks. His parents often came but rarely participated, which in some ways was a good thing—the last thing he wanted to witness was his parents fucking. The same goes for most of the "parents" of his cousins. But it didn't stop his other cousins from taking part. Charles was Aunt Charlotte's son, and he was at the club more than he wasn't, but luckily, he behaved from what everyone could tell. There had been no complaints about him, anyway. His wife was hardly ever here, but from what Christian knew, she didn't care if he took part in the activities here. Christian had always wondered why she was still with him, but then he only had to look at his own situation to see that she probably had a similar issue to him.

"You okay?" Freddie asked in his ear as they weaved through the crowds in the main club area.

Christian nodded and aimed for the raised platform at the back of the room. Before he traded places with the current Monitor, he turned to Freddie. "Have fun, okay? Don't worry about me."

Freddie gave him that look and rested a hand on his shoulder. "I'll always worry about you, but I heard you. Come find us if you need anything."

Christian smiled. "Will do." He stepped up onto the platform and checked in with his sister Elizabeth. "Hey. How have things been?"

Elizabeth pursed her lips and continued to look straight ahead. "Good. No issues so far."

"Except for the locked door," he said.

She glanced at him with raised eyebrows, then looked away and nodded.

Christian sighed, glad for the music that would hide it from her ears. Elizabeth was more like his parents than he liked, and she didn't like him one bit. Apparently, she thought he was spoiled, getting all their parents' attention. As far as he was concerned, she could have their attention if she wanted it. He didn't.

"Well…" He held out his hands. "Have a good evening."

Elizabeth glared at him and stepped down, disappearing into the crowd. Christian surveyed the room, checking with the different stages and ensuring everything was calm. He crossed his arms over his chest and stood still. He'd received plenty of practice at staying still for hours on end, and people seemed to forget he was there when they couldn't see him moving. It was how he'd found out plenty of information, more than he needed sometimes, when people hadn't realised he was there.

Despite his body being still, his mind wasn't. He ran through every piece of information he had on his family, his aunts and uncles, his cousins, the bombing that killed his aunt and the attempts to ruin his cousins' lives over the past few months. He was concerned that whoever was behind it all—which he was certain was Aunt Charlotte—was stepping up the ante.

In his research, Christian had gone back years, trying to

remember every little incident that had happened to anyone within the royal family. He was stunned to realise there were a lot more than he'd expected: food being tainted by something someone was allergic to, causing them to go to hospital; falls that couldn't be explained; even bullies who had put someone in hospital. Christian had it all, and it didn't leave a pretty picture.

The following morning, he had a meeting to get to, and he had to do it quietly without anyone realising it was happening. No one could know who was helping him. They would be in too much danger. It was the reason Christian had taken over the research for it; he didn't want this person to put themselves in the line of fire any more than they already were.

"Master Christian?"

He glanced down at the submissive standing in front of him. Christian stepped down to be level with him. "How can I help?"

"Would I be able to set up a time with you soon, please, sir?"

Christian smiled. "Of course, Ricky. See Clarice on your way out. She knows what times I have available."

Ricky lowered his head. "Thank you, sir."

"You're welcome." He tilted his head. "Have you found anyone else to help you when I'm not available? Please be honest with me."

Ricky shook his head. "No, sir. Well, I've tried with a few, but none that I feel I can..." He stopped.

Christian rested a hand on his arm. "I understand. Good boy for telling me. I'll see what I can do for you."

"Thank you, sir."

"Enjoy your evening, Ricky."

"I will, sir."

Christian watched Ricky weave through the people and returned to his platform. The boy had been unlucky with a previous relationship that had turned for the worse, and it had taken Christian a long time to get him to where he was now. Neither wanted more from each other except the opportunity to be themselves for a few hours. He'd done Ricky an injustice by not doing more for him before now. The problems with his family were overtaking his other responsibilities, and he couldn't have that. He needed to find a balance.

Unfortunately, there were only so many hours in a day, and most of them were used on trying to keep his family alive.

4

OSCAR

"No," Oscar said.

Hilary whined. "Come on! Just because the last time didn't work doesn't mean the next will be the same."

"Hilary, he called me stupid. Daddies don't call their boys stupid. He shouldn't have even been there. He had no idea what I was talking about when I told him what I wanted. He ignored everything I said and did whatever he wanted to do. I'm not going through that again."

Hilary put a hand on his shoulder. "I know he was an asshole, but they're not all like that. Besides, I told Elton about it, and he said he'd speak to the guy."

Oscar threw his hands in the air. "Wonderful! Now the guy knows I tattled on him. That's one way to make sure I never find a Daddy. Thanks."

Oscar pushed through the door to the front of the store and came to a halt, ice freezing in his veins.

"Good morning."

Oscar couldn't say anything as he stared in horror at the

man standing in front of him. How much had he heard? If his smirk was anything to go by, everything. Oscar closed his eyes and thought about turning around and going back the way he'd come, but he had a business to run. He swallowed and pasted a smile on his face.

"Good morning. Can I get you a coffee?" He didn't acknowledge if his voice was too high and squeaky, and his cheeks heated.

"Sure. Black, no sugar."

Oscar turned away and focused on making the drink, though it didn't take as long as he wished it had. Would he pretend he hadn't heard, or would he say something to bring attention to it? It was Oscar's fault. He shouldn't have been talking so loudly about his personal life when the store had just opened.

Inhaling, he carried the mug to the counter and placed it in front of him, refusing to make eye contact. "That'll be three ninety-five, please."

Christian held out a note, and Oscar returned his change. He gasped when their hands touched, and a spark went through him. His gaze met Christian's and saw an answering...something in his eyes. Oscar pulled his hand away and closed his fist around the sensation.

"Feel free to grab a book," he said.

Christian stared at him for a moment, then nodded. "Thanks."

Oscar watched him trail over to the same table he'd sat at on his previous visit. He placed the mug on the table, then wandered over to the books. Oscar had to tear his gaze away and try to remember what he was supposed to be doing. He checked the stock and made sure they had everything they needed for the morning rush.

After half an hour of serving customers, Christian came back to the counter. "Could I have another coffee and a slice of cake, please?"

Oscar lowered his eyes. "Of course. We have chocolate, carrot, vanilla and red velvet."

"Let's go wild with some chocolate, please."

Oscar's cheeks heated as he plated a slice of chocolate cake. What was it about the man that made his body so unsteady and shaky? Was it because Oscar was scared he'd heard them talking earlier? Or was it something else?

He rested the plate in front of Christian and turned to make the coffee. He blew out his breath slowly as the coffee dripped into the mug. He glanced up, unable to stop himself from checking the mirror to see Christian. He nearly dropped the mug when he realised Christian was already staring at him through the mirror. He lowered his eyes again and swallowed hard. He concentrated harder than usual on keeping the coffee within the mug and rested it on the counter.

"Eight-twenty, please."

Christian handed over a tenner but didn't let it go when Oscar reached for it. Christian tugged on it gently, pulling Oscar closer. "When do you have a break?" he murmured.

"Ten o'clock."

Christian nodded. "I'll be waiting." He let go of the money, and Oscar watched him carry his things back to the table.

Oh, god.

His hand trembled as he put the money in the till. For the next hour, he tried to concentrate on serving customers and making small talk with the regulars and not on watching the clock count closer to ten o'clock. He wasn't sure if he wanted it to speed up or slow down. Could he sit with him and talk? He didn't have much choice, did he?

When Sam came in, Oscar's heart sped up. He made a drink for himself and another for Christian, then told Sam and Hilary where he'd be. They both raised their eyebrows at him, and he shrugged. He carried the mugs over to Christian's table, smiling at the customers as he passed by.

"Hey, have a seat," Christian said, closing his book and resting it on the table.

"I brought you another drink. I wasn't sure if you wanted one, but…" Oscar set it in front of him, then sat opposite.

"Thank you. I can never have too much caffeine." Christian lifted the mug and took a sip. "Perfect." He nodded at Oscar's. "I see you have it black, too."

Oscar gave a small smile. At least he hoped he did. His hands were shaking.

Christian huffed a laugh. "You don't have to be scared of me."

Oscar chuckled at that. "Don't I? You're a prince. I'm just…" He shrugged.

"A person like I am."

"I know. It's not every day someone like you asks to speak with me. I'm nervous about why."

Christian leaned forward in his seat, closing the distance between them, and lowered his voice. "I'm sorry if I made you uncomfortable. That wasn't my intention."

"What was your intention?" Oscar couldn't believe he'd said the words, and his eyes widened as if he could take them back. They sounded completely different from the way he'd meant them to sound.

Christian grinned, the expression making him look happier than Oscar had ever seen him. "I want to get to know you. Your bookstore is a new favourite of mine, and I want us to get to know each other so you don't feel uncomfortable around me."

Oscar gripped his mug and brought it to his mouth, taking a big swallow. "I'm not so much uncomfortable as unsure. I'm trying to treat you like a regular person, but it's difficult to forget. I feel like hiding and burying myself in my numbers."

Christian tilted his head. "Numbers?"

Oscar's cheeks heated. "I like working with numbers. It relaxes me."

Christian nodded and sighed, staring at the table. "I know it's difficult to be around me." He lifted his gaze. "Okay. Ask me anything you want. Anything at all. If I can answer it, I will."

Oscar raised his eyebrows. "I wouldn't know the first thing to ask."

"Let me start then." He leaned closer again. "You're looking for a Daddy?"

Oscar covered his face and sighed. "That's what I was expecting you to talk about." He groaned. "Please, can we forget those words ever left my lips?"

Christian chuckled. "Oh, no, we can't. Let me help."

Oscar frowned. "What?"

"Let me help you find someone. I have contacts. I know people."

Oscar held up one hand. "No, I'm fine, thank you. Hilary has done enough, and I want to pretend everything is perfect without having to go through that again."

"He was an asshole. Hilary was right. He didn't know the first thing about how to be a Daddy. The first rule is don't call your boy names. You're supposed to cherish them, care for them, give them what they need, and eventually, love them. Nothing else is worth fighting for than having the best."

Oscar stared at Christian, whose gaze seemed far away. Something about the way he'd spoken made Oscar feel like Christian knew what he was talking about. Was he a boy? He thought over their interactions, and he twitched when he realised the truth.

"You're a Daddy," he whispered.

Christian blinked at him, not moving a muscle as they stared at each other until a barely-there nod came from the man. His gaze took in their surroundings, breaking Oscar of the hold he'd had over him. Oscar hadn't expected it, and he wasn't sure what to say. Obviously, it wasn't something that was advertised, so Oscar would have to keep it quiet, but that wasn't a problem. If Christian knew about the lifestyle, then maybe he did have contacts and knew where Oscar could find someone.

"What type of boy are you?" Christian asked, keeping his voice low.

Oscar's cheeks heated, and he focused on his cup. "A little. In public, about age four or five. In private, two or three," he whispered. He covered his eyes. "Why am I telling you this?"

Christian covered his hand with his own. "Don't be embarrassed. I've been told I'm very easy to talk to."

Oscar snorted, which he was sure was Christian's intention. "You are. Even for an almost stranger."

Christian spread his hands. "How can I be a stranger when the world knows who I am?"

Oscar wasn't sure the bitterness of Christian's tone was supposed to be as apparent as it had been. For the first time, he wondered what the man had to go through being part of the royal family. "Do you not get any peace at all?"

Christian's mouth quirked. "It's not too bad for me. I'm far enough away from the throne to be inconsequential most of the time. Doesn't stop my private life from being plastered across the newspapers, though."

"I can't imagine."

Christian checked his watch and grimaced. "I must go. Think about what I said. I know people." He stood, slipping on his coat, then leaned down with his back to the rest of the room, hiding them from sight. He brushed his finger down the side of Oscar's face. "Thank you for the coffee and cake, little one. They were delicious."

Oscar's eyelids fluttered, then Christian was gone. Oscar gathered up the mugs and plates and carried them behind the counter, trying to ignore the stares of his customers and employees alike.

"I need to get some work done. Let me know when you get busy," he told Hilary.

"Sure thing."

He pushed through to the back, smiling at Jonas as he passed, then closed the door to his office. Sinking into his chair, he stared at nothing, his mind whirling with the information Christian had trusted him with. Why did Christian tell him that when Oscar could turn around and let the entire world know? He wouldn't, but he could have. Did Christian trust him already? He hardly knew him. Oscar's mouth curled at the idea that Christian trusted him in such a short time.

"Boss, we're getting busy," Hilary called.

"On my way."

He stood. He needed to push thoughts of Christian aside

for the moment. He'd dissect it later.

"I'm here!" Oscar called as he closed the front door of his parents' house, juggling boxes. "Who's up for pizza?"

"Me!" Tina shouted, followed by a thundering of feet as she ran down the hallway.

"Hello again, princess." He bent down and passed her a smaller box than the others. "This is just for you. Hide, quick!"

Tina giggled and ran off the way she came. Oscar winced, wondering if the pizza would stay in the box or if it would end up on the floor. He should've waited until they were in the kitchen to give it to her. He shook his head. As he wandered towards the stairs, Gemma came down, and he passed her a box with a wink. She gave him a small smile in return that faded within a second.

He entered the kitchen and saw his parents dressed up to the nines. "Wow, look at you. Where are you going again?"

His mother, Sally, kissed his cheek. "There's a charity event at the Denver Hotel. All proceeds go to..." She glanced at Tina. "Go to children who need it."

Oscar understood what she didn't say. Since their cousins had moved in with them, they'd found out there wasn't as much help out there for people in their situation as they'd thought there would be, but with some research, his parents had found a charity that was working to gain better help for orphaned children who'd been sent to extended family members.

"I'm sure you'll have great fun." Oscar glanced at the two girls. "We'll be fine with a movie or two, won't we?"

"Yeah!" Tina shouted, pumping her arms in the air. "Can we have *Descendants* again?"

Gemma groaned. "No! Come on! There must be something else we can watch. We've seen it six times in the last three days!"

Jim chuckled and clapped Oscar on the back. "Good luck."

Sally gave Tina a hug and patted Gemma on the shoulder. "Be good, girls. Stephen is in his room. You might need to lure him out with food."

He hefted the last three pizzas. "That's the plan."

Sally raised her eyebrows. "How many are for him?"

Oscar laughed. "Two."

"Good call." She waved and followed his father.

"Right, girls. Eat up while I grab your brother."

Oscar put the pizzas on the counter and removed his coat, draping it over the back of a chair before heading for the stairs. Stephen was a typical fifteen-year-old, wanting nothing more than to hide away in his room and play video games all day. They were lucky enough that he enjoyed school, so he always did his homework on time, but he focused the rest of his time on video games.

He knocked on Stephen's door. "Hey, Ste? We have pizza."

"I'll be down in a minute."

"Don't be too long because I *will* let Tina get her hands on them."

He chuckled and returned downstairs to grab his own box. "Okay, movie night. Everyone gets a choice. Tina, I know yours. Gemma?"

He sat at the head of the table and opened his box, the steaming scent of meat, vegetables and pineapple always making him smile. They talked while they ate, with Stephen arriving shortly after. His parents had a rule that takeaway was not allowed in their rooms, so Ste had to eat it with them. By the time they'd finished, they'd decided on two films, with a third in reserve in case they changed their minds. The first one was *Ella Enchanted*, which was a compromise for everyone. It was funny but still a princess movie to make Tina happy. Then, once Tina had gone to bed, they'd put on either *Jumanji* or *Honey, I Shrunk the Kids*. It was Oscar's role to show the kids some decent films from his childhood.

The evening had lots of laughter and several bowls of popcorn, and his parents joined them for the end of *Honey, I Shrunk the Kids* when they came home. Once it finished, his mother asked him if he would stay over, but Oscar declined.

"I'm okay to drive home, don't worry."

Sally huffed. "I know, but I like you being here."

He hugged her. "I like being here, but I'm thirty, Mum. I have a place of my own now, and you have enough to handle without me cramping your style."

They laughed.

"Okay. Let me know when you get home," she said.

"As always. Love you."

"Love you, sweetheart."

"Bye, Dad." Jim smiled and put his thumb up.

Oscar left, driving home with a near constant yawn. He loved his family, but looking after those three kids was exhausting after having worked for ten hours.

By the time he got home, he needed a shower and bed. He undressed, throwing the clothes in the corner of his room that he used as a washing basket because he didn't have an actual one to use. He strode, naked, into his bathroom, switching the shower on and stepping straight under. The water pounded down on him, and he closed his eyes, letting it relax his muscles, hoping it would help him sleep. His thoughts drifted to Christian and the offer he'd made. Oscar had known he wanted a Daddy after a visit to The Den several years ago. Hilary and Wally had taken him when he'd been pissed off after another relationship had ended because he "couldn't give him what he needed." Oscar had never understood what that had been, and each time an ex-boyfriend had told him that, he felt like screaming.

The Den was an eye-opening experience, one he'd found a home in as soon as he'd visited. It had still taken him a few months to figure out where he stood within the variety of kinks, but when he'd experienced a Daddy dynamic, he'd cried. Literally sobbed his heart out because he finally knew what he'd been missing. His first Daddy—a temporary two-night Daddy—was Brian, and he'd been amazing. In the few hours they'd had before Brian was due to go back to the Army, he'd taught Oscar so many things. The main thing was not to settle for something that wasn't working and to communicate *all the time*.

He'd seen Brian once more after that, but he'd broken the news that he was being transferred. Oscar had wished him well, and since then, hadn't been able to find a Daddy for more than a night at a time. It wasn't like he was asking for much. Just someone who would take care of him when he was in his little space. Most of the Daddies he'd met had wanted just the sexual aspect of the lifestyle, which Oscar wasn't against, but he wanted more. He wanted the odd day of being little and experiencing everything that came along with that.

Which brought him back around to Christian's proposal. Could he take the chance? Or rather, what did he have to lose?

5

CHRISTIAN

"Well, look what the cat dragged in."

Christian curved one side of his mouth at his cousin's voice. "Charles. Pleasure as always."

"Mother wanted me to ask you to visit with her today. If you have time, of course." He sneered, his handsome features marred by the cruel twist to his lips and glint in his eyes, visible even on the video call.

"Of course. I have an errand to run, then I will drop by. I shouldn't be more than an hour."

"She'll be waiting."

Charles ended the call, and Christian sighed and dropped his head. Visiting Aunt Charlotte was the last thing he wanted to do, but when she asked, it *wasn't* an ask. It was an order.

He continued to his destination, knocking on Randall's office door.

"Come in."

He entered with a smile. "Good morning, Randall. How are you?"

Randall stood and held out his hand. "I'm good, thanks, Your Highness. You?"

Christian shrugged. "Getting along as always."

The corners of Randall's mouth curled slightly. "I can imagine. He's waiting for you."

"Thank you."

Christian wandered over to another door and knocked, waiting for permission to enter before doing so. He closed the door behind him.

"Christian."

His uncle stood and wrapped him in his arms, gripping him. It took everything in Christian to keep his composure at the easy display of affection. He received nothing of the kind from his immediate family, and he refused to let Uncle Andrew know that, though he probably knew already. The longer Andrew held him, the more his muscles relaxed.

King Andrew stepped back, holding Christian's upper arms, and shook his head. "How are you holding up?"

"I'm good, Uncle."

"Do you have anything for me?" Andrew sank into the leather sofa in front of his desk, and Christian sat beside him, lifting his knee to the cushion to face him.

"Nothing more than before. Neil thought we had something with the last batch of information that came through, but so far, it hasn't panned out as anything other than what it appears to be."

Andrew tapped his knee. "Don't worry. They won't get away with this forever."

"But the longer it takes, the more likely they will!"

"The longer it takes, the more confident they become because they think they got away with it. In the end, the truth will prevail. I truly believe that."

Christian rubbed a hand over his forehead. "I wish I had your confidence."

"I have enough confidence for the both of us." Andrew smiled. "How are you apart from that?"

Christian rolled his eyes, his uncle being one of the few people he felt comfortable doing that around. "I have orders to see Aunt Charlotte after being here."

Andrew rubbed his chin. "Do you know why?"

"No idea. I've heard nothing from Father or Mother since I returned from the barracks the day before yesterday. I had planned to head home after this to see if I could find anything if they weren't there."

"Be careful, Christian. I know we spoke about this a few months ago, but I don't like the idea of you searching the house in case they find you. I don't want to think what they could be capable of even if you're family."

Christian kept his face blank, not giving away any of the stomach-churning memories that flashed in his mind. He tucked them away, using them as training for when he needed to study their behaviours. When not if.

"I'll be fine."

Andrew stood, rounding his desk. "I do have something that was sent to me. It might be of interest to you." He picked up a USB and handed it to Christian. "I don't know if any of it will make sense to you—it certainly makes little sense to me—but maybe you can get your experts to look at it."

"What is on it?"

Andrew shrugged. "As I said, it makes no sense to me. It's just a bunch of numbers."

He pocketed it. "Okay, I'll look into it."

Andrew stopped in front of him again. "You don't need to

keep doing this, Christian. You can pull out whenever you want to. I hate you going back to them. I wish I could trust them with you."

Christian smiled. "I've dealt with them for this long; I'm sure I can manage a little longer." He headed for the door, feeling better than he had in several days. "I'll call you after I've spoken with Aunt Charlotte if there's anything you need to know."

"Call me no matter what. I want to know you're in one piece."

Christian dropped his head and breathed through his nose at the love tinging his uncle's voice. Something that had always been missing in his father's. "Okay."

He left, raising his hand in goodbye to Randall, who was on the phone. Walking the halls of Windsor, he hoped he didn't run into any of the Outrageous Eleven, as George had coined them. He hated being so close and unable to visit, but he couldn't let Aunt Charlotte wait too much longer. As it was, she'd want to know what errand he had to run. Uncle Andrew had given him permission to tell them he was planning a surprise party for Freddie, George and Patrick in August. As much as he wished it wouldn't come to it, they could use it as bait if they needed to, but Christian hoped they were behind bars by that time.

He'd just started his engine as Freddie's car entered the area. Christian cursed silently but put a smile on his face and wound down his window.

"Morning," Freddie said.

"Good morning. Been anywhere exciting?"

Freddie chuckled. "Just back from brunch with the Secretary of State for Education."

"Enlightening?"

"Very. We have a lot of work to do."

"Better get to it, slacker." Christian grinned, winked and gunned the engine. As much as he wanted to stay and talk to Freddie, he couldn't. One because he didn't have time, and two because Freddie saw too much of him.

The drive to Kensington Palace took three-quarters of an hour, and although it was lunchtime, he refused to eat before he saw his aunt. His stomach was roiling enough without adding food into the mix. He would've preferred to be sent to the worst war-torn places on earth instead of meeting with her, but he had a job to do.

He parked and inhaled deeply before climbing out of the car. From this moment forward, he couldn't show any hesitation in what he saw or had to do. He'd been hiding his true job for six months now, and though it was getting harder, he refused to put anyone else in danger.

The door opened as he strode closer, and he nodded at the butler without stopping. He aimed for his aunt's residence, locking everything down deeper until he was an empty shell of a man. His empathy, his care, his love were not welcome in this place, and he didn't want those areas tainted by what was to come. By the time he stood at her door, Christian was a different man.

He knocked.

Another butler opened the door and waved him inside. "Her Highness is waiting in the drawing room."

Christian didn't reply, just strode in that direction. The decoration was luxurious and hideously expensive and not to Christian's taste, but it didn't surprise him that Aunt Charlotte went for that. She had expensive taste in everything.

He stopped outside the drawing room and knocked.

"Come in." He entered, closing the door behind him

before he met her gaze. She stood, holding her arms open. "Christian! I'm so glad you could make it."

He stepped forward, wrapping his arms around his aunt and resting his hands on her back. She rubbed a hand up and down his back, then pulled away.

"How are you, Aunt Charlotte?" He sat, crossing his legs and leaning his elbow on the arm of the chair, a picture of ease.

Charlotte beamed. "I'm doing fantastic, young man. Charles and Juliet are expecting again! Isn't it wonderful?"

He smiled. "That's great news! I'm so happy for them. Do they have a due date?"

"November twentieth. I can't wait to have another grandchild to spoil." She clapped her hands together and pressed them to her mouth, eyes sparkling.

"An early Christmas gift for you," he said.

"Yes!" She picked up her cup, then put it down again. "Would you like a drink?"

He waved her away. "I'm fine, thanks. I had one in the car on the way here."

"Anything to eat?"

"Honestly, I'm fine. Thank you, Aunt Charlotte."

"Well, we have to keep your energy levels up, don't we? Working as hard as you do. You spend so much time there, I'm surprised you're not being promoted more often." She chuckled, but he could hear the question behind the ruse.

He smiled. "I'm more than happy where I am at the moment. Four or five days working with the other days off unless I'm called in—it's a win in my book. Especially as I enjoy it, too." None of that was a lie.

"What do they have you doing at the moment?" She sipped from her cup, her eyes on him.

He wagged a finger. "You know I can't tell you. You ask every time, and every time I tell you the same thing."

She hid her grin behind her hand. "I know, but I'm hoping one day you'll let it slip."

Didn't she just.

"Charles said you needed to see me urgently?" He tried to turn the conversation to the reason he was there, so he could get out of there quicker.

She nodded, replacing her cup in the saucer and folding her hands on her lap. "I did. I have a favour to ask of you." He raised his eyebrows, waiting. She stood and went to the window overlooking the gardens. "I appreciate all the information you have been able to give us about what your uncle and cousins have planned, but we need something more." She faced him, her hands and arms becoming extensions of her words. "They seem to have contingency plans in place, and we're not chopping the head of the beast off. We're only hacking away at what we can reach. We need to go bigger. We need to think like Jack."

Christian frowned. "Jack?"

Charlotte grinned. "Jack and the Beanstalk. He had a solid plan, chopping the beanstalk at the base." She nodded, eyes wide. "It certainly stopped everything from above." Christian was not convinced she hadn't lost her mind. She waved her hand. "Anyway, we need to know who's fanning the flames of the resistance. Who's deciding to divert off the main track and take the unhygienic route?"

Christian swallowed. "I understand." And unfortunately, he did. "I will see what I can find out. Is this time-sensitive, or can I take a few weeks to gather my intel?"

"We have time, Christian. We just need the information to be correct, understand?"

"Of course." He stood. "I will get started on it right away."

"Wonderful! Oh, I'm so glad we could have this chat." She cupped his face and kissed his cheek. "You're such a wonderful man. Just like Charles. So willing to do what's needed to make sure the royal line stays pure. I'm so glad you're with us."

Christian smiled. "I wouldn't want it any other way."

He accepted another hug, then bid goodbye, but before he closed the door, his aunt called his name. He glanced over his shoulder.

"The end is nigh."

He nodded and closed the door, keeping his blank façade in place until he had driven twenty minutes away from a place he never wanted to return to again. He pulled over on a deserted stretch of road he often used to decompress and climbed out of the car. He shoved the keys in his pocket and stalked to the field he'd parked beside. It stretched as far as he could see, meaning he could see if someone was coming, but at that moment, he didn't care.

He walked to the centre of the field and dropped to his knees in the dry soil, emptying his stomach. He retched until he had nothing left to give, then fell to the side and rolled to his back, staring up at the blue and white sky. Tears dripped down his temples and into his hairline. As much as he'd told Uncle Andrew he could manage, every time Charlotte or her cohorts asked him to do something, it took another piece of his soul. His cousins couldn't understand why they had to cancel or rearrange some of their plans because of unforeseen circumstances. He hated lying to them. His uncle was the only one who knew what he was doing, but he felt awful.

The charities his cousins supported were some of the

worst, according to Aunt Charlotte. So whenever they had an event set up, she did something to sabotage it. Christian had given her so much information about them that he wouldn't be surprised if his cousins never spoke to him again when they found out the truth.

If what Charlotte said was true, and the end was coming, it wouldn't be long before he found out the truth of the matter. He could lose everyone he ever cared about.

He inhaled and sat up, wiping his face. He didn't have much left to give, but he would give everything he had to ensure those pieces of shit were put where they should be.

He stood, brushing off as much dirt as he could, then drifted back to his car. Opening the boot, he unzipped his bag and pulled out a fresh shirt. He didn't care that he was replacing his Army shirt with a T-shirt. As much as his father insisted he should stay in his Army uniform, he couldn't help it if it got dirty. That would offend his father more than not wearing his uniform. Checking the road to ensure it was empty as far as he could see, he stripped off his trousers and replaced them with jeans, then slammed the boot shut and climbed into the car.

Switching on the engine, he pressed the button to continue with the audiobook he'd been listening to. George had an amazing voice, and although it was uncomfortable to listen to him read a sex scene, his voice was perfect for every aspect of narrating. Christian hadn't understood why he hadn't told them what else he had done. They knew he was a speechwriter—at least, they did now. That was a recent development they hadn't known about before. What other jobs did his cousins have that they didn't know about?

He pulled into Windsor for the second time that day, but instead of searching for his cousins, he left Windsor on foot and strode for Book Drunk. He'd only been there that morning, but he needed to get lost in the fictional world.

When he entered, Oscar glanced up, smiled and looked away as his cheeks heated. Christian hadn't forgotten their conversation the previous morning, though it felt like it had happened weeks ago, not a day. He wanted to help the man find someone worthy of him. No one should put up with assholes who had no idea what they were doing.

He waited in line, and when he was at the front, the other staff member tapped Oscar on the shoulder and switched places with him, although Oscar tried to push her aside. Christian hid a smile when Oscar, lost and flustered, came to serve him.

"Hi. Your usual?"

Christian nodded. "What do you recommend for lunch?"

Oscar raised his eyebrows and checked his watch. "A late lunch, as in a snack, or lunch itself?"

"Lunch itself. I've not eaten yet." He wasn't sure if his stomach would take much, but he needed to try.

"Any allergies?"

"None."

"Anything you don't like?"

"No."

"How about a jacket potato with cheese, coleslaw and salad?"

"Sounds good." And it did. "Go for it."

"All right." He turned and set about making his drink, and Christian leaned his elbows on the counter, watching him in the mirror above the counter. His movements were methodical and efficient, and within minutes, he had his coffee and had paid. His usual table—if you could call it usual when he'd only used it twice—was taken, but he found another close to the books and out of the way. He didn't plan on doing anything but reading and eating, so he wanted to ensure he was out of the way. He'd found that if he looked busy, people left him alone more than if he didn't.

He searched for the book he'd started earlier that day, then sat and found his page. He lost himself in the pages of the book until Oscar brought his food.

Christian made room on the table for the plate. "Thank you. It looks delicious."

"You're welcome." Oscar rubbed his hands together and lowered his voice. "If you were serious about helping me, I would appreciate it."

Christian smiled at him. "Of course, I am. Let me know when you're next free, and we can sit and chat about a few things before I set something up. I need to know about you before I can find someone suitable."

Oscar nodded. "I work all week, except Sundays, but I can always take some time out of the day if I need to. Hilary could manage for a bit."

"How about I come here at the end of business on Saturday? We can chat over coffee?"

Oscar nodded again. "Okay. Thanks."

"Oscar?" He waited until Oscar looked at him. "I won't bite."

Oscar flushed and stumbled back to the counter, and Christian grinned before tucking into the food. Watching Oscar's cheeks heat was a new favourite pastime.

6

OSCAR

$\mathcal{H}$ilary slid into the space between Oscar and the wall, raising her eyebrows. "You're clumsy today. What's going on?"

"Nothing." He avoided her gaze, swallowing to combat the dryness of his mouth. He had forgotten she would be working that day because Anna was on holiday. Hilary usually worked weekdays only, but Anna had booked the day off months ago because her boyfriend had surprised her with a week-long holiday.

"Nothing, my ass. You keep watching the door as if..." She paused, and Oscar glanced at her and wished he hadn't. "You're waiting for him. I didn't realise he was gay. There's nothing on the news about it."

Oscar sighed. "He's not. At least, I don't think he is. He said he could help me find a Daddy. He's coming in later so we can discuss my needs." He stretched himself taller and breathed through his nose, not wanting her to discount his words.

Hilary tilted her head. "I'm glad," was all she said before wandering back to the counter to serve a customer.

Oscar frowned. He'd expected some fight about it, but she'd let it go. Hilary never let things go. He palmed his face. What was she going to do? He would bet his entire annual takings that she was up to something, and it wouldn't be in his favour, but she was a force to be reckoned with. There was no stopping her when she decided something.

He finished making the toastie for a customer, plated it and took it over to the table, smiling as he set it down. On his way back, he picked up a few empty cups and plates, setting them on the side to take back into the kitchen for washing. She was right in some respects. He was nervous, and it was making him clumsier than usual. He was surprised he hadn't dropped any of the items he'd carried—it wouldn't have been the first time that day—but it only seemed to happen when Christian distracted him.

Did the guy already have someone in mind for him? Would he be bringing someone to meet him tonight? They hadn't discussed anything like that, but he couldn't rule it out. There had to be more people out there that had the same likes he did. They were probably already taken or living somewhere else. Like Brian. He shoved the thought of Brian out of his head, not wanting to become melancholy before he saw Christian. Undoubtedly, he'd have to explain his previous relationships, but he didn't want to think about it now.

As the hours passed slowly, Hilary didn't say another word, and that worried Oscar more than her annoying the hell out of him. When the bell tinkled just before five-thirty, Oscar glanced up, his throat closing at the sight of Christian. Now that the time was here, he was nervous as hell. What if

Christian didn't understand what he needed? Everyone was different. Were his needs too much?

He watched as Hilary wandered over to the prince and greeted him. Christian smiled at her and nodded, then weaved through the tables to what Oscar was becoming to think of as *his* spot. Hilary rounded the counter and set about making a drink, he assumed, for Christian.

"What were you talking about?" he asked her.

She shrugged. "I just asked if he wanted his usual."

Oscar narrowed his eyes. "What are you up to, Hilary?"

"Nothing. I'm just serving the customers."

"Well, it's nearly time you finished, so I can finish the drink off for you."

Hilary pushed his hand aside. "It's fine. I'll do this, and then I'll clock off. No problem."

Oscar lowered his eyes, trying to understand what was going on. He felt completely out of his depth and snuck a look in Christian's direction, seeing him engrossed in a book.

"Excuse me?"

Oscar turned to the voice and smiled. "How can I help?" He helped the customer, and by the time he'd finished, Hilary had disappeared. He glanced over at Christian again, and his heart thumped when he saw Hilary sitting at the table with him, chatting and drinking coffee as if nothing were amiss. Going over there and ordering her to go home was not something he could do, but the need was there. Instead, he focused on tidying up and serving the last customers. There were only five people left when Hilary stood and collected her cup, carrying it to the counter.

"What are you doing?" he hissed.

Hilary smirked. "I'm getting to know your friend. He's nice. Anyway, I'm out of here. I'll just grab my stuff."

She disappeared into the back, returning a few minutes later, then waved goodbye and left. The last woman brought the books she wanted to buy to the counter, and Oscar rang them up, putting them in a bag and following her to the door once the transaction was complete. As soon as she'd exited, Oscar locked the door and flipped the sign to closed.

He and Chloe worked together to finish cleaning up and lowering the blinds, and Oscar tried his hardest to ignore the looks Chloe kept giving him. When there were only the bins needing to be put out the back of the building, Oscar told her she could go.

"See you next week, Oscar."

"Have a wonderful week, Chloe. Good luck with your exams."

"Thanks." She waved, and he let her out, locking the door again behind her.

His hands were shaking when he turned to Christian, who looked like he was engrossed in the book in front of him, but Oscar was sure he was aware of everything. A shiver ran through his body as he studied the prince.

"I'm just going to finish up, then I'll be with you," Oscar said, trying to sound confident.

Christian smiled across the room at him. "No rush. I'm good." He held the book up for a moment, then went back to it.

Oscar's mouth twitched at the relaxed appearance of the man. He wished he could be as chilled as he was. He finished up the bins and put the cash into the safe—he'd count it after his discussion with Christian. After several inhales, he made them more drinks and carried them over to the table.

"Thanks." Christian closed the book and pushed it aside, dragging his cup closer. "I can never have too much coffee."

Oscar chuckled. "I can. That's why mine is decaf."

Christian's eyes widened. "Traitor! I don't know how you can drink that stuff. It has always tasted horrible to me."

"I can't tell the difference anymore."

Christian shuddered dramatically. "I can't even…"

Oscar laughed, knowing Christian was trying to put him at ease. "It's a good job you get the good stuff."

"I think I'd have to arrest you if you did."

Oscar paused. "Can you do that? I thought you were in the Army."

Christian paused for the briefest second that Oscar wouldn't have noticed if he hadn't been looking at him at that exact moment. A smile graced Christian's lips as he said, "I might not have the authority, but I could certainly detain you until the police got here."

"Good to know." He sipped his coffee, trying not to fidget at the silence that descended.

"I won't bite," Christian repeated the words he'd said earlier that week.

Oscar sighed and put his mug down. "I know. I find it difficult to talk about all of this, even to my friends."

"I can understand that. It's such a taboo subject in general conversation, although it's easier than it used to be." He leaned forward on his arms. "You mentioned you were a young little. Can you tell me what that looks like to you? It will help me see what your Daddy needs to be able to do."

Oscar inhaled through his nose, held it for a couple of seconds, then exhaled and took a chance. "I know everyone is different, but this is what I need. I like to spend a good couple of hours in littlespace whenever I can. It doesn't happen often because I can't always find a Daddy at The Den, but my best friend helps me sometimes." His cheeks heated.

"Your best friend?" Christian tilted his head. "Is he a Daddy?"

Oscar chuckled. "No, but he's a nanny, and he says it's no different from looking after the kids. He's happy to do it, but it's just the caring aspect, not..." He coughed, lowering his eyes as his cheeks heated further.

"Not the sexual aspect." Oscar nodded. "That's kind of him."

Oscar inhaled, steeling himself for the next part. "In private, I like to wear nappies, have baths, play with toys, have bottles..." He trailed off, shrugging.

"You like to leave the heaviness of adulthood behind and enjoy being free of responsibilities."

Oscar flicked his gaze to Christian's, eyes wide. "How did you...?"

"I'm a Daddy. The impression I get from you is that you have a lot going on in your life. You need someone to help you relax, to lower your stress levels, to care for you for a change. You need to forget about the burdens weighing on your shoulders to be able to have a clear head to continue with your adult life in the next moment."

At that moment, Oscar believed Christian was a god. There was no other way the man could understand him so well without being able to see right inside his soul. No one had ever understood him like that. No one had ever figured it out without it having to be explained in minute detail. The only person to have ever realised what Oscar needed had been Brian.

"Brian?"

Oscar frowned. "Sorry?"

"You said 'Brian.' Is he important to you?"

Oscar shook his head. "No. Well, kind of. No. He's..."

Oscar rubbed his face and inhaled. "Brian was a Daddy I met a few years ago. We only had two nights together, but he understood me like you do."

"What happened to him?"

"They transferred him to another barracks."

"He was Army?"

"Yes. It was just my luck that I found him before he moved. It has always been that way." He lifted his mug to his lips, sipping the black brew.

"You mentioned The Den earlier. Is that where you go?" Christian leaned back in his chair, a small smile playing around his mouth.

"Yes. Do you know it?"

"I do. A…friend of mine goes there often. I'm also friends with the owner."

"You know Elton?" Was there anyone this guy didn't know?

"Yes. We've spoken several times about the club. I like the place, and Elton is a good owner. He looks after everyone." Christian gulped his coffee. "So, you need someone who can give you time as a little as often as possible."

"It doesn't have to be often. Just…more than now." Oscar chuckled.

"As often as possible," Christian repeated. "Are there any hard limits?"

"No sex when I'm a little," he blurted. Oscar's cheeks heated again, and he cursed his complexion, knowing it would be visible, and rubbed at it. "It confuses me. I can't flick the switch in my head from little to being able to have sex without coming out of my space fully. It…it happened once, and it scared me," he admitted.

Christian stood and rounded the table, pulling his chair to

sit next to Oscar, and wrapped his arm around his shoulders. "Did someone force you?"

Oscar shuddered but shook his head. "No. No one forced me, but a Daddy asked if it was something I wanted, and as I'd never done it before, I wasn't sure if it was something I'd like. I told him that, and we agreed to try." He swallowed, staring at his mug. "He changed my nappy, and the minute he touched me like that, I freaked out. I kicked out, hurting him."

"That wasn't your fault, Oscar. He didn't blame you, did he?"

"No, but after that, I couldn't stand his hands on me, and he was unable to complete the aftercare. He had to call Wally —my best friend—to help because I was so shaken."

"Your head will have been trying to figure out which direction it should go in. Should it go back into littlespace, or should it go back to being an adult? This is why coming out of subspace slowly is so important."

The brushing of Christian's hands over his shoulder and back was calming, and Oscar felt his muscles relaxing. He hadn't realised he'd closed his eyes until his head rested against something warm. He pulled back, though Christian didn't remove his hand.

"Sorry. I must be more tired than I thought."

Christian smiled. "Look at me, little one." Oscar swallowed, then lifted his gaze, meeting the startlingly blue eyes. "You don't need to apologise. I'm happy to comfort you." He pulled Oscar towards him again until Oscar rested his head on Christian's shoulder. "Relax for a moment. I need to think about who I know who could help you."

Oscar remained stiff as Christian continued to rub his shoulders and back until he had no choice but to sink into his side. He closed his eyes, inhaling the spicy scent of Christian's aftershave or shower gel or something. Christian's hand moved to the base of his head and pressed into the muscles there, and Oscar groaned as his face nuzzled forward into Christian's neck.

"That's it, little one. You've had a hard day, and you need to relax for me."

Oscar's eyelids felt so heavy, as did his body, and he tried to grasp onto the thoughts that kept floating through his mind. There was something he needed to remember. The thought flitted away again, and he sank deeper into the sensations bombarding his body. He was so tired.

A firm rubbing against the base of his head brought him to the surface. The pressure moved to his upper arm, then his shoulder, then his back before returning to his head again, getting firmer each time.

"Good boy. Come back to me, little one. Slowly does it. That's it. Here's a drink for you."

Oscar felt what appeared to be a straw press against his lips, and he opened his mouth, sucking the liquid into his mouth, then more when he realised how thirsty he was. The water wasn't particularly cold, but it soothed the dryness in his mouth, and he still felt it slide down his throat and into his stomach.

"Well done, little one. Can you open your eyes for me?"

The voice was intoxicating, and Oscar felt himself responding without thought. He blinked open his eyes, and the first thing he noticed was the warmth against his side and beneath him. He wanted to sink back into it, but the rubbing on his back stopped him. He rolled his head back so he could see what he was leaning against and met a bright blue gaze.

"Hello, little one."

Oscar was startled and sat upright, almost clipping the underside of Christian's jaw. They were sitting in one of the armchairs the cafe had for those wanting to relax and read. He glanced around him, taking stock of their mugs still on the table several feet away, the bottle of water with the straw sticking out of it on the small table beside them, and Oscar sitting on Christian's lap. He scrambled to get off, but Christian's hands held him steady.

"Wait, little one. Get your bearings first."

Oscar stopped moving, closing his eyes as heat flowed through him, and he wanted to hide from the embarrassment. "I'm so sorry. I must've been more tired than I thought."

Christian smiled. "It's not a problem. I've missed holding someone like that. I don't get the chance as often as I used to."

Oscar studied him, noticing the dark circles under his eyes, the strain of his features, and wondered, not for the first time, what Christian was dealing with to be restraining his need. Without thinking, Oscar smoothed a thumb under Christian's eye and down his cheek.

"You need this as much as I do," Oscar whispered.

Christian's expression didn't change, and he didn't tense, but Oscar saw what he tried to hold back. "I don't have the ability to take care of anyone at the moment."

"Don't you need the release of being a Daddy as much as I need the release of being a little?"

Christian smiled, though his eyes didn't sparkle as they had done earlier that day. "I can manage."

Oscar realised his thumb was caressing Christian's jaw and pulled back. "I'll…" He motioned getting up, and Christian held his arms as Oscar got to his feet. He swayed a little, grateful Christian held him, then he stood tall. "Thank you. How long was I out?"

Christian rose, standing before him. "About half an hour. I didn't want you to sleep too much and ruin your night. And you're welcome."

Oscar covered his face with his hands. "I'm sorry. I didn't mean to fall asleep on you."

Christian cupped his cheek. "You obviously needed it. I'm happy to help. I have more information now, so I can find someone who could help you."

"You don't need to. I've taken up enough of your time."

Christian chuckled. "I'm happy to. I'll find someone worthy of you. Don't worry." He pressed a kiss to Oscar's forehead and strode to the table, sliding his jacket on. "I'll be in touch." When Christian opened the door, he said, "Come lock the door, little one."

Oscar hustled over and whispered, "Thank you, Christian."

Christian put his finger under his chin and lifted it slightly, then smiled and stepped back. Oscar closed and locked the door, then watched as Christian left. He rested his forehead against the cool glass and closed his eyes. What the hell had happened?

7

CHRISTIAN

Seeing the ease at which Oscar had relaxed against him reminded Christian of what he was missing. He had told Oscar he didn't have the ability to care for anyone, and it was true, but it was because he didn't want to put anyone through what he went through with his family. Nobody deserved to be subjected to his parents and siblings. And if Christian brought home a man? It was the last thing he'd ever do. His father would make sure of it.

After leaving Oscar and pushing thoughts of the man as far into the recesses of his mind that he could, he aimed for his parents' house. He couldn't call it home because it had never felt that way. The minute the butler closed the front door behind him, John called his name. Christian sighed silently and strode to his father's office. He knocked, waiting for the confirmation he could go in, then stood to attention opposite the man.

John made him wait, and Christian concentrated on his breathing to stop him from getting annoyed. Another knock sounded, and his father called for them to enter. Christian couldn't see who it was, but after a few seconds, the scent of his mother invaded his nostrils. How she could smell like vanilla and be like she was, he never knew. He understood one wasn't linked to the other, but to him, it seemed unfair that she smelled so nice when she was as evil as his father.

"Miranda, you're right on time." John clasped her hand as she came to stand beside him. "Christian just arrived home." He focused on Christian. "Now, what have you found out so far?"

Sweat gathered along his spine, but he kept his gaze above John's head. "They are preparing for a triple birthday party for Frederick, George and Patrick on 13 August. They're going to open up Windsor for the all-day event."

"All-day? What do they have planned?"

Christian stopped himself from shrugging. "I don't know as yet. There have been a few ideas thrown around, but nothing has been confirmed yet. As soon as it is, I'll let you know."

John snorted. "I bet it will have some theme or something to do with those perverting our line. They would have to make sure they were 'inclusive' to show everyone they care." John used air quotes, which under other circumstances would have been funny, but Christian held his tongue. "How Douglas, George and Henry could think it was okay to touch another man *that* way was beyond me."

Miranda patted John on the shoulder. "It won't be for long, sweetheart. Remind yourself of the future, and it will help you see past the atrocities happening now."

John smiled at her. "Thank you, dear. You're right. It makes me sick to my stomach to think of them."

"They're in love."

As soon as the words left his mouth, he knew he'd been

wrong in saying them. His father's expression soured, his eyes narrowing. "Love? Abominations like them cannot feel love. They're twisted inside, feeling things that aren't possible." John stood, rounding the desk, stepping closer to Christian. "Are you on *their* side?"

"No, sir. I was just trying to explain—"

"You don't need to explain anything. I don't want to know what *you* think of them. If it wasn't necessary to help the cause, I wouldn't have you anywhere near them. Every time you get close, I worry they will turn you. That their sickness will rub off on you. The idea that you could become one of them wears on my mind. Douglas, George and Henry have a lot to answer for, but I blame their parents. If they took a firmer hand in their upbringing, this wouldn't have happened."

Christian kept his mouth closed, staring at the wall in front of him. He was used to these rants.

"Look how our children turned out, Miranda. And Charlotte's children. With a firm hand, they can keep themselves on the right path. We will not allow those tainted ones to fester in the family for long."

Christian felt himself cracking. "What about at the club?" he asked. When his father glared at him, he continued, feeling braver than he should. "Men are allowed to play with men there. Why is that any different?"

John rounded on him, backhanding him hard enough to knock him from his position. Christian caught himself on the wall. He hadn't been expecting the hit and hadn't kept himself braced, hence why he fell. He wiped at his mouth, his fingers coming away red. He tongued the cut in his mouth, tasting the metallic liquid and stood tall once more.

"Do you dare question me?" John shouted, standing in front of him.

Christian swallowed, knowing what he did next could ruin everything he was working towards. "I don't understand how you can allow one but not the other."

John stepped closer still. "You don't *need* to understand. You need to do as you're told. The people in the club are inconsequential. The loyal members of this family don't engage in those activities."

Christian snorted. "When was the last time you visited the club?"

John stepped back, and Christian braced, knowing he was poking the bear, a phrase he found true to form when it came to his father. The punch, when it came, took the wind from him, and he braced his hands on his knees, trying not to throw up. Unfortunately, his father threw another punch, catching him on his left eye and taking him to the ground. Christian could fight back. He knew how, but what would that accomplish?

"I don't need to visit the club. My children and Charlotte's children are there enough to gather all the evidence we need to know who needs...training to become better members of the family."

John kicked him in the stomach, a move Christian hadn't been expecting. He breathed through his nose to stop the nausea. It surprised him John was taking this for himself. Usually, he called in a guard to do the beating for him. Christian must've pissed him off good.

"And Douglas, George and Henry will be the first to feel our wrath."

At that moment, Christian broke. He climbed to his feet, stood tall and met his father's gaze. There would be no going back from this, and he hoped Uncle Andrew would forgive him for ruining their plans.

"You'll have to go through me first."

John frowned at first, but Christian saw the moment he understood what he was saying. "They've got to you already. I thought you, of all people, would be able to withstand their influence."

"It has nothing to do with them. My body, my life. I'm bisexual, Father. I would love nothing more than to have my dick ramming into another man."

His heart thumped as happiness and fear ran equally through his veins. This was the first time he'd vocally acknowledged his sexual orientation. He had no idea what his father would do with this knowledge, but looking at the mottling of John's face, it wouldn't be good.

"Guards!" Christian braced himself again as two guards flew into the room. "Take him downstairs," John said.

The guards grabbed Christian's arms and wrestled him towards the door.

"You know what, John? You're trying to hang onto Charlotte's coattails, trying to grab whatever crumbs she deems you worthy to receive. You are not worthy. You are as worthless as she is, and I will make sure you go down for it!"

Christian fought the hold the guards had on him, but they were as well-trained as he was. At least, physically, they were. There would be no getting out of this unless one of them made a mistake, and it wasn't worth the man's life to make a mistake like that. Another guard opened a door for them, his eyes widening at the scene. They dragged him down the stairs to the cells they had built. He knew they wouldn't be easy to escape from, but he would try. He had to let Uncle Andrew know what had happened.

The guards threw him into a room, one purposefully putting his foot in front of Christian and making him slam into the floor, then closed the door behind them.

Christian winced as he rose and checked himself over for injuries. He had the cut lip, bruised eye and ribs from his father, and now he had a throbbing knee, cuts on his hands and a bruised jaw, if he wasn't mistaken. He had seen the cells before but had never been inside one himself. They had always excluded him from taking part in the torture his parents inflicted on the people they brought down here.

He flexed his knee, knowing it would hurt like hell to run on, but he'd do it anyway if he could. One thing the guards hadn't thought of doing was checking his pockets. He had his car keys on him, which included a lock pick, though he had little faith it would work on these particular locks. He also had his phone, but he knew he wouldn't get a signal because the walls were too thick.

He heard a noise and put the keys in the corner of the room, not wanting them to be found should they come back and search him. The door clicked, and Christian braced himself, ready to fight for his escape, but nothing happened. The door didn't open, and there was no more sound. He frowned. Was it a trick? Were they letting him think he could leave, then throw him back in again when he exited and saw guards surrounding him?

He waited, but still no sound. Stepping closer to the door, he put his ear to it, and again, nothing. He shrugged. He had nothing to lose. Pushing against the door, it slid open quietly, but nothing came towards him, so he stepped out, glancing around and seeing no one there. He had no idea what was happening, but he wasn't going to stop his attempt to escape. Going back into the cell, he grabbed his keys and shoved them in his pocket before exiting the room. There was no one he could see, and he climbed the stairs, one foot at a time, pausing each time there was a small amount of noise.

When he reached the upper door, he took a breath. This would be the trickiest part. Every guard probably knew what had happened now, and the moment they saw him, they would be after him. He needed to get to his car, which meant he needed to get to the front of the property. How he would get there unseen was another thing.

He turned the handle and pushed it open a small amount. All seemed quiet, apart from distant voices and noises from the nearby kitchen. He chose to head towards the kitchen, knowing his family rarely set foot in there, and slid out of the door, closing it behind him before turning and drifting towards the noise. When he appeared in the doorway, a man stood at the island facing him. He didn't seem surprised to see him but gave him a small shake of his head, his eyes flicking to the right.

Christian froze, stepping closer to the wall and into the shadows.

"Can I get you anything else?" the man said to someone.

"No, thank you. I'll be going back to my post now."

A guard stood and put his plate on the counter, then pivoted towards where Christian was and stalked past him without even being aware he was there. It would piss John off to know the man wasn't doing his job, but it made Christian's life easier. He didn't want to hurt anyone if he didn't have to, and if someone found out he was missing, it would end up with people being injured and him possibly dead.

Christian glanced at the man in the kitchen, who nodded and jerked his head to Christian's right. He slipped into the kitchen and to the right, where the man had indicated.

Before leaving through the side door, Christian studied the man.

"Did you do it?" The man paused, then nodded once. "Thank you. I won't forget that. What's your name?"

"Rodriguez."

"Come with me?"

The man shook his head and went back to what he was doing as Christian left the house. He crept through the gardens, keeping to the bushes as much as he could, avoiding whatever guards he came across and ignoring the pain in his body. At any other time, he would've been pissed that the guards weren't more alert, but right now, he couldn't have been more grateful. He reached the corner of the house and saw his car parked where he'd left it. He'd have to take the chance and run for it because he'd have no cover, and undoubtedly, they would see him, but if he could get to his car, he could get out of there. His parents' house had no gates keeping people out or in because they didn't believe they needed it with the number of guards they hired. Another thing that worked in his favour.

He stayed in place for several nail-biting moments, watching where the guards were, then removed his keys from his hand and got them ready. Seconds later, he sprinted across the gravel towards his car, the beep of it unlocking alerting the guards to it. It took them several seconds to react, but then they were shouting and running towards him.

He slammed his door shut, shoved the keys into the ignition and roared the engine as soon as it started. He gunned it away from the house and towards the exit, not knowing if he would make it or not. The guards had guns and could easily pop his tyres, but no guns were raised in his direction, just the guards running towards him as his car sped along the driveway and onto the main road. Why hadn't they shot at him?

The car raced forward as he gained traction on the asphalt, and he continued, putting as much distance between them as he could. He knew they would come after him, but not today.

He'd just made it to the top of the shit list.

By the time he pulled into Windsor, his body was crying at him. He could feel his ribs were bruised and see his face was already discolouring. He hadn't wanted to arrive looking like he did, but what choice did he have? He needed to speak with Uncle Andrew urgently.

Climbing out of the car with a wince, he strode towards Randall's office. The king's personal assistant would know where his uncle was. Luckily, in some ways, he didn't see anyone but household staff on his way. He knocked on Randall's office and was called to enter.

"I wasn't expecting…Good god. What happened?" Randall came around the desk to pull Christian towards a chair, but Christian stood firm.

"I need to see Uncle Andrew."

Randall nodded. "Wait here."

Randall strode for the king's office door, knocked and stepped through. Christian kept himself upright by tensing every muscle in his body, which hurt enough to keep him conscious. He had a feeling that as soon as the adrenaline faded, he would sleep for a while, but he couldn't allow that to happen before he told his uncle everything that had happened.

"Come in, Christian," Randall said, holding his arm and steering him onto the sofa. "I'll get the doctor."

"Thank you, Randall," Andrew said, coming towards

Christian and kneeling in front of him. "What happened, Christian?"

Christian snorted. "My father happened."

Andrew stared at him. "This isn't the first time he's done this, is it?" Christian shook his head. "Why didn't you tell me? I would've stopped this a long time ago."

Christian glanced at him when his voice cracked. "I could manage, and we needed the information."

"Not at the risk of your life!"

"Yes, Uncle Andrew. I'm willing to sacrifice myself to save others."

Andrew took Christian's hand. "No, you're not. Not anymore. You are not worth less than anyone else. You've taken on so much responsibility, but it's over now. You're done."

Christian shook his head. "No, I'm not. They won't stop. If anything, this will make them work faster, harder. I know things they wouldn't want me to know. I've just become their number one enemy."

"We'll get you protection, and you will stay here with us. We will beat this, Christian. I promise you."

"I know we will, but we need information, and we've just lost our spy." He frowned. "I'm sorry. It's all my fault. I couldn't keep my mouth shut this time, and it spiralled out of control. I've messed up."

"It doesn't matter. All that matters is that you're here. You're safe, and we'll get you patched up. There are other ways to get information, Christian. You don't need to worry about that."

"I told them about the birthday plans as we'd agreed, but I don't know if they will take the bait because of what happened afterwards."

"Tell me." Andrew sat beside him, keeping hold of his hand.

Christian rested his head back, tiredness wracking his body. "He threatened them, and I snapped. Told him he'd have to go through me first. He accused them of turning me against him, and I told him I was bisexual." He swallowed down the lump in his throat. "It didn't go down well because I ended up in a cell."

"And they beat you there?"

Christian chuckled humourlessly. "No, that happened before. My father is mean when he's angry."

"How did you get out?"

"A kitchen staff member let me out. They'll kill him when they find out, but he wouldn't come with me."

"We'll try to get him out." The door flew open. "Doctor, please check over Christian. Randall, could you get a room set up for Christian close to Frederick, if possible, please?"

"Yes, sir."

Andrew ran a hand over Christian's head. "You belong to *my* family now, Christian. I won't let you down like they did."

Christian closed his eyes as tears leaked from the corners of his eyes.

8

OSCAR

"**A**nd you haven't heard from him since?" Wally asked, bringing his glass to his lips.

Oscar finished his mouthful. "No. We spoke, and he said he would be in touch. How long do you think it would take to find someone?"

Wally shrugged. "It depends if he has someone in mind or if he needs to ask around, I suppose."

Oscar groaned and dropped his head back against the sofa. "Argh. I hate waiting."

Wally grinned and threw some popcorn at him. "You're so impatient."

"I know." He groaned again. "I just want to be able to live how I want, but I need someone for that."

He put his bowl of popcorn on the table and leaned his arms on his legs. He couldn't understand why he was as impatient as he was, considering he usually had a lot more. Was it because it was so close that he could almost taste it? Christian had given him hope, and he wanted it more than anything.

Wally clasped his shoulder in his hand. "You will find someone. I have faith. Not just in Christian—though why I do, I have no idea as I've never met the guy—but also in you. You might not believe in yourself, but you have people around you who do."

Oscar stood, wandering to his kitchen and grabbing a couple of beers. He passed one to Wally when he sat back down.

"Should you be drinking when you want to be little?" Wally asked.

"I don't know if I can do this today. I'm too wound up."

"Even more reason. Come on, Oscar. Let's do this."

Wally stood, taking the beer from Oscar's hand and putting them both on the table. He sat on the table in front of Oscar and held his hand, rubbing his thumb over the back of it. The soothing gesture settled him as not much else could, and he closed his eyes, letting the worries of adulthood wash away.

"Ozzie, I think it's bath time." Wally squeezed his hand and stood, pulling him to his feet. "Do you want to choose some toys to play with while I fill it up?"

Ozzie clapped and bounced on his toes, and Wally smiled, leading him to the bathroom. Ozzie loved having baths. The bubbles made mountains, and he could pretend he was Santa with a white beard. They entered the bathroom, and he dropped to his knees, opening the plastic box full of toys.

"Boat!" He waved it in the air, pretending it was bouncing over the waves. He put it on the floor and grabbed his bubble wand. "Bubbles!"

"Are you going to make bubbles for me, Ozzie?" Wally asked.

"Bubbles!"

Wally laughed. "Water's ready. Let's get those clothes off you."

Ozzie stood while Wally removed his clothes, then he grabbed his boat, bubbles and his yellow duck and climbed into the bath, the bubbles covering his tummy. He pushed the boat around. "Chug, chug." Wally sat beside him and poured water over his back. "That tickles," Ozzie said, chuckling.

"Do you want me to blow some bubbles?" Wally asked.

"Yeah!" Ozzie spun around to face Wally, water splashing over the edge of the bath.

"Woah, slow down." Wally unscrewed the bottle and pulled the wand out.

Bubbles floated through the air, and Ozzie giggled, popping them with his fingers. They were such fun to watch. "Ouch," he said when a bubble popped into his eye.

"Oh, dear. It's okay. It's okay."

"Hurts."

"I know, Ozzie. Here. Press this to your eyes." A cold flannel rested against his face, stopping the hurt.

"Out, Wally."

"Okay. Let me grab a towel. Hold the flannel on your face for a minute."

Ozzie pressed it over his eyes and sniffled.

"Is it feeling better?"

"A little."

"Okay. Take it off now."

Ozzie climbed out of the bath, and Wally wrapped a towel around him. It was warm and soft, and Ozzie snuggled inside. He ran through the door to the bedroom, laughing.

"Come back here, you little monkey."

Ozzie jumped onto his bed and bounced, holding tight to the towel. "Bounce!"

"Don't bounce on the bed, Ozzie. Come down, and I'll help you get dressed in your PJs, okay?"

"Boat?"

Wally chuckled. "You can have the boat PJs, yes."

"Yeah!"

Ozzie jumped off the bed and ran over to Wally, laying down on the mat. He wriggled as Wally dried him with the towel.

"Lift up," Wally said, and Ozzie chewed the edge of the towel as Wally put a nappy underneath him. He dropped down again and glanced around as Wally closed the sticky pads and pulled his trousers on. "Arms up." Ozzie dropped the towel, sat upright and lifted his arms. "Okay. Would you like to watch *Boss Baby*?"

"Popcorn?"

"Yes, we can have popcorn."

Ozzie stood and raced into the living room, jumping onto the sofa. He loved popcorn. It was one of his favourite foods. And *Boss Baby* was his favourite film. It was so funny. Wally came into the room and sat beside him, picking up the remote, and Ozzie cheered when the film started, then again when Wally passed him a small bowl of popcorn.

Ozzie held the bowl close, bouncing his legs and wiggling his toes. His eyes were sore, and he kept rubbing at them. Was it from the bubbles?

"Are you okay, Ozzie?"

"Eyes hurt."

"Let's have a look." Ozzie rose to his knees and looked at Wally. "Hmm. I don't think it's from the bubbles. I think I have a tired little boy on my hands. Are you tired, little man?"

"No." Ozzie sat down and crossed his arms, knocking some of his popcorn from his bowl when he did.

Wally chuckled. "Okay. If you say so."

Ozzie let his arms drop to his sides and snuggled into Wally's side, watching the TV. He yawned and blinked.

"Come on, little man. Time to wake up, sleepyhead."

Ozzie pushed away the hand on his head. "Sleeping."

Wally snorted. "Yes, you are, but we need to get you to bed. Have a drink, little man."

Ozzie pushed his hands beneath him and lifted to sitting. He rubbed his eyes, blinking several times before he could see properly. He held the cup to his lips and drank. He was thirsty. Hands rubbed his back and neck while he drank the whole cup, then he gave it back to Wally.

"Well done. Are you hungry?"

Oscar yawned and shook his head, dropping his head into his hands. Wally pulled him into his arms and kept rubbing his limbs. As Oscar came out of his littlespace, he understood more and more of what Wally was doing. This was the routine of bringing Oscar out slowly and not jerk him from it too soon. A drink and getting the blood flowing in his body. He had no idea how long he'd been there, but he was grateful as ever because he felt relaxed and energised at the same time. Not energetic enough to do anything but go to bed, but it always made him have a new lease of life.

It was the reason he wanted this more often than he had at the moment. He didn't need this twenty-four-seven, but he needed it at least weekly, and he couldn't ask Wally every weekend. It wasn't fair on him to be "working" on his day off.

Oscar let his head drop to Wally's shoulder. "Thank you."

Wally kissed his head. "You're always welcome. Do you want me to help you with getting changed?"

Oscar was over the embarrassment of his kink, and it was easy to talk about with his friends. "No, I'm good. I'll have a shower, then get into bed." He yawned again. "Are you staying over?"

Wally shook his head. "Not tonight. I have to be up early tomorrow to take Summer to her dentist appointment."

"Okay." He stood, grabbing the bowls and cups, but Wally took them from him.

"I'll do this. You get yourself into the shower and bed. It won't take a minute."

Oscar hugged him, more grateful than ever that Wally was his best friend. "Thank you."

"Not a problem. Now go."

"Yes, boss."

"Glad you're finally admitting it." Wally winked and pushed him in the direction of his bathroom.

"Night, Wally."

"Night, little man."

After his shower, Oscar snuggled under the covers with Rexie and slept.

"Holy shit," Hilary murmured. "What happened to him?"

Oscar followed her gaze and gasped when he saw Christian striding towards them, his eye and jaw covered in yellow and purple bruises. His focus remained on him as Christian stopped at the counter.

"Morning. Could I have coffee and cake, please?"

Hilary bustled behind him, but Oscar stared, following the shape of the bruises until he met Christian's gaze.

"Are you okay?" he whispered.

The corner of Christian's mouth quirked up. "I am, thank you. Sorry I haven't been around much lately. Things have been crazy. I haven't forgotten, though."

Oscar didn't need to ask what he was talking about, and he felt his cheeks heat and lowered his eyes. "Thank you. There's no rush. It's fine if you're busy. I know you must have royal duties to attend to."

Christian leaned forward, resting his forearms on the counter, winced, then stood upright again. His hand rested against his ribs.

"Go sit down and rest. I'll bring your things over," Oscar said, not wanting Christian to cause himself any more pain.

"It's okay."

"Go sit down." Christian raised his eyebrows, and Oscar flushed. "Please sit down. Let me help in the only way I can," he whispered.

"Okay."

Oscar watched him weave through the tables and settle at his usual table, then straighten with a grimace. Did he have bruised ribs as well? It certainly seemed so. What the hell had happened to him? Oscar wanted nothing more than to insist he tell him everything, but he knew he couldn't. It wasn't any of his business. They might be becoming friends slowly, but that's all they were. Oscar would never have the ear of a prince.

Hilary finished Christian's order, and Oscar carried it over. He set the tray down and unloaded the coffee and cake in front of Christian before realising there was more on the tray. He glanced at Hilary and pointed at the items. She pointed at him and mouthed, "Yours," and waved her hand. Embarrassed, he dropped his head.

"Would you like some company?" he asked.

Christian smiled. "Sure. Have a seat."

"I don't have to if you want some peace. I didn't realise Hilary had…"

"Sit down, little one," Christian murmured.

Oscar slid into the seat opposite him, pulling his cup and cake towards him. He was quiet for a moment before he peered at Christian again. "Does it hurt?"

Christian chuckled. "A little. Eating is tiresome because it makes my jaw ache, but I can manage."

"Are your ribs the same?" Raising his eyebrows, Christian tilted his head. "I saw you wince a couple of times."

"Yes. My ribs are decorated like a rainbow at present."

Oscar gasped. "Should you be resting?"

"If I didn't get out of there, I would've gone mad. I've been 'resting' for days already." He focused on his coffee, taking a sip.

Oscar bit his lip to stop from asking what happened. Instead, he used his fork to cut a piece of his cake and slide it into his mouth. The chocolate cake was delicious, and the reason he always had his supplier make an extra cake so he could take one home. He counted it as part of his wages. It didn't help that he had a sweet tooth, something his Daddy would need to help him with when he had one who stayed longer than a night.

"What are you thinking about?" Christian asked.

Oscar opened the eyes he hadn't realised he'd closed and studied him. Then he stared at his cake, pushing crumbs from one side to the other. He huffed a laugh. "I was thinking that I needed my Da…" He glanced over his shoulder. "I needed my Daddy to make sure I didn't eat too many sweet things. I have something of a problem."

Christian laughed. "Working in a cafe is probably not the best idea."

"Don't I know it. I'm sure my trousers are getting tighter by the day."

"You look fine to me. I bet being on your feet all day balances the sweet addiction. I bet it's not as bad as Henry and George, anyway."

"Why?"

Christian put his mug down and curled his hands around it. "Henry loves fudge. Any flavour, any shape. Just fudge. If he had his way, he'd eat it every day. As for George, his addiction to love heart sweets easily pays a factory worker's annual salary."

Oscar chuckled. "I don't feel so alone now."

"You'd fit right in, don't you worry."

Oscar's heart jumped with Christian's words, though he knew the prince didn't mean anything by them. There was no way he would fit in with royalty.

"I will be speaking tomorrow to a couple of people who might be interested in your...situation," Christian said. "I will hopefully have more news for you tomorrow."

Oscar swallowed hard, ignoring the pang in his stomach when he thought about someone else being with him. He couldn't have a prince. "Thank you." He drank his coffee, shoving down the feelings his traitorous body was bringing to the surface.

"What's wrong?"

Oscar glanced up. "What?"

"You seem sad. Has something happened?"

"No, nothing. I'm okay."

Christian narrowed his eyes on him, and Oscar fidgeted in his seat, wanting to make himself smaller. Not because Christian was intimidating, but because Oscar's brain was already associating Christian with being a Daddy and someone he didn't want to upset. He wanted to be good for him, even though they didn't have that type of relationship.

"Oscar?"

He lifted his gaze to where his name had been called, and Hilary waved for him. He stood. "I have to get back to work. I'm glad you're okay." Oscar stepped away but turned back when Christian said his name softly.

"I'll find someone. I promise."

Oscar sent a smile towards him, then hustled towards Hilary. "Sorry, hun."

"Don't be sorry that you're chatting away to royalty. It doesn't happen enough, especially as we work so close to them."

"Close?"

"Position wise. We work opposite their home!"

Oscar chuckled. "That means nothing. I live near a pet store. It doesn't mean I'm going to go in there just because I'm close to it."

"Aww, but think of all the cute bunnies you'd see."

Oscar opened his mouth to reply and realised she was right. "Okay. Bad example. And now you've made me need to see what they have in there. That's unkind, Hilary."

Hilary laughed. "I'll come with you, and we can get all soft over the cuteness together."

"Thanks."

He turned to serve a customer, the time ticking by. He'd just finished with an order when the door opened, and the cafe went quiet. He glanced up, his mouth gaping when

Prince Frederick came in with his bodyguards. Oscar's throat dried up, and he had no idea what to do. He stared as the heir to the throne strode over to Christian, pulled him in for a hug and sat in the seat Oscar had vacated. His bodyguards split up. One stood behind Christian's chair, near the door to the backroom. One stood beside the entrance door, and the other sat at a table close to the princes.

"Go," Hilary said, nudging his arm.

"What? No! They don't want to be interrupted by me." He transferred his gaze, his heart racing at having two princes in his cafe. He couldn't believe they'd just been talking about royalty visiting, but having Prince Frederick in there was overwhelming, to say the least.

"Oscar, Prince Christian is trying to get your attention," Hilary said.

He focused on Christian, and the man beckoned him over. "Oh, fuck. Oh, fuck. Oh, fuck. How can I meet the heir?" he whispered, his hands shaking.

"Just go."

Hilary pushed him away from the counter, and he continued moving, one foot in front of the other until he reached them.

"What can I get you, Your Highnesses?"

Christian chuckled and raised his eyebrows. "I've managed to get him to call me Christian, but the minute you show up..." He shook his head.

Prince Frederick laughed. "I can't help it." He glanced at Oscar. "Christian tells me you own this place."

"Yes, sir."

"It looks great. Could I have a tea, please?"

"Of course. Can I get you anything else...Christian?"

Saying just his name felt wrong, but he knew Christian wanted him to.

The pride in Christian's eyes made the uncomfortable feeling dissipate. "Another coffee, please, little one." Oscar gasped and glanced at Prince Frederick, then back again. "Don't worry. Trust me."

Oscar gulped but nodded. "I'll be back with your orders shortly."

"Thank you, Oscar."

"You're welcome…" Oscar bit his lip to stop the name from exiting. He had nearly slipped up and called him Daddy. What was it about the man that made him lose his head?

He returned to the counter and made the drinks, breathing deeply to stop his hands from shaking so much. The cafe had become busier, which he knew was due to the princes being there, and once he'd put their drinks in front of them, he stepped towards the bodyguard behind them and lowered his voice.

"If you feel the need to close the cafe, by all means, go ahead."

The bodyguard tilted his head and nodded, a small smile playing on his lips. "Thank you."

He glanced at Christian, seeing a smile on his face, and returned to the counter. He had never imagined one prince would visit his cafe, let alone three now, what with Prince Douglas having visited first.

9

―――

CHRISTIAN

"What's brought you out here?" Christian asked as he lifted his coffee to his mouth.

Freddie stared at him. "You need to have a guard with you, Chris," he said, voice low. "I know you're well trained, but I want you as safe as can be."

"They won't come after me. Not yet, anyway."

Christian hadn't spoken to his cousins about everything yet. Uncle Andrew had asked him to wait until that night so he could be there as well. He was sure they wouldn't be as understanding as the king expected them to be, but there was no point in keeping them in the dark any longer.

"They might, and that, as far as I'm concerned, is a safety issue." Freddie nodded towards the guard behind Christian. "Brett will be your tail from this moment forth. Do *not* try to lose him; otherwise, you'll hear from me."

"Yes, sir." The sarcasm was apparent in Christian's voice, but he smiled. "You need to chill."

Freddie chuckled. "Chill?" He gestured around them. "This is as much of a chill moment as I've had in the last...I

91

don't know how long." He took a drink, staring across the cafe. "He seems nice."

Christian glanced at Oscar. "He is. A bit lost, but he'll be fine."

"Little one?" Freddie raised his eyebrows.

Christian hid his smile in his mug. "Caught that, did you?"

"Yours?"

"No. I can't, Freddie. You know I can't." Christian crossed his arms and leaned on the table.

"Why? Your family is out of the picture now."

Christian snorted. "Do you, of all people, think that matters?" He thumbed over his shoulder. "You've just been complaining about me needing security. If you didn't think there was a problem, I wouldn't need a guard." Freddie clenched his jaw, and Christian's point hit its mark. "I'm helping him find a Daddy. I know he's not part of the club, but I want someone he can trust. He's had some shitty luck at The Den."

"Is Elton not looking after him?" Freddie frowned.

"Oscar hadn't told him."

"And you did."

It wasn't a question. Of course, Christian had spoken to Elton. He hadn't wanted to inadvertently pick the same person because some of their members visit The Den, too. Elton had been furious that he hadn't known about the behaviour and had promised he would get to the bottom of it and provide additional training for those who wanted it. It would become mandatory for those who wanted to stay as a member of the club. Christian knew Elton was a good man, but that solidified it.

"Who did you have in mind?"

Christian sat back, finishing his coffee before answering. "Noah, or possibly Carter."

Freddie tilted his head. "Noah's a good choice, although he might be out of the picture because I've noticed him with the same guy a few times."

"Shit. I was hoping he would be the best bet." He rubbed a hand over his mouth. "Any ideas?"

"You didn't like my idea, remember?"

"Freddie, you can't deny I'm right. Why would you put him in danger like that?"

Freddie leaned forward, lowering his voice, though it still whipped across the space between them. "I wouldn't put anyone in danger. You know that." He inhaled and sat back.

"I'm sorry. That was uncalled for. I know you wouldn't." Christian glanced at the counter, watching Oscar smile at the customer he was serving. His stomach fluttered when the smile was turned on him, unwittingly. He couldn't deny his attraction to the man, but did he want to put him in the line of fire?

"I wouldn't have suggested it if I didn't think you were capable of taking care of him, Chris." Freddie's words had Christian turning to him. "Yes, he might be a target, and you would need to sit down and talk to him about the situation to get his agreement before you do it, but I can see you care for him already. He's as much a target because you come to the cafe." He lowered his voice again. "Why put yourself through seeing him with someone else when it's clear you want him?"

Christian gazed out of the window, letting himself think about it. He'd taken himself out of the equation for the reason he'd told Oscar. He didn't want to put him in the middle of this...disagreement. It wasn't fair to Oscar, but with Freddie making him face it, he could admit he wanted to be Oscar's Daddy, even if it ended up being the short term until he found someone better. Was it the best idea? No. Did he want to? Hell, yes.

He refocused on Freddie, seeing the small smile on his face. "You don't need to say anything," Freddie said. "Explain the situation to him. Give him the option to say no before you take the choice from him."

Christian's body froze as emotions overwhelmed him. He'd learnt the hard way that showing emotions was a sign of weakness, and it was difficult to forget the training. A hand touched his shoulder, and he glanced to the side.

"Are you okay?" Oscar asked, blocking the customer's view of them with his body, slight as it was.

Christian blinked at him. How had he known? The hand increased its pressure, calming Christian in a way he hadn't expected.

"Yeah, I'm okay."

Oscar didn't believe him, but he nodded. "Would you like anything else?"

Freddie stood. "Not for me, thank you. I appreciate your hospitality, but I'll go so you're not inundated with people wanting to see us."

"You don't have to. You're more than welcome to stay."

Freddie smiled at him, and Christian felt himself bristle, which had him sitting back in his chair. He was jealous? Fuck, maybe now that he'd let himself think about the possibilities of him and Oscar, he was going to be this protectively jealous asshole.

"Thank you, but I have work to do, too. I will be back, though. I really like what you've created here, Oscar. Please, if you need anything at all, let one of us know. If it's within our power, you'll have it."

Oscar gasped and held up his hands. "You don't need to do that."

"I know, but you've created something special." He flicked his gaze to Christian, then back to Oscar. "That's important." He fastened the buttons on his jacket. "I'll see you soon," he said to Christian, putting his finger under his own chin and lifting slightly before turning and exiting with two of the guards. It was a similar gesture to what they did to each other, but it showed the same meaning when they couldn't do it in public.

"Wow, he certainly has a fan club," Oscar murmured as they watched several customers leave in Freddie's wake. Christian chuckled, and Oscar spun around. "Sorry, that was rude."

"Not at all. It's true. I'm sorry people are leaving, though."

Oscar waved his hand. "It's fine. You two might be good for business, but I'm happy with how it is normally." He glanced at the guard standing behind him. "New friend?"

Christian laughed and glanced over his shoulder. "Brett, meet Oscar. Oscar, this is my new tail, Brett."

Brett nodded once. "Nice to meet you, Oscar."

"Likewise. Are you allowed to sit?" He glanced between them.

"I'm allowed, yes, but I prefer to stand."

"Okay." Oscar turned back to him. "More coffee?"

"Do you know what? Yes. I haven't had the chance to read yet."

Oscar chuckled. "On its way."

Christian watched Oscar walk away and barely stopped

himself from holding him back. Why had Freddie opened the box? Now, he couldn't stop thinking about Oscar being his, and it was going to become a problem unless he decided what to do about it. It was only after he'd settled in to read that he realised he'd had an entire conversation with Freddie about being a Daddy for Oscar when Christian had never told anyone he was bisexual. How the hell had he known? And how had Christian not picked up on that until now?

He sighed. He'd get through the meeting tonight before he made any decisions about his future. The outcome of that night would determine what else happened and if Christian was allowed to stay at Windsor.

Andrew had called the meeting to happen in Freddie's living room at Windsor, and Christian knocked on the door and entered without waiting for an answer.

"Woohoo! We're up to eleven!" George shouted, throwing his arms in the air from where he sat on Timothy's lap. "The Outrageous Eleven are in session!"

Christian snorted. "You're an idiot."

"I resemble that remark," he said with a smile.

"What do you want to drink, Chris?" Patrick asked. "I might be able to find something to match your outfit." He circled a finger around his face and grinned.

"Accessories are not required. Coffee, please."

"Not drinking tonight?" he asked.

"Not yet, but maybe before the end of the night." He grinned and dropped into a chair.

"Do you know what this meeting is about?" Henry asked. "No one else seems to. Not even Freddie."

Christian considered lying, but they'd find out as soon as his uncle arrived. "Yes, I do, but we need to wait for Uncle Andrew."

He could feel Freddie staring at him, but he averted his gaze, thankful when Patrick brought his coffee. "How are you doing, Paddy?"

Patrick glared at him. He hated the name Christian called him but refused to tell him to stop, so Christian kept doing it.

"Good, thanks. Father has given me more accounts of my own now, so I'm running free." He chuckled.

"That's great news! Well done. I knew it wouldn't be long before he let you have at it. You're an asset to him, and he can see it."

Patrick smiled, though it didn't reach his eyes, and Christian wondered what secrets he was hiding. As much as the Outrageous Eleven had each other's backs, they were known to keep things quiet. Douglas had kept his help for the submissives a secret, Henry had kept his puppy and submissive side a secret, George kept his job a secret, and Christian kept his entire *life* a secret. It wasn't unreasonable to think Patrick and Freddie had secrets, too.

The door opened before he could say anything more to Patrick.

"Good evening, gentlemen," King Andrew said with a smile. He held the door, and Uncle William entered behind him. Andrew stopped and put his hands on his hips, glancing around the room. "It's nice to have you all here together."

"Would you like a drink, Father, Uncle William?" Freddie asked, wandering over to the drinks table.

"Bourbon on the rocks will do nicely, please," William said.

"Nothing for me." Andrew settled himself into an armchair next to Christian, resting his hand on his shoulder before focusing on the rest of the room. "How is everyone?"

"Busy," Patrick said, sipping his drink.

"Amazing," George replied, resting his head on Timothy's chest and gripping Eddie's hand.

"Great," Henry said, looking at Robert with a smile.

"Crazy," Douglas said, rubbing a hand over his face while Mav patted his shoulder.

"I second crazy." Freddie chuckled, handing Andrew his drink.

Christian remained quiet, knowing his answer would cause concern, though his quietness didn't go unnoticed.

Once everyone was sitting, Andrew cleared his throat. "I called this meeting because we have a few things to discuss, and I brought William in because he's been involved with some of it." He sighed. "You know what happened to Christian, but there's more."

When his cousins had found out what John had done to him, they were livid and ready to fight his corner, but Christian had held them back. They hadn't had all the information, and going off half-cocked was not the way to settle it. The first couple of days he'd spent at Windsor had been in the company of one cousin or another. He had heard nothing from his siblings and didn't expect to, but he didn't need them when he had these people.

"Do you have news about Mother?" George asked, sitting upright.

Andrew shook his head. "I'm sorry, but no."

None of them believed the bodyguard and driver were responsible for the bomb that killed the queen. Despite the police having charged and sentenced them, they knew someone else had a hand in it. Christian hadn't been able to prove anything, no matter how much spying he'd done.

"Christian has been doing a tough job these past few months, and unfortunately, it ended with what you see here." Andrew waved a hand at Christian's face, though he knew about the rest of his injuries. "That had never been my intention when I agreed to this plan. I'm sorry, Christian."

"You have nothing to be sorry for. It was my idea."

Andrew sighed and crossed his legs. "When Christian found out his parents were working with Charlotte, he approached me and explained everything. I knew some of what each of you had been through, but Christian told me everything. Every little detail." He stared at his hands as he spoke. "It broke my heart that this has been happening beneath my nose, and I knew next to nothing about it. I know Charlotte hates homosexuals and the LGBTQ+ community in general, but I never knew her hatred would cause her to turn her back on her humanity. Everything she's done..." He shook his head. "We know she's responsible for so many things, but we couldn't find any evidence." He covered his mouth, staring at the table between them.

Christian took some of the burden and sat forward. "I went to Uncle Andrew because I wanted to help. Finding out my parents were part of it made me feel sick, but I was in the perfect place to gather information."

Freddie stood. "Tell me you didn't suffer for our sake," he whispered. Damon rose and slid a hand to Freddie's nape. "Tell me we weren't the cause of these injuries."

"You weren't the cause. I was." Christian inhaled when Freddie sat again. "After dropping hints for several weeks, John finally brought me into some apparent home truths. Nothing that pointed to them breaking the law, but enough for me to understand what he wasn't telling me. After that, I contacted my old commanding officer, Neil, and explained the situation. He offered to take me back into the Army—officially, in the same position I left, unofficially, as an undercover officer."

"That's why you had more leniency," Patrick said. "I wondered why you were able to come and go a lot more than you used to. I thought they had promoted you."

Christian smiled. "As far as my family knew, my working hours were the same. I just left them to visit you lot before heading back to work."

"Sneaky." Patrick chuckled.

Andrew sighed again. "Every stone we uncovered came up as a dead end. When Christian came to me saying his father wanted him to spy on us, I agreed he could."

"What?" Freddie said.

"Christian has been passing information about our schedules to his father. We had to make it look real."

"Is that why several events were cancelled last minute?" Douglas asked.

Andrew nodded. "We gave them the information, fully expecting something to happen, but I refused to let you become the targets. Every time there was even a whiff of something at an event you were attending, I cancelled it."

"I didn't know anything about the bomb," Christian said, staring at George. "There was nothing anywhere that I found. I searched every day for something, even afterwards, but there was nothing. I couldn't pin it on them, even though I know, deep inside, they were at fault."

George climbed off Timothy's lap and dropped to his knees in front of Christian. "It's not your fault, Chris." He hugged him, and Christian inhaled deeply to stop his emotions from overflowing.

"It's no one's fault but theirs," William said. "No, we don't have any proof, but we all know it. How many incidents have there been now?"

"Five since we've been counting, but there are others we haven't been sure about but could easily be them," Christian said.

"Six," Freddie said. "Remember the helicopter crash?"

Andrew tilted his head. "That was seven years ago. They said it was a mechanical failure."

Freddie nodded. "I don't think it was. I checked that chopper over and over before I climbed into the pilot seat. You know how *anal*," he glanced at George with a smile, "I am about it. There was nothing wrong with it. When I handed the reins over to the co-pilot, suddenly, things went wrong. I wish he'd survived so we could find out the truth."

"Bloody hell. How long have they been trying to get the throne?" William asked.

"Come on, Will. You know what they've always been like. Every time we have meetings about the club, they fight tooth and nail to get things approved, then storm out when they don't get their way. Charlotte has never kept quiet about wanting to do things her way. I just never thought she'd go against us all and try to kill us." Andrew sat back.

"What happened, Chris?" Damon asked.

Christian put his mug on the table and clasped his hands, elbows on his knees. "He spoke so calmly about removing you. Permanently. I broke. Told him he'd have to go through me to get to you because I was bisexual, and if he wanted to dispose of *us*, he had to do it to his own child first."

Andrew settled a hand on Christian's back. "He beat the shit out of him, then had him locked in a cell beneath the house. Luckily, a staff member let him out, and Christian was able to escape and come to me." Andrew pressed a kiss to his head. "You're never going back, Christian. You're *my* son now."

Christian closed his eyes against the tears and lost track of the conversation. How could they forgive him?

"You don't need to be forgiven, Chris. You did nothing wrong." He peered up, seeing Freddie standing in front of him. "You are the bravest, most selfless man I know, with the exception of Father." The smile he sent Andrew was fleeting. Freddie pulled Christian to standing, cupping his head. "Thank you for everything you've done. Everything you've been through. I wish I could make it up to you, brother."

Christian's legs caved, but Freddie held him strong. The tears he'd held back for years came to the surface and dripped down his cheeks, soaking into Freddie's shirt. He'd never been this emotional in front of anyone before, but he couldn't stop himself. He'd never felt more at home than he did at this moment, and it scared him that his parents could take it away.

10

FREDERICK

Holding Christian as he broke had Freddie holding back his own tears. How could his parents be such assholes? Who would want to be so mean to their kids? It was completely unfathomable to him.

He held Christian tightly, not wanting to let him go until he'd composed himself. It was the least he could do after everything Christian had been through for them. For him. He was grateful that his *brother* was now out of that situation. It didn't matter if they'd lost something important by not having him undercover there. He preferred Christian safe with them.

Christian pulled back and wiped at his face, then Freddie's shirt. He chuckled. "Sorry."

Freddie cupped his face. "You don't need to be sorry."

He pulled away when he felt Christian's strength return, letting him sink back onto the sofa. Freddie returned to his chair and leaned back, catching Damon's gaze as their shoulders met on the narrow, uncomfortably small sofa. Damon's eyes glittered, and Freddie knew he was angry, as was Freddie. There wasn't much they could do right then. They needed to support Christian, but once they finished, they needed to figure something out. They would not let Aunt Charlotte and Uncle John get away with their treatment of him.

Damon repositioned himself until he sat sideways, with his arm behind Freddie's head. It was a position they'd taken many times, but when Damon's hand touched Freddie's neck, goosebumps travelled down his spine. It was a fleeting touch, but one that lingered.

Freddie refocused on the conversation, trying to ignore the thoughts running rampant in his head.

"What's the plan now?" Douglas asked.

"Should we concentrate on trying to find out who else could be involved with them? Do some more security checks on staff?" Patrick said.

William nodded. "I think that would be beneficial, even if it's just to assuage our fears. Adding in checks on phone calls would be good, but I know that's not allowed." William winked in Freddie's direction, and he pursed his lips to stop his smile.

Freddie knew for a fact that Uncle William had used his contacts to do that when one of his own household staff had been under investigation for one thing or another in the past, but it was all hidden tightly behind closed doors. Freddie only knew because William had needed his help.

"What about going through the events that you have booked and checking their security measures as well?" Damon said.

"Good idea." Freddie nodded. "I'd feel better if I knew everything had been triple-checked. We don't have an event planned for a while, so we have some time."

Damon moved his hand again, and Freddie shivered with the proximity. What was wrong with him? Why had he somehow become so attuned to Damon's position? They always spent time together, but now, he felt...aware, which was confusing.

They threw about ideas for a while longer, then Andrew called an end to the meeting when Christian's eyelids began dropping. George took hold of him and marched him out of the door with Timothy and Eddie beside them.

When there was only Andrew, William, Damon and Freddie left, Freddie cleared his throat.

"Can we do anything in retaliation?" he asked.

Andrew sighed. "Not really. As much as I wish I could wrap my hands around John's throat, there isn't much we can do without gaining even more backlash."

"What about stopping some of their so-called charity events?" William said.

"Maybe. Look into that, Will. Let's see if that's something that can hurt them without it becoming too obvious the reason for it." Andrew stared at Freddie. "I know you're angry and hurt, but we need to keep a level head. Charlotte is not stupid. Far from it. She doesn't seem to have any reservations about what she's doing. That makes her even more dangerous."

Freddie nodded, though he wasn't happy about it. He stood, hugging his father and uncle before they left, too, leaving him and Damon in silence. He paced the room, rubbing his hands together, his mind going a mile a minute. He made a couple more passes before Damon caught him.

He stared at him, his gaze taking in the strained lines around Damon's eyes, the grip he had on his arms, the closeness of his body.

"It's not your fault," Damon whispered. Freddie swallowed hard and shook his head, unable to say anything. "It's not your fault," Damon repeated, cupping his face, rubbing his thumbs underneath his eyes, wiping away tears Freddie hadn't even realised he'd been shedding.

Freddie closed his eyes, and Damon wrapped his arms around his shoulders and head, letting Freddie bury his head in Damon's neck. He slid his arms around Damon's back and held him tightly, trembling. This time, it was Damon holding Freddie up instead of Freddie holding Christian up.

And why did Freddie never want to let go?

11

OSCAR

Seeing Christian's blank expression had sent Oscar over to him before he realised his feet had moved. It wasn't his place to check up on him or interrupt his meeting with his cousin, but he couldn't help himself. Hours after Christian had left, he tried to work out what he was doing. Yes, he was drawn to the man, but was it because he was a Daddy and was helping him? Or was it another reason? His mind circled through the unanswered questions repeatedly until he felt like screaming. Christian had said he would speak with someone the following day, and Oscar needed to be patient.

Easier said than done.

All during his working hours that day, he was a mess. He got orders wrong, he took the items to the wrong tables, and at one point, he was aiming for the door with a tray before he realised he didn't have any outside tables. He hadn't seen Wally the previous evening and hadn't been able to get rid of his tension by being little. Hyped up and distracted didn't look good on him.

"Oscar!" He glanced at Hilary, and she pointed to the door leading to the back. "Go get some work done in your office."

"Why? We're busy."

She stepped closer. "And you're making things worse. We've had to remake more drinks today than we ever have. I say this with the nicest possible meaning…go take a break. Get some of that paperwork done that you keep putting off."

He opened his mouth to argue but stopped. "Okay." He held out the cup he had hold of. "Just a short one."

"I'll call you if it becomes too busy for us. Go." She pushed him towards the door, and he went.

When he sat in his office chair, he sighed and checked his watch. He had four hours until the shop closed. Would Christian visit him before the end of the day, or would he wait until the following day? He hadn't said what time that day he'd be talking to someone, so it could be that night, and then Oscar would've been worrying all day for nothing.

He rubbed his hands over his face and through his hair before leaning back to stare at the ceiling. Who would Christian find? He would have to be nice, otherwise, he didn't think Christian would let him help him. Christian seemed nice enough to want someone good for Oscar; therefore, the man he chose would have to be kind and considerate. It eased something inside of him to know he didn't have to find someone himself. He was so over that part of a relationship, even a solely kink relationship like this would be.

He grabbed a bottle of water from the mini-fridge and drank half of it in one go. The cold water chilled his insides, cooling the heat of his worry. Trusting in Christian was easier than he'd expected it to be, and he reminded himself he could always say no.

Opening his laptop, he logged in and diverted his attention to the stock numbers and accounts. As Hilary had so rightly said, he had enough work here to last him a month without taking any breaks. It wouldn't hurt to bury his head in it for a while.

"Boss, you have a visitor," Jonas poked his head into the office, jerking Oscar from his work.

"Huh?"

Jonas grinned and moved aside, letting Christian slide past him. Oscar's mouth opened and closed, but he couldn't say anything. Christian held a tray, and if he wasn't mistaken, there were two cups and two plates with slices of chocolate cake on them.

"Good afternoon, Oscar. I was told you might need sustenance for your brain as well as your body." Christian smiled, and Oscar was glad he was sitting down with how weak that expression left him.

"Hey," he said, trying to sound more composed than he was.

He moved a few things aside, allowing Christian to place the tray on his desk. "After your mention of loving sweet things, I thought chocolate cake might be in order," Christian said, sliding the visitor's chair closer to the opposite side of the desk.

"There's always a place for chocolate cake," Oscar replied, dropping his gaze when his cheeks heated.

"Says the little one with the sweet tooth." Christian winked, and it drew Oscar's attention to his bruises.

"How are you feeling?" He waved his hand in front of his face.

Christian tilted his head back and forth and probed his jaw with his finger. "Not bad. As with all bruises, the gentle ache when you press it is addictive." He smiled. "Please tell me I'm not the only one who presses bruises to feel them hurt."

Oscar chuckled. "The only one who would admit it, probably."

"The rush of endorphins that are released when the pain receptor activates makes it worthwhile to some. Not much different to a BDSM scene, though less intense, and I'm in control of when it starts and stops."

"Good point. What about your ribs?"

Christian laughed. "I'm fine, Oscar. I promise."

Oscar lowered his gaze again. "I don't like seeing you hurt."

Silence followed his words, and he felt the flush travel down his neck to his chest. He had no right to say such a thing, but he could hardly take it back now.

"Oscar, you—"

"Did you speak to the person you were going to?" He glanced up with a smile, interrupting the prince, not wanting to hear what he was going to say.

Christian narrowed his eyes on him, and Oscar licked his lips and focused on his plate again, picking up his fork.

"Wait for a minute, little one." Christian's voice stopped him before he speared the cake, and Oscar froze. "Look at me." Oscar inhaled and lifted his head. "Please don't interrupt me when I'm talking. I understand there are some things you find uncomfortable, but you don't need to stop me from speaking. If you don't want to talk about it, we can decide on a better way for you to express your feelings."

"Yes, D—" Oscar cleared his throat.

"Go on," Christian encouraged.

Oscar swallowed hard, staring into Christian's eyes and

seeing something he hadn't expected. He frowned, trying to understand what was happening. Why would he want Oscar to say…? His eyes widened, and Christian's mouth curled as he nodded slightly.

"Yes, Daddy," he whispered.

"Good boy. We have a lot to discuss, but for now, enjoy your cake and coffee, and tell me about your business."

Grateful for the diversion and the easy topic, Oscar ran with it. He took a sip of his coffee and ate a piece of his cake, closing his eyes as the sweetness melted on his tongue. His shoulders lowered, and he smiled. Opening his eyes, he opened his mouth, pausing when he saw the small smile on Christian's face. Oscar's cheeks heated again, and dropping his head was a temptation he could barely resist, but he inhaled instead.

"Well, the shop opened five years ago, and I've been working hard ever since."

"I can't believe this place was here, and I didn't know about it. I thought I knew about every book shop and cafe within a ten-mile radius." Christian shook his head. "When Douglas told me about it, I couldn't believe it and visited as soon as I could. This place is amazing, Oscar."

"Thank you." He forked another piece of cake into his mouth to hide his pleasure at the praise.

"What made you decide on a cafe *and* book shop. Most people decide on one or the other."

Oscar shrugged. "I couldn't decide which one to open. Few people had done this, and I wanted to see if I could make it work."

"It worked."

Oscar chuckled. "Yeah, it did."

"Adding in the library-style idea was a fantastic idea.

People are more likely to buy a book if they've read some of it beforehand and know what they're getting."

Oscar nodded. "I agree. Before I opened this place, I would go to bookshops and read the first chapter of a book before I bought it because I didn't want to be disappointed. I don't think the shop owners were happy with me, but I refused to spend money on something as important as books without being sure."

Christian threw his head back. "I can just imagine you standing for hours in the shop, flicking through pages. This place suits you down to the ground."

Oscar did drop his head at that, hiding his face in his mug. They finished their cakes while talking about the different aspects of the business. Christian had a few ideas for events Oscar could hold to increase the visibility of the shop, and a tingle thrummed through him.

"I'm sorry to bother you. Oscar, we need some help. It's quite busy now." Jonas poked his head through the door again with a grimace. "Sorry."

Oscar rose, collecting the empty plates. "It's fine, Jonas. I'm supposed to be working, anyway." He glanced at Christian. "Sorry, we didn't get to talk about..." He didn't finish the sentence, knowing Christian would understand what he was saying.

"It's fine. I'll find a book to lose myself in, and we can talk when you have time."

Jonas had disappeared, and Oscar paused before exiting the office. He bit his lip and focused on the floor, where he scuffed his shoe against the carpet. "You could come to mine later if it's easier for you?"

"Oscar, look at me." He raised his head. "You don't need to lower your eyes for me. I know you find it difficult, but I love seeing your eyes. It helps me to understand what you're asking."

Oscar got lost in the blue depths and leaned back against the doorframe.

Christian moved closer and cupped Oscar's chin between his forefinger and thumb, gaze roaming over his face. "I will stay here until you close, then you can decide what you would prefer to do. Okay?"

Oscar nodded, or at least, he tried to. Christian raised his eyebrows, and Oscar swallowed before saying, "Yes, Daddy."

Christian smiled and brushed his thumb under his lower lip. "Come on, then." He rested his hand on Oscar's lower back and led him from the office, where Oscar found Christian's guard waiting, towards the front of the shop. Oscar kept his head high, but he felt the touch all the way to his toes, even through the fabric of his shirt. Christian held the door open for him, and Oscar stepped through with a smile. They separated, Oscar going behind the counter and Christian heading for a table—not his usual one.

Oscar felt as light as the foam on a cappuccino. If he wasn't mistaken—and he hoped he wasn't—Christian had offered to be his Daddy, and his brain wanted to explode at the idea. He could tell Christian was an amazing Daddy even before they had done anything.

"How are you doing?" he asked Hilary.

She blew out a breath. "Ready for a break." She laughed. "Ever since the 'popular kids' came around, business has picked up, hasn't it?" She had tilted her head towards Christian when she'd said "popular kids," and Oscar chuckled at the idea.

"It has. People are expecting to see them, I think. It's not like they live here, though."

Hilary snorted. "Are you sure about that?" She raised her eyebrows and looked over at Christian, who had found an armchair near the bookshelves and now stared at the pages of a book.

Oscar smiled and pulled his gaze from the man, scared his emotions would be visible on his face. He focused on the next customer, smiling and chatting while he worked. The afternoon flew by, but he knew where Christian was at all times and had been sure the man's gaze had been on him several times throughout the day.

Checking his watch for about the ten-thousandth time, he saw it was half-past five, Hilary's home time.

"Go on, then, Hils. Get home to your cat."

"God, you make me sound like an old cat lady or something."

"Definitely something." He sniggered at her gasp.

"I'll get you back for that, Mr I'm-Waiting-For-Mr-Right-When-Mr-Right-Is-Right-In-Front-Of-Him."

Oscar stared at her, eyes wide. "Say that twice as fast," he murmured.

Hilary burst out laughing and drew her apron over her head. "Yeah, I was lucky it came out right the first time."

She disappeared into the back, and Oscar set about cleaning up the coffee machine. He only had half an hour until the place closed, and Sam was currently wiping down the tables and piling empty cups and plates onto a tray. As he lifted it, the tray wobbled, and Oscar flinched, waiting for the crash, but raised his eyebrows when Christian jumped up and grabbed it before it fell. Christian took it from Sam with a smile and carried it to Oscar.

"Thanks for the save," he said, sliding the tray towards him from where Christian had placed it on the counter. He transferred the contents to the dishwasher, a steady thrum of something buzzing through his body.

"You're welcome." Christian leaned his elbows on the counter. "Things were really busy for a time there. I was worried you wouldn't have enough staff."

Oscar chuckled. "We're a well-oiled coffee machine now."

"I saw that. You all work well together."

"I wouldn't still be here if it wasn't for my staff. They're the ones breathing life into my dream."

Hilary appeared through the door with her coat and bag. "I'm off. Don't do anything I wouldn't do." She winked.

"That doesn't leave me much, Hilary."

"I know! Have fun!"

Christian chuckled. "They love this place as much as you do. You can see it while they're working. There's always a smile on their faces, a quick word of hello, a longer chat if time allows, and they always do their jobs. You couldn't have picked better people."

Oscar's chest expanded with the praise, and he fought to keep the smile from breaking his face. He finished loading the dishwasher and set it going, taking the few things that couldn't be put in there into the kitchen. Jonas dragged his coat on.

"I'll see you tomorrow, boss."

"Have a good evening, Jonas."

Oscar returned to the front. Christian was behind the counter, staring at the coffee machine with a frown.

"Everything okay?"

"This lady wanted a latte to go, so I thought I'd help." Oscar glanced at the flushed face of the woman and knew having Christian make her drink could well be the highlight of her year. "The machine looks a lot different from what I use at home."

Oscar chuckled. "I'm sure it is. Here."

He stepped closer, explaining quietly what Christian needed to do while Christian followed his instructions. After laying the plastic template over the top of the cup and sprinkling the cocoa to make the shop emblem on the surface of the drink, Christian carried it over to the woman. The woman beamed and thanked him while Oscar took her payment. The smile on Christian's face sent Oscar's stomach somersaulting. More so when he turned it on Oscar.

"I'm closing up, Oscar!" Sam called.

He glanced at him, blinked and nodded. Focusing on the till, he signed it off and took out the tray.

"I just need to count this and finish up, then I'll be ready."

Christian smiled. "No rush. Are you okay if I sit and read?"

"Of course."

Oscar carried the money to the office and set it on his desk. Ignoring everything else, he concentrated on counting the money and inputting the figures into the spreadsheet. Sam came and said goodnight, then he finished up, locking the money in the safe to take to the bank the following day. Once he was sure everything had been done, he grabbed his things, locked the office door and headed for the front of the shop.

Christian was sitting in the armchair again, a book opened in front of him, but he was staring straight ahead. He must've lost himself in his thoughts because there was nothing to look at in that direction except for the lowered blinds. Oscar glanced at the guard, who stood unobtrusively to the side. The man nodded at him but didn't say a word. Oscar made a bit of noise to ensure he didn't make him jump, but all Christian did was close the book, turn and smile at him. Oscar's heart thumped painfully.

"Would you like to talk here or...?" He didn't make the offer again in case Christian didn't want to join him at home. He'd offered to have him at home because it meant he had things he could show Christian, like his toys and his "little" things.

"If the offer still stands, I'd love to visit your home."

Oscar let his smile roam free. "I'd love to show you."

Christian stood, returning the book to the shelf. "Lead the way."

"Do you have a car...a silly question." Oscar shook his head as they exited the shop.

"I do have a car parked at Windsor. If it's okay with you, I'll get it and follow you?"

Oscar nodded. "Of course. I parked my car just behind here. I'll pull out onto the road and wait for you."

Christian smiled. "I'll see you in a minute."

Oscar watched as the prince and his guard strode across the road and towards Windsor. He raised his eyebrows at the thought of being able to come and go from a castle as he did, then snorted. Shaking his head, he wandered to his car and parked on the road as he said. While he waited, he checked his phone.

WALLY: I'm free tonight if you need me.

OSCAR: I have a guest tonight, so I'll have to say no.

He chuckled, knowing that not giving Wally any more

information would drive the man nuts. Throwing his phone towards his bag, he waited until a car pulled up beside him. Oscar's mouth dropped open and, with difficulty, pulled his gaze from the beautiful sight the car was to the man grinning behind the wheel. Oscar shook his head and smiled, pulling out in front of him. He led the way home, wondering if he should be doing this. The closer he got to his destination, the more he considered the implications.

Would Christian expect them to play elsewhere? Oscar had only ever played at home or a club. Questions whirled around his head, but he shook them off. Tonight was about talking. He was sure Christian would answer all his questions before they started anything. If he hadn't read things wrong in the first place.

He needed to chill out; otherwise, he'd end up unable to think or talk about anything.

12

CHRISTIAN

Christian didn't know when he'd made the decision to become Oscar's Daddy, but Freddie's words must've hit home. When he'd thought about the Daddies he could ask, he'd found each of them wanting and couldn't fathom how they could be right for Oscar. In the end, he'd chosen to do it himself. He wanted to give Oscar what no one else had managed to. He wanted to give him the perfect experience. But to do that, they needed to talk and get on the same page.

They arrived at a small semi-detached house with a grassy front garden, and Christian parked on the road outside, whereas Oscar pulled into the driveway. There was a steady heat blooming in his stomach, and he breathed through it, calming his need to show Oscar everything at once. Christian had spent many hours playing with littles and boys and girls, helping them through the first steps to becoming their true self and being a surrogate to others who were in between Daddies. He had always felt the rush when teaching, and now was no different, except his awareness of Oscar was unusual. He could already tell when the man was upset and confused.

He watched Oscar climb from his car and glance over at him, then head for his door. He knew he wouldn't push Christian to come inside; it wasn't Oscar's way. Christian felt his mouth curve at his unintentional knowledge of the man. He'd never experienced it as much as he had with Oscar. Not this quickly, anyway. Once he'd interacted with a submissive for several sessions, then he could gain clues from their body language and words, but with Oscar, it seemed almost instinctual.

He got out of the car, locked it, and wandered to the house. The front door was almost closed but not latched, so Christian opened it and called out.

"In the kitchen!" Oscar said.

Christian wandered towards his voice, down the hallway to the back of the house, which opened into an open-plan kitchen and dining room. Oscar was standing at the counter with two mugs, pouring hot water into them.

"I wasn't sure if you were going to come in or not, but I made coffee, anyway.

"Sorry. I got lost in my thoughts."

"It's okay. You're as entitled to change your mind as anyone else is."

Despite Oscar's assurance, Christian could hear the strain in his voice. "I wasn't changing my mind." He inhaled. "I was trying to understand why I felt such a pull towards you. I've never experienced it before."

He laid it all out, knowing if he didn't, their communication would suffer.

Oscar glanced at him from the corner of his eye while he

concentrated on making the drinks. "I know what you mean," he whispered finally.

Christian waited for Oscar to finish the drinks. When he had hold of his, he said, "Where are we sitting?"

Oscar hesitated, then drifted back down the hallway to a room Christian had passed on his way in. He opened the door, and Christian gaped when he saw it. He'd been expecting a similar look to the kitchen, but this was a wonderland. For Daddies *and* littles. There was a single bed, low to the floor in the far corner of the room, the neatly made covers having stars and planets on them. Next to it was a bedside table with a lamp and a small clock with a bright sun on it—he'd seen those before. It stayed as a sun until they changed it to bedtime or naptime, and then a star came out instead. Along one wall was a cube unit, two boxes high and four boxes long, with wicker baskets in each cubbyhole. On the opposite wall was a sturdy-looking wooden changing unit complete with nappies, wipes, changes of clothes and everything else he could think a Daddy would need to take care of his little. A small two-seater sofa was under the window. Finally, there was a small set of shelves full of books and a small table and chair with colouring pencils in a pot.

Christian couldn't get over how much like Oscar the room felt. He put his drink on a higher shelf near the door and held out his arms. Oscar stepped closer, put his drink in the same place, and almost fell into Christian's arms.

"Thank you for showing me this part of you. I can tell this was a difficult thing for you to do, but I'm so pleased you found the courage to show me." He pressed a kiss to Oscar's head and tightened his hold. "Let's sit on the sofa with our drinks, and we can have a talk, okay?"

Oscar nodded into his chest, then sighed, Christian

feeling the heat of his breath and the movement of his body, and moved back. His cheeks were pink, and his bottom lip was puffy from where he must've been biting it. He curled his legs underneath him as he dropped onto the sofa, his hands surrounding the mug as if he needed the extra warmth. He didn't meet Christian's gaze once. That wouldn't do at all.

Christian sat beside him, one knee bent and resting on the seat to allow him to face Oscar. He tilted his head and studied the man. "Oscar, when you're feeling uncomfortable about something, be it the situation, the conversation or whatever, what I want you to do is take a deep breath and imagine you're in your favourite place or with your favourite people. Allow yourself to sink into the feelings of being there and knowing that you're safe. That your opinions matter. That you are wanted and loved. And once you have those feelings inside you, open your eyes and keep that feeling on the surface. No matter what your opinions are on a subject, they are valid, even if they counter what other people think or feel. Do you understand?"

Oscar let his eyes close, and Christian watched as his eyelids fluttered closed. Studying him, Christian saw the moment Oscar found his favourite memory because the tension left his body and the lines on his face smoothed out. When Oscar opened his eyes and met Christian's gaze, the serenity in them eased Christian's mind.

"Well done, little one," he whispered, leaning forward and brushing a thumb down his cheek briefly. He sat back again. "I would very much like to become your Daddy, be it for a short time or a longer period. Before we agree to this, I need to let you know about a few things that are happening which could affect you." He hated seeing the tension creeping back into Oscar's body. "There are some issues surrounding the royal family at the moment. After Aunt Louisa died, other things have happened which the media does not know about. These...problems are being handled, but it's not impossible for you to be affected by your association with me. If you don't want to be a part of this, I can find you another Daddy. I would hate for you to suffer because of me."

Oscar cleared his throat. "Can you tell me what's happening?"

Christian averted his gaze to the window. "Nothing specific at the moment. I'd need you to sign an NDA before I can give you details, but know that the media presence will increase, and they could use you to get to me. It sounds bad, and I won't sugar-coat it, but I need you to understand what you're getting yourself into."

Oscar focused on his mug, not saying anything for a few minutes, and Christian let him think. It wasn't easy to ignore the instinct to ask questions. When he spoke, Christian wasn't surprised by his words.

"Could we discuss our...relationship first? Then if we decide we're happy with it, I can sign the NDA, and you can give me more information before we agree to anything further?"

Christian smiled. "That sounds like a good idea."

Oscar's cheeks flamed under Christian's scrutiny, and he fidgeted. He inhaled and sat still again. "I've already mentioned that any kind of sex is off the cards when I'm little. I can't..."

Christian leaned forward, laying his hand on Oscar's knee. "That's fine. You know your body, and I refuse to make you uncomfortable. I don't need sex when you're little. I don't need sex at all when it comes to this dynamic. If you don't want it, you don't have to have it. No means no, Oscar."

Oscar bit his lip. "And what if I want it outside of being little?" he whispered.

Christian kept a leash on his smile. "Then that's something we'll discuss and decide together."

Oscar nodded, putting his cup onto the windowsill, then repositioning himself. "I like baths. The more bubbles, the better. I wear nappies but don't always use them. It depends how little I am."

"Okay. What is the most prevalent age you seem to be when you're little?"

"Two years old, pretty much. That's what Wally said, anyway."

"Wally? Oh, your best friend."

"Yes. I think I told you he's a nanny, and he has been helping me be little for as long as I can remember. He can't do it every night, but most weeks, he can come over for a couple of hours and give me my freedom."

"Is that how you see it? Freedom?"

Oscar nodded, gazing at him. "It is freedom. When I'm like I am now, I feel almost caged. Not in a bad way, but sometimes, when I'm coming out of my littlespace, it feels like I'm closing the door on it."

"That's a good analogy. I can understand how you see it that way. Is there anything else you don't like to do when you're little?"

"Not really. I don't go outside, except sometimes into the back garden, but that's more when I'm feeling three or four years old."

Christian loved that Oscar had different sides to his little.

It wasn't always easy to explain how they felt when they were in that space, but Oscar seemed to have a handle on it.

Christian sipped his rapidly cooling coffee. "In an ideal situation, what do you envision your littlespace looking like?"

Oscar chuckled. "You don't pull punches, do you?"

Christian smiled. "We need to be on the same page before we go ahead with this. I want to know everything. I'm curious."

That was the understatement of the century. Everything about Oscar called to him, and Christian found himself wanting to promise him the world. He had no idea why Oscar affected him as he did, but he wasn't going to look a gift horse in the mouth as Aunt Louisa would've said.

"Okay, ideally, I would like to spend a whole day as a little. I've never experienced that, so it might not be for me, but I'd like to try. I don't know if I'd transition from one age to another during that time." He glanced at Christian as if he would have the answer to that.

"Every person is different, so I can't answer that. Until we try it, we won't know. What else?"

"It would be nice to wake up as a little." Oscar frowned. "I seem to slip out of littlespace whenever I sleep, and when I wake, I'm back to being me."

Christian tilted his head. "You're still you, even when you're little, Oscar."

"I know, but I don't know how else to explain it."

"You're doing well, little one." He put his mug alongside Oscar's. "For me, I'm an extremely hands-on Daddy. I will look after you in all ways. I'll clean you up, I'll feed you, and I'll play with you. If you want to try being little outside, I can do that, too, although we would need to carefully organise it for obvious reasons. No one besides family and past partners knows that I'm a Daddy."

"I wouldn't tell anyone." Oscar's eyes were wide.

Christian repositioned himself on the sofa and held out an arm for Oscar to snuggle into his side. "I know that, sweetheart. I wasn't saying you would, but we would need to figure out what we could get away with outside."

"I'm happy staying home. I've only ever been little here or at The Den." Oscar peered up at him. "I won't tell a soul."

Christian kissed his head. "I know, but sometimes, the media doesn't give us the option of hiding."

"That's horrible. I wish they would leave you alone."

Christian smiled. "Do you have any questions for me?"

Oscar remained silent, and his hand smoothed over Christian's shirt, and Christian wasn't even sure the man knew he was doing it. He let Oscar have his silence, knowing it was how he thought through everything—though how he knew that, he wasn't certain.

"The only question I can think of is punishment. I'm not a fan of pain, so I don't really want to be spanked or anything like that. If I do anything wrong, what would you do?"

"There would be no physical punishment. I might choose a time-out type or the withdrawal of your favourite toys or TV time or something similar. I've seen and dealt with all types of punishment, but we will do whatever you think will work, and if it doesn't, I'll think of something else. No humiliation or anything like that." Christian inhaled. "You won't give me any problems, though, will you, little one? You're too excited about being free from responsibility, aren't you?"

Oscar nodded, the movement warming Christian's chest.

"I don't like being punished, but I don't know if I'll start anything if I stay as a little longer than a couple of hours."

"We'll find out as we go along. It's not something we can't discuss when it comes up." Oscar went silent again, and Christian wondered what the cause was. "Do you have another question?"

Oscar inhaled deeply. "Not so much a question. I suppose it is a question, really." Oscar gripped Christian's shirt in his fist, and Christian rested his hand on the top. "When I come out of littlespace, I sometimes have an erection. I never feel it while I'm a little, but afterwards, I do."

"Thank you for being brave enough to tell me. That must've been difficult to admit, but it means I can help. If you agree, we can deal with that however you want to. If you want to go to the bathroom and handle it yourself, or if you want me to help. Either way, there is no right or wrong answer, and there is nothing to say you can't do it one way the first time and change things each time after. The way we do things is not set in stone when we sign on the dotted line. Whenever something comes up, we discuss it and find the best way forward. There is no point in making things more difficult for both of us when words can get us where we need to be."

"Thank you."

"You're welcome. Would you like to go ahead?" Oscar nodded, his cheek brushing Christian's chest. "Okay. I will get a contract and NDA sorted out, then we'll go through it together, then we know where we stand. I will also explain what else is happening, so you can make an informed decision. As soon as we're happy and it's signed, we can decide when we'll start. And if you decide not to go ahead, that's fine, too."

Oscar pulled back, lifting his gaze to Christian's. "From what I've heard so far, I'm happy, but I know you want me to know everything."

Christian cupped his jaw. "You're amazing. Don't ever forget that."

Oscar's cheeks heated, and he tried to lower his gaze, but Christian held him in place. "I'll try," he whispered.

"Good." Christian pressed a kiss to Oscar's forehead. "I have to go, little one. Will you be okay?"

Oscar moved back. "I'll be fine."

They stood, and Oscar opened the door, resting against it while Christian exited. "I'll see you tomorrow, no doubt," Christian said with a wink.

Oscar smiled. "See you tomorrow."

"Close and lock the door, little one. I need you safe."

"Yes, Daddy," Oscar whispered.

The serenity that flowed through him at those words was almost more than he could handle, but he kept from breaking down. He didn't deserve that feeling. He waited until he heard the lock click, then jogged down the path to his car. He waved at his bodyguard and climbed in, racing off towards Windsor. He had work to do, and not all of it was to do with the man he'd left inside that house.

13

OSCAR

All Oscar wanted to do was run to the phone and call Wally, but he couldn't. Christian was a prince, and as much as Oscar trusted Wally with everything in him, he wouldn't take the chance with Christian's trust.

He picked up the mugs from the windowsill and carried them back to the kitchen. He'd expected them to have more to talk about, but Christian was right about needing to be sure about what Oscar wanted before they continued. He could mull over Christian's words tonight and have a clearer picture by morning. There wasn't much he could give Christian in return, but whatever he *could* give, he would.

It was too early to sleep, however much he wanted to, so he made a hot chocolate with cream, marshmallows and grated chocolate and settled onto the sofa in the main living room, putting a film on. He pulled a blanket over his legs, tucked it around him, then cradled the mug while thoughts of Christian swirled around his head.

Christian seemed...tired, for want of a better word. Fed up. Something was going on, and Oscar hoped he'd be able to explain it all when Oscar had signed the NDA. He hated not knowing what was wrong with him. Hated the pain in his eyes that he couldn't always hide. It wasn't Oscar's place to do anything about it, but he hoped it would ease some when they played.

Oscar frowned. Played didn't seem the right word. It didn't fit what they might have. Play inferred it was for recreation and not a serious purpose, but Oscar didn't feel that way. Being little was a way of life for him, not something that wasn't serious. He shook his head and chuckled, though there was no one with him. His thoughts were too deep, and he hadn't acknowledged the film at all.

Turning off the TV and the lights, he put his cup in the sink and filled it with water. He'd wash it in the morning. Then he trudged up the stairs. The closer he came to his bedroom, the more his body heated, and his breathing increased. Would Christian want a sexual relationship as well as a Daddy and little one? Oscar wouldn't be averse to it. Christian's body was a temple he'd willingly worship, but would it mess with everything else?

He stripped off his clothes and headed for the bathroom. He switched on the over-bath shower, stepped into the tub and enclosed himself with the curtain. The water pounded down onto his back, and he closed his eyes and lifted his head to the ceiling, wetting his hair completely. He rubbed his hands through his hair, trying to ignore the way the droplets streamed down his torso, catching on his nipples and cock. His groin tightened, and he pushed the images away, focusing on getting clean rather than where his traitorous thoughts were going.

It was no good, though. As his hands slid across his skin, it pebbled, sending electrical sparks in their wake. He glanced down at his shaft, the deep purple looking decidedly angry at Oscar's refusal to touch it. Dropping his head back again, he chuckled at where his thoughts went, then wrapped his hand around his dick, stroking leisurely despite the hissing sound coming from his throat.

He braced himself on the tiles, the cold holding him steady against the need to curl and buck into his hand. Panting, he took his pleasure higher, images of someone behind him, pounding into him while he stroked himself, taking him to the precipice. The fictional man sinking into him grabbed his jaw and turned Oscar towards him. Christian's face swam into view, and Oscar called his name as his cock spurted his release onto the tiles.

He rested his forehead and waited until his breathing had returned to normal, then washed again. A leisurely, floaty sensation followed him out of the shower and into bed. His dreams were already taking him away before his head hit the pillow.

His alarm clock woke him the next morning, and he groaned, reaching his hand out to switch it off. When he couldn't find his phone on the bedside table, he reluctantly opened his eyes and searched for it. He found it still in his trouser pocket. Switching it off, he turned to his back on the bottom of the bed and spread his arms, uncaring of the cool air brushing his skin. It might help wake him up. A morning person he was not.

His stomach complained enough to rouse him, and he stumbled to the bathroom to do his morning business, then jumped into the shower for a quick rinse before dressing and grabbing a banana to tide him over until he got to the shop.

He froze in the middle of the hallway when he remembered the conversation he'd had with Christian the previous evening. His cheeks heated when he thought of what might happen between them. Swallowing the bite of banana he'd shoved into his mouth, he bit his lip and smiled. With an extra pep in his step, he locked up his house, climbed into his car and aimed for the cafe.

He parked in his usual spot and stared at Windsor with a small smile as he wandered to the front door. He let himself in, locking up behind him as it was only seven-thirty in the morning, and got to work getting the shop ready for opening.

The morning flew by, especially as he tried to ignore the many looks Anna sent his way. He avoided her like he would avoid an author he'd given a critical review to. He couldn't tell her anything, anyway, and that would just annoy her. Lunchtime came and went, and he tried not to think about Christian and whether he would make it into the cafe like he said he would. Christian did have a life of his own.

Avoiding Anna ended when she stretched her arms from one edge of the counter to the other so he couldn't get past.

"What's going on?" she said.

"Nothing." He tried to go around her, but she wouldn't let him.

"I know something's up because you're never *this* quiet."

He snorted. "I think there's a compliment in there somewhere."

She rolled her eyes and waved her arm, allowing him through. He grinned at her and handed out the drinks he'd made. When he turned back to the counter, Christian was standing there, waiting. How had he missed him entering the shop? His cheeks heated, and he cursed his inability to hide his feelings.

"Good afternoon, Oscar," Christian said, eyes on him the entire journey from the table to the counter.

"Afternoon." He smiled. "Your usual?"

"As always. I'm nothing if not a creature of habit."

"Have a seat. I'll bring it over."

Christian nodded and settled at his table, dragging the book from the shelf beside it and opening to a page at least halfway through. How did he remember where he was without a bookmark? Did he have more information for Oscar? Was the NDA ready? He glanced at his bodyguard, who was back in his usual spot behind Christian.

He finished making the drink, grabbed a sliver of chocolate cake, and headed over to him. When he placed it on Christian's table, the man asked, "Do you have five minutes to spare?"

"Anna? Five minutes!"

"Okay, boss! I'm counting!"

Oscar rolled his eyes and sat opposite Christian. Anna could give Hilary a run for her money on who is the bossiest. "Everything okay?"

"Yes. Everything is ready for us. Unfortunately, tonight I have somewhere I need to be, but we could catch up tomorrow after you close?"

Oscar smiled, though his excitement waned a little with the delay. "Of course. We close on Sundays, too. So it can be any time."

"Fantastic. Shall I meet you at your house, say, five-thirty?"

Oscar nodded, despairing of having to wait the entire day to speak to him. "Sure."

"One minute left, boss!"

Oscar shook his head and chuckled. "I better get back to it."

"Don't work too hard."

"I'll try not to."

He strode behind the counter, and Anna hip-checked him. "Everything okay?"

"Yeah, everything's good."

The afternoon dragged, especially after Christian left, not even an hour after he arrived. When he finally settled into his office chair an hour before closing time, he checked his phone and cursed when he found several messages from Wally.

WALLY: You can't leave me hanging. Come on!

WALLY: No fair. I tell you all my secrets.

WALLY: What are you doing, Oz? Tell meeeeee!

WALLY: I'm not telling you anything anymore. You're a meanie.

WALLY: Are you okay? You never normally go this long without messaging me.

WALLY: You said you have someone coming over. If you don't reply soon, I'm going to assume you've been kidnapped and murdered.

WALLY: Seriously, Oz. Message me.

The last one had been ten minutes earlier. He immediately replied.

OSCAR: Sorry, sorry. I got sidetracked and hadn't checked my phone all day. I'm fine. Everything's fine. Are you free tonight for a movie marathon?

WALLY: Fucking hell, Oz. You scared the shit out of me. I was seriously contemplating calling the police to check on you.

WALLY: Yes, to the films.

OSCAR: Sorry.

WALLY: You should be. You will have to make it up to me by bringing cake.

OSCAR: Any preference?

WALLY: The more chocolate the merrier.

OSCAR: Understood. Let yourself in if I'm not there.

Oscar returned his focus to the spreadsheet in front of him and tried to understand what they were telling him, but he couldn't. His mind was busy with Christian and his words. What was Christian doing? He probably had some royal duties to attend to. Come to think about it, he hadn't seen Christian in his Army fatigues for a while. Did that mean he'd left the Army? He'd have to remember to ask, although he needed to be prepared for him to not answer. Hopefully, when Oscar signed the NDA, he would be privy to more information.

"It's time, boss," Jonas called.

"On my way." Oscar put the computer into sleep mode and closed his office door, heading for the front of the shop where he would take over now Anna was leaving for the night. Chloe was still working for the next half an hour, but that was it. They spent the time cleaning the tables, mopping the floor, and readying for Monday morning. Oscar had considered opening on Sundays, especially with the tourists around, but for the moment, he was doing enough, and he was making a profit. He didn't want to jinx that just yet. Maybe in a year or two, he might consider opening on Sundays, but he'd reassess the decision then.

"Have a good evening, Chloe."

"You, too, boss."

He snorted at how they all called him "boss." Hilary had started it, and everyone else had followed suit shortly after. He locked the front door, grabbed the till tray and carried it back to the office. He cashed up, switched everything off, locked up, and headed home. If he was lucky, Wally would already be there with takeaway on its way.

He *was* lucky.

"Chinese is on its way," Wally said in lieu of an alternative greeting.

"Perfect. I'm starving." Oscar waggled a bag back and forth. "I have cake."

Wally made grabby hands, but Oscar shook his head. "Not until after the Chinese. You don't let me do that, so I won't let you."

Wally groaned. "I knew that rule would come back to bite me in the ass."

Oscar chuckled and headed for the kitchen, putting the cake in the fridge and grabbing the milk. He poured himself a glass and drank it while he sought comfort in being at home and able to relax for a full thirty-six hours. The doorbell rang, but he let Wally get it, as he'd been the one to order it. When Wally brought it into the kitchen, the scent wafted towards him, and his stomach growled in response. Wally snorted. They divided the food between them—after years of similar evenings. They ordered several items off the menu and shared them, giving them a small taste of everything—then headed for the living room to eat it in front of a film.

"How about a TV show tonight? There are loads we haven't seen," Wally said.

"Which ones are you thinking about?" Oscar said around a mouthful of chicken chow mein.

"*Good Omens, Supernatural, Grey's Anatomy…*" Wally raised his eyebrows. "Tell you what? Let me scroll through the list and see what we can find."

They spent half an hour arguing over which ones were worth their time and ended up watching *Scorpion*. Oscar had watched the first few episodes before, but it had been a while.

"What made you not want your little time today?" Wally asked.

Oscar knew the inquisition had been coming, but he still had no idea how he was going to explain without explaining. Although he could tell him he signed an NDA already and couldn't talk about it, but that would give away more information than if he kept quiet.

"Too many thoughts I need to sort through." It wasn't the best answer, but it would have to do.

Wally frowned. "But that's when you need it most. We still have time if you want to?"

Oscar shook his head. "No, I'm good. I just want to watch TV tonight."

"Okay."

Oscar could tell from Wally's voice that it wasn't okay, but he knew the man wouldn't push. "Tell me about the kids. Is it still working out?"

Wally hadn't planned on becoming a nanny, but after a

friend had asked him to help as a favour until they could find someone else, he had fallen in love with the job. Oscar knew Wally was struggling a little, but it was more because he was attracted to their dad—his *single* employer. He'd kept it under wraps for the whole two years, but the strain was apparent whenever they spoke about the family.

"Yeah. The kids are growing up fast. They're going away for two weeks in August, so I won't be working. I have no idea what to do with myself." He laughed, though it sounded choked.

"We'll sort something out. I can take a day off from the cafe and leave Hilary in charge. Maybe we could go to Brighton or Southampton for a day or two."

Wally raised his eyebrows and stared at him. "Who are you, and what have you done with Oscar?"

"What?"

"You're offering to leave the cafe in someone else's hands. You haven't done that in the five years it's been open. What gives?"

"Nothing. We don't have to." Oscar cursed his inability to hide his feelings.

Wally faced him fully. "You can tell me if something has happened, you know? I'm still your best friend."

Oscar sighed. "I know. It's difficult."

"Is it to do with this *someone* you had over yesterday?" Oscar nodded. "The prince?"

Oscar snapped his head towards him. "How did you...?"

Wally grinned. "Hilary tells me everything."

Oscar rubbed a hand over his face and groaned. "She should know better when it comes to royalty." He sighed. "Yes, it has to do with Christian. I can't say anything because there's an NDA. Please don't say anything to anyone about this. The media has enough ammunition about them without adding this to the mix."

Wally's expression softened. "I'll ignore the fact that you think I would break your confidence like that. I won't say a word, you know that. Ask him to get another NDA for me if it will make you both feel better. I wouldn't do anything to hurt you."

Oscar felt like shit. "I know. I didn't mean it to come out like that. I just know how gossip can be, and words are out before anyone realises. Hilary is proof of that." He frowned. "Maybe I should get my entire staff to sign NDAs, then we wouldn't have to worry so much."

Wally nodded. "That might not be a bad idea, even if nothing comes of whatever you're talking about."

Oscar chuckled. "Sorry. I know I'm being cryptic. Let me speak with Christian first, and then I'll know exactly what I can and can't tell you."

"Deal." Wally faced forward again. "Can we start this episode again? I have no idea what's going on."

Oscar snorted. "Sure."

While Wally sorted the TV, Oscar fetched the cake, and they sat in companionable silence with the occasional comment about the programme. When Wally stood to leave, he pulled Oscar into his arms and gripped him.

"Whatever you decide and whatever happens, I'll always be here. There's no getting rid of me."

"Thanks. I appreciate that more than you know." Oscar winked. "Say hi to Donovan."

Wally narrowed his eyes. "Leave it alone, man."

Oscar smirked. "I still say he bats for our team as well."

Wally lifted his middle finger and left, and Oscar laughed. Despite his teasing, he knew Wally wouldn't do anything to rock the boat with his employer. He loved those kids as if he were their dad, and he wouldn't mess with that. Oscar wished he would take a chance, but it wasn't his place to push. Just a gentle nudge now and then was all he could do. He had his own drama to sort through and too many hours between then and Christian's visit the following day to think about the potential outcomes.

Instead of heading to bed, even though tiredness pulled at him, he snuggled under a blanket in front of the TV and put on his favourite film.

14

CHRISTIAN

"What's happened?" Christian asked as soon as he entered the room they'd been using as a hub in the barracks.

Neil, his commanding officer, Daniel, his second in command, and Gia, his tech wiz, all stared at him, and for once, he couldn't translate their expressions. He moved closer to the screen they were congregating around. He leaned down, scanning the information but couldn't understand the symbols and numbers.

"Tell me."

Daniel cleared his throat. "We've been decoding that USB you gave us. It's locations."

His stomach churned. "Where?"

"Too many to count."

Christian rubbed his forehead. "Please tell me in simple terms."

Neil sighed. "We can divide the locations into two groups. The first are places that have been known to have had incidents in the past. The second are places where no known incidents have occurred. Yet."

"It's a hit list."

Gia nodded. "It seems to be. I've cross-referenced all the known incidents, and they all happened to royal members. High up royal members."

"The helicopter accident?" Gia nodded. "The fire?" Gia nodded. "The bombing?" She nodded again. "What about the smaller incidents like Douglas's arrest or the attack on Timothy?"

"Those locations are listed, but as there are no dates or other identifying markers, we can only assume that's what they mean," Neil said.

"What are the locations of the unknown incidents?"

Gia glanced at Neil, who nodded, and she clicked a few buttons. Dozens of dots appeared on the screen. "These are the ones within the south of England," Gia said. "There are more all over the country and a few in other countries, too."

Christian stared at the screen, his hands pressed to his mouth as the full meaning of the information settled inside him. There was no way they could guess which target was next. From the locations he could see, they were places they visited regularly. It would be impossible to figure out their plans.

"Shit." He sank into a chair and closed his eyes. "It's…"

"Next to impossible," Daniel said, echoing his thoughts.

"Where do we go from here?" Christian asked, looking at his commanding officer.

Neil grimaced. "We delve deeper. Go into each incident listed here and see if there are any comparable factors. Cross-reference every detail, however minor. See if any people or companies show up more than once." He sighed. "I'll see if I can get you some more people."

Christian shook his head. "Don't bring anyone else in. It's bad enough that you three are involved. We can't put anyone else's life in danger." He exhaled the emotion too close to the surface and tried to take back control of his body. "Can you show me the locations closest to Windsor for both groups?"

Gia typed something, and the map zoomed in, stopping with the whole of Windsor in view. Dots highlighted Windsor Castle, St George's Chapel, Freddie's house, Timothy's house, Windsor College and Eton College, as well as Eddie's old house, Robert's flower shop, Mav's father's house, Eddie's cafe, and...

"Fuck!" Christian jumped off the chair and pulled his phone from his pocket. "Freddie," he said once his cousin answered, "We need to get a guard over to Oscar's house."

Freddie murmured into the background, then came back. "Done, but why?"

Christian's heart slowed, knowing his cousin would get someone over to the house as soon as possible. "There are targets painted on all our backs, Freddie. Literally. We have evidence of locations that match up with past incidents and locations that have not been hit but are close to our hearts."

Freddie was silent for a moment, and Christian gave him the space to digest the information. "How bad is it?"

"It's bad. Real bad."

"Get me a list of every single location. I'll speak with Father."

"I'll be there soon."

He ended the call and ran his hands through his hair. "This is fucked up."

"Who's Oscar? He's not listed as a person of interest," Neil asked.

Christian stared at him but said nothing. Neil's eyebrows rose, and if Christian wasn't mistaken, his mouth curled slightly.

"Understood." He turned to Gia. "Divide the list into four and send them to us. We'll get started now."

"Could you print off several copies of the complete list? I need to get them to Uncle Andrew. I'll be back after I've spoken with them."

Neil nodded, settling into a chair at a different desk. Daniel followed suit, and Gia nodded at Christian, letting him know he could collect the printouts.

"I'll be back shortly."

"Take your time, Christian. Make sure everyone is okay." Neil stared at him, understanding flowing between them.

He nodded and pivoted away. He jogged down the corridors towards the exit. His room was his first visit, and he closed the door behind him. The moment the door latched, a click sounded to his left, and he froze.

"Do you know how easy it was to get into your room, Christian? All I needed to tell them was that I was visiting my cousin because he was feeling a little under the weather."

Christian slowly turned until the gun rested against his left temple, and he could see Charles in his peripheral vision. "To what do I owe this displeasure?" he asked.

Charles smiled. "I have it on good authority that you're a loose end now. One that needs to be tied up." And he didn't mean with rope. Christian understood that.

"What are you waiting for?"

Charles chuckled. "You're really not bothered about dying, are you?"

"Nobody's dying today, Charles."

"Oh, somebody is, but it's by his own hand. Or at least, that's what it will look like. One bullet through the temple is all it will take to stop the plans from unravelling."

"You won't get out of this building if you shoot." Christian's eyes roamed the room, trying to find something he could use as a weapon.

"I won't need to. I came here to see my dear cousin because he'd been so upset about the argument with his parents. I did what I could to reassure him, but he was adamant he would take his own life. I couldn't stop him."

Charles's version of events was flimsy, but for all intents and purposes, they were family and close at that. Without evidence, they wouldn't be able to prove it. The gun pressed harder against his skin, but Christian wasn't concerned because he had a plan.

"There's one problem with this idea, asshole."

"What's that?"

"I'm right-handed. No one will believe I shot myself with my left hand."

Charles stayed silent. "You're ambidextrous."

"Am I?" He was, but if he could get Charles to doubt it, he would have him where he needed him.

Charles slid the gun across Christian's forehead as he stepped around him, intent on changing sides. Within seconds, Christian threw his arm out, grasping Charles's wrist, just below his gloves, and knocking the gun away from his head. Christian manhandled Charles to the floor with his arm twisted behind his back and rested his feet on either side of him. Charles groaned, undoubtedly in pain from the position.

"Not today, asshole," Christian said.

"You'll regret this."

He probably would, but he also couldn't do anything about what Charles had done. It was his word against Charles's because there was no video evidence. There would be no way he could prove Charles came into his room intending to kill him. The gun was free of fingerprints due to Charles's gloves, and he could bet it was either new or second-hand, so no one could say it belonged to Charles.

Charles would be going home that day, and Christian would need to be on guard even more.

"The only thing I'm going to regret is letting you go." Christian let go of Charles's arm and stepped back, sliding the gun to the other side of the room with his foot. He wouldn't be picking it up without gloves. They might be able to track it to Charles and use it as evidence, but Christian doubted it.

Charles climbed to his feet, forehead creasing as he rubbed his shoulder. "Letting me go?"

Christian smiled. "I'm not like you. I don't kill for power. I kill to protect."

The warning hung in the air, and Charles swallowed hard. Christian tried not to find that amusing.

"Leave. If you know what's good for you, you'll stop this."

Charles snorted. "Stop it? There's no stopping anything." He walked to the door, turning the handle but not opening it. "You'd be better leaving, Christian. Cut your losses and leave. If you stay…"

Charles closed the door quietly behind him, leaving Christian to mull over the words. He pushed them aside to dissect later and put a call into Neil, asking him to come to his room with gloves and evidence bags. When he arrived,

Christian explained what had happened, giving him a verbatim report of the conversation.

"Son of a bitch. Who let him in?" Neil pulled out his phone, shouting at the person on the other end to ensure the people responsible were in his office by the time he finished with Christian.

"He's ex-RAF and a prince, Neil. They'll let him here, even if they don't like the idea."

Neil blew out a breath. "You came close, Christian. This is escalating."

"It is. Let me get this to Uncle Andrew. I'll fill him in on what happened."

"Don't come back today. Stay with your family. Let us work on this information and see what we can find out."

"Yes, sir."

Christian packed a few things in his bag and headed out. As he passed Neil's office, he heard the shouting from behind the closed door and was grateful to be on the right side of it. Climbing into his car, he took a deep breath, centring himself as best he could. That hadn't been the first time a gun had been pointed at him, but it was the first time a family member had done it. He hoped the guard had already been posted outside of Oscar's house. He didn't want him to feel the wrath of Charles if he decided to take his anger to his door. He would need to remember to call him, but he didn't have his number. A failure he needed to rectify.

He started the engine and started the journey to Windsor.

"Call Gia," he told his phone, which was attached to his car speakers.

"Christian?"

"Could you find out the phone number for Oscar Hall, owner of Book Drunk?"

"Bear with me." He heard clicking in the background, then she recited the number, and he heard the beep of his phone, signalling a message had come through.

"Thank you."

He ended the call after a goodbye and dialled Oscar's number.

"Hello?" His voice was wary, as it should be when he didn't know who was on the other end of the phone.

"Oscar, it's Christian."

"Christian? What's wrong?"

Christian's shoulders lowered at his voice. "Nothing. Everything's fine. I wanted to let you know that I have requested a guard to wait outside your house."

"Why? What's wrong?"

Christian sighed and wished he could make things simpler for him. Although, maybe he could. "We've increased security across the board, and since you've been involved with us, I thought it would be better to make sure you're safe."

"Is this something to do with what you haven't been able to tell me yet?"

"It is. I promise I will give you more information this afternoon."

"It's okay. I understand."

"Is the guard outside?" Christian asked.

There was silence for a moment, then Oscar said, "I can see a black car with someone in the front seat, but I can't really see."

"That's probably them. Please don't go anywhere without a guard. Please, Oscar."

"I won't."

Christian felt the knot ease in his chest, and he sighed. "Thank you. I will be there at five-thirty."

"Take care of yourself, Christian. Stay in one piece, okay?"

"I will." Christian paused, not wanting to end the call but knowing he needed to. "I'll be there soon," he murmured.

"I'll be waiting."

Christian couldn't stop the smile from spreading across his face as he raced towards Windsor. He tried to tamp down on his feelings because he had a difficult meeting to get through before he could relax in Oscar's presence.

By the time he arrived at Windsor, he was ready for battle. He strode through the hallways and knocked on Randall's door, opening it straight away.

"He's waiting for you."

"Thanks."

Christian knocked on Andrew's door and was given the command to enter. Andrew was sitting behind his desk, and he was with Christian's group and Uncle William. It was a little cramped, despite the size of his office.

Andrew stood and pulled Christian in for a hug. "How are you doing?"

Christian snorted. "I'm better now I don't have a gun pointed at my forehead."

Voices clamoured over each other as they tried to ask questions, but Andrew held up his hands. "Stop. Let him talk."

Douglas pressed a glass into his hand, and Christian downed the whiskey without hesitation. "Thanks."

"Right, sit down." Andrew ushered him into a seat that had appeared from somewhere, and he gratefully sank into it. "What's going on?"

Christian huffed a laugh. "How much time do you have?"

He waved away his words. "We decoded the information that was on the USB you gave me."

"What was it?"

"Locations." He sighed. "Locations of past incidents and places where we congregate, however regularly or not. The team is working on comparing the information and seeing what we can come up with."

"The guard is stationed outside Oscar's house," Freddie said.

"Thanks. His house isn't listed, but his cafe is. It makes me wonder how up-to-date that USB is because it's only recently we've been visiting Book Drunk."

Douglas rested his ankle over his knee. "If the cafe is on there, it must be fairly recent unless someone else had visited without us knowing."

Mav spoke up, "From what I heard from conversations, Douglas was the first to visit, and that was only a month ago at maximum."

"Recent enough then," Christian said. "Did you ever find out who sent the USB to you?"

Andrew shook his head. "It was tested by the security team before they allowed me to have it, but they had delivered it with nothing but my name."

"We have a spy, though we don't know who it is," George said.

"Possibly." Christian wouldn't agree until he had more information. From what he could tell, the information seemed good, but until they had researched more, he was withholding his opinion.

They discussed the USB for a little longer, then Andrew turned to him. "What happened with the gun?"

Christian explained his meeting with Charles, and he could feel the tension rise in the room.

"What the hell? Why did you let him go?" George asked, flying to his feet.

"How could I prove it, George?"

"We could've spoken with him!"

"George." Andrew stood, rounding the desk and taking his son into his arms. "It's not his fault. We need to get evidence, then we can lock them up and throw away the key."

"It's not fair!"

"It's not fair, but it's not Christian's fault. It's Charles's fault. It's Charlotte's fault. It's John's fault." Andrew's voice became harder with each name he uttered. "Don't let us fight between ourselves."

"Sorry," George said to both Christian and his father.

"You're right to wonder, George." Christian gave a small smile. "I couldn't have proved he used the gun on me. No one was with us. He made sure of that."

George hugged Christian, then returned to his seat beside Timothy and Eddie, the former wrapping his arms around his shoulders. Christian looked around the room, seeing the pained expressions on his family, and wished he could do more. Life wasn't fair, as George had said.

Christian faced Andrew. "We need to figure out what events they might target and who is visiting them. We know they've tried for Freddie, Douglas, George and Henry, and that's just recently. Going through this list might show more members of the family who have had brushes with death."

"I'll get Neil onto it. He can send any information he finds directly to you and me. We have a good team working on it, Christian. We'll figure it out."

"I wish I was still in there. I could've found out more—"

"No, you couldn't. I think they suspected you all along, which was why they only gave you certain information. If they were really bringing you into the fold, they would've trusted you with more," Patrick said.

The man wasn't wrong, but it didn't appease Christian any. He needed to keep his family safe. He needed to keep Oscar safe, and he couldn't do that when he had no information to work with.

15

PATRICK

As Patrick had listened to Christian's story, he'd come to the conclusion that Uncle John and Aunt Charlotte were stringing Christian along. The information Christian had wasn't enough to do anything of consequence to the pair of them, and that was what they'd planned on. Had they been doing it just to see what they could make him do? How far he was willing to go to stay undercover? Probably.

"Any ideas on who the spy could be?" Patrick asked, glancing at his cousin.

Christian shrugged. "The guy who helped me escape, Rodriguez, could be, but I can't see how he'd get the information, to begin with. I barely saw him outside of the kitchen or dining room."

"Anyone else you can think of?"

Christian shook his head. "No one. They run a tight ship, as the saying goes."

Freddie leaned forward. "Hold on. How did Charles know you were at the barracks?"

Christian sat upright. "Either there's a tracker in my car or someone at the barracks told him."

"But it takes, what? Forty minutes to get there? More? How long had you been there?" Patrick asked.

"That's a good question. I'll ask Gia to look into it," Christian said.

Patrick checked his watch. "I'm sorry, but I need to get going. Can you fill me in later with what I've missed, please?"

"Of course, Patrick. Thanks for being here." Andrew hugged him, and Patrick left the room, closing the door behind him.

He wandered down the corridor, his mind on the conundrum that was this entire situation. When he reached the front door, a hand shot past him and opened it for him, and he glanced at Kieren.

"Thanks. Sorry. I was lost in my thoughts."

"It's fine. Would you like me to drive?" his bodyguard asked.

Patrick frowned. "If you don't mind."

"Not a problem."

They arrived at the car, and Patrick passed Kieren the keys. He slid into the front passenger seat—he never rode in the back when it was just the two of them unless he was attending a function.

Kieren left him to his musings as he drove smoothly through the streets towards Bagshot Park. He could do with talking it out with someone, but he didn't want to put the burden on Kieren. He'd signed an NDA, of course, but to have this information was dangerous to them all. He knew he could trust him, but *could he*?

"Is everything okay?" Kieren finally asked when they pulled up outside Patrick's home.

Patrick lowered his head, tapping his thumbs together, needing to feel an instrument beneath his fingertips. "Not really."

He climbed out of the car on that unhelpful phrase and headed for his music room, Kieren on his heels. Patrick entered, uncaring if Kieren stayed or went. He needed... He gazed around the room at his collection, knowing he would understand which one he wanted to play as soon as his gaze landed on it. And he did. He reached for the violin—his pride and joy, the Stradivarius.

He settled it into place, picked up the bow and closed his eyes. He played before he even knew what music he would play, the notes flowing out of him as if on autopilot. As usual, he started slowly, changing the beat with the end of each song, faster and faster until the bow and his fingers sped across the strings.

He had no idea how long he played, but when he finally stopped, he was dripping with sweat, his entire body ached, but he felt free again.

His eyes flicked open when someone took the violin and bow from his hands. Kieren. Always there, protecting him not only from outside enemies but also from himself.

Patrick tensed his legs, knowing the moment he tried to move, the pain would become unbearable. Kieren had seen this too many times to count and returned with paracetamol and a glass of water. Patrick washed them down and handed back the glass.

Kieren set it aside, then wrapped his arm around Patrick's waist. "Ready?" he whispered.

Patrick nodded and let his knees bend, thankful Kieren was there to take his weight when his legs didn't hold him up. Kieren's strength kept him from collapsing to the floor, and they made their way to Patrick's rooms. When they were locked behind closed doors, Kieren took him to the bathroom, settling him on the closed toilet seat, and began running a bath.

"Why do you do this? It's more than you're paid for."

Kieren sighed. "I don't like to see you suffer," he murmured. "Besides, the music you make is too beautiful not to be repaid."

Patrick stared at the side of his face, the strong features, the concerned expression he couldn't—or wouldn't—hide. He always went far beyond what his job description was, and Patrick shouldn't take advantage of that.

When Kieren turned off the taps, he faced Patrick. "Do you need help, or can you manage?"

"Helping anymore is far beyond your pay grade."

Kieren sighed. "Do you need help, or can you manage?" he repeated.

Patrick closed his eyes, his cheeks heating. "I need help." And those were the most truthful words he'd spoken in months.

16

OSCAR

Oscar checked out the window more times than he could count, impatiently waiting for Christian to arrive. He wasn't concerned about *his* safety, especially with the guard stationed outside, but he didn't know if Christian had been hurt, which might have been the reason for the guard in the first place.

When he saw Christian's car pull up, he raced to the door, flinging it open. Christian jogged down the path and into the house, closing the door behind him.

"Hey—" He grunted when Oscar slammed into him and threw his arms around his neck but held him tightly in return. "Everything's okay." He brushed his hand through Oscar's hair in a soothing motion.

Oscar couldn't bring himself to let go. He must've been more worked up than he realised.

"Sorry. I got worried after your call."

Christian pulled back a bit and cupped his jaw. "I'm the one who's sorry. I shouldn't have dropped the bombshell on you like I did. I should've come and explained the situation."

"It's not me I was worried about." Oscar checked him over as much as he could with how they were standing, and he appeared to be in one piece. "Are you hurt again?"

Christian smiled and shook his head. "I'm fine. I promise."

Oscar dropped his forehead to Christian's chest for a moment, then stepped back, but Christian held him. Their gazes locked, and Oscar's breathing increased as much as the butterflies taking flight in his stomach. He licked his lips, and Christian's focus dropped to them. Oscar wanted to kiss him, but he wasn't sure he could, as they hadn't signed the NDA. But as Christian lowered his head, all reasoning left.

Their lips brushed, and Oscar mewled, gripping Christian's shirt. It was the softest touch, barely there but sending sparks through Oscar's body. Christian returned, sipping gently from his upper lip, then repeating his action on his lower lip. Oscar opened a fraction, dropping his head back, and Christian gave tentative licks to the inside of his mouth. Oscar's head spun. He could do nothing but hope Christian could hold him up as the man sensually explored his mouth in the softest, most earth-shattering kiss he'd ever received.

When Christian pulled away, he gently pressed Oscar's cheek to his chest, and Oscar relaxed into him. He could feel Christian's heart racing, matching his own. If that was their reaction to a kiss, what would it be like with more? Oscar didn't think his heart could take it.

"I apologise. I got carried away," Christian's voice sounded as if he'd just woken from a long sleep.

"Don't apologise for *that*. That was..." He blew out a breath and lifted his head. "Amazing."

Christian smiled. "It was." He cupped Oscar's jaw, something Oscar had noticed he did a lot, and brushed his thumbs over his cheeks. "You make me forget myself."

Oscar covered Christian's hands, holding them to him. "I'll help you remember," he whispered.

Christian pressed another kiss to his lips, then sighed. "I've brought the paperwork, although I need to collate it again." He chuckled, and Oscar looked at the floor, seeing papers strewn across his hallway.

"Sorry." He crouched and helped pick up the sheets.

"I'm not."

Oscar glanced at him and smiled, though his cheeks heated. He hated that his embarrassment was visible and rubbed his cheek against his shoulder. He stood, straightening the paper he held.

"Are the pages numbered?"

"They should be."

Oscar handed the papers to him. "Shall we get a drink?"

"Please. I feel like I've barely had enough to keep me awake today," Christian said as they wandered down the hallway to the kitchen.

"I can imagine. You sounded busy when you rang." Oscar wouldn't push for more information until the NDA had been signed, so he concentrated on making coffee. "Have you eaten?"

"Ye… No."

Oscar glanced at him, a frown creasing between his eyebrows. "Are you okay?"

Christian blinked and refocused on him. "Yes. I hadn't realised I hadn't eaten." He rubbed a hand over his face. "It's been a day."

Oscar didn't reply. He handed Christian the coffee and drifted to the fridge, pulling out the fixings for spaghetti carbonara. It was a meal he could make in fifteen minutes, and it felt good to cook for him while Christian sorted the paperwork into the correct order. Oscar refilled his coffee once, then when the food was ready, he placed a plate in front of him.

Christian startled, lifting his gaze to him. "You didn't have to cook."

"I know. I wanted to."

"I didn't even realise you were cooking," he said in a distracted voice.

Oscar rested his hand on Christian's shoulder. "Any kind of relationship is a two-way thing, you know. I don't expect you to give all the time. You can take when you need to."

Christian covered his hand with his own and closed his eyes. "Thank you."

"You're welcome." He handed him some cutlery, and they both tucked into the food once Christian moved the paperwork aside. They made small conversation, Oscar telling Christian about his day and Christian telling him about his favourite movies. Innocuous topics until they satisfied their bellies and could move on to the subject at hand. Oscar filled the dishwasher, then sat beside Christian after replenishing their coffee.

"Let's get it done," Oscar said with a smile.

Christian chuckled and handed over the NDA. "Have a read-through, and if you have any questions, ask before you sign."

"Okay."

The information was fairly standard. He'd not had to sign an NDA before, but he'd seen one when Wally had started work as a nanny. Wally had wanted him to read it over with him to make sure he wasn't signing something he shouldn't.

This NDA seemed similar, asking him not to reveal any information that was discussed while Christian was present. There wasn't anything he thought was dishonest, so he picked up a pen and signed.

"You didn't have any questions?" Christian asked, eyebrows raised.

Oscar put the pen down again, sliding the paper over to him. "No. I've read one before. It appeared standard."

"You understood it?"

Oscar narrowed his eyes. "Yes. Why wouldn't I? It's not worded in undecipherable legal jargon."

"Sorry. I didn't mean that you wouldn't be able to understand it, but you're the first person to not have a single question about some aspect of it."

Oscar shrugged. "I'm good."

Christian's mouth curled. "Now for the fun part." He slid another set of papers towards him. "This one I want you to have questions about. Even if you think you understand something, I need you to make sure. I would hate for something to happen because you agreed to it in this contract, but you were unsure about it."

"I won't do anything I don't want to. I promise." Oscar held his gaze, hoping he showed how true his words were.

Christian nodded. "Good." He tilted his head. "While you read, can I have a look at your room again? I'd like to familiarise myself with it."

"Sure."

Christian leaned over, pecked a kiss on his lips, then slid out of the seat, disappearing down the hallway. Oscar's face felt sunburnt, and he closed his eyes and sank into the feeling of being cared for, even though they hadn't started yet. He focused on the paperwork, reading through the terms of the contract and filling out his parts, including what his hard limits were. He put a dot next to the parts he wanted to ask Christian about, which weren't many. He wasn't concerned about anything listed, and if anything, he wanted it desperately. He wanted to start that night but knew it was unlikely.

When he'd finished going through it, he picked it up and headed to his room. He stood in the doorway, watching Christian peer into boxes and drawers, a small smile on his face.

"Does he have a name?" Christian asked.

Oscar jumped, not having realised Christian knew he was there. "Um." He looked at the elephant Christian held as if it were new, then blinked and cleared his throat. "Elliot."

Christian smiled over at him, and Oscar's legs went weak. He was a sucker for a gorgeous smile, and he leaned against the doorframe to stop from sinking to the floor in a puddle.

Returning the elephant to the shelf, Christian said, "Any questions?"

"A few."

"Good." Christian sank into the sofa, resting his arm along the back of it. "Let's go through it."

Oscar sat beside him and handed over the papers. "The ones with dots are my questions."

Christian nodded and read through what Oscar had filled in, asking his own questions along the way to clarify Oscar's wants and needs. It was more than any other Daddy had ever done for him, but then if this was to be a long-term relationship, he supposed it needed more thought going into it.

"Despite what you've agreed to here, the moment you change your mind, you can say so. This isn't set in stone. If at any point you don't want to take part in an activity or anything, just say."

"Is that like a safe word?"

Christian nodded. "I would like you to have one. Is there a word we can use?"

Oscar thought about it. "Gherkin."

Christian raised his eyebrows. "I'm assuming you don't like them."

Oscar shivered and grimaced. "No. Disgusting things."

"Okay, gherkin it is." Christian checked the paper again. "Your favourite cuddly is a dinosaur called Rexie? I didn't see a dinosaur here."

Oscar's cheeks heated—again; would they ever stop—and he fidgeted. "He's upstairs."

"Do you sleep with him every day?" Oscar nodded, pulling at his cuffs. "That's nothing to be ashamed about, Oscar." Christian's hand covered his, stilling his movements and setting the butterflies fluttering again. "Will you show me?"

Oscar nodded. "I'll get him." It gave him an excuse to hide upstairs for a few minutes and gather his confidence from where he'd obviously left it. He raced up the stairs and into his bedroom, grabbing Rexie and sitting on the edge of his bed, cuddling him while he closed his eyes and regained his equilibrium. He wasn't embarrassed as much as excited. With every question, every answer, he grew closer to beginning something with Christian, and it scared him that Christian wouldn't want what he had to offer. He couldn't understand why someone like him could want anything to do with him.

"Oscar?" Christian's voice was close but not near his room. "Are you okay?"

"Yes. I'm coming back."

"Take your time. I just wanted to make sure you were okay."

Oscar closed his eyes, and tears soaked into Rexie's fur. Apart from his friends, no one had ever wanted to just "check" on him. The feelings filling his body were overwhelming, and he needed to squash them back into the box that held them when he needed to keep his cool. He wiped his face and stood, holding Rexie tight to him as he drifted down the stairs.

Christian waited for him in the doorway of his room, and the moment he saw him, he strode for the stairs and bundled Oscar into his arms.

"I'm sorry if I upset you, little one." He rubbed a hand up and down his back.

Oscar gripped his shirt. "No! You didn't upset me. Sometimes, my emotions get the better of me. They get too big, and I have to shut them back in the box. I'm so happy that you're willing to be my Daddy. I couldn't ask for better."

"Oh, Oscar. Emotions are a tricky thing, and you need to deal with them however you can, but bottling them up won't help you come to terms with them. Does being little help you work through them?"

Oscar nodded into Christian's chest. "After spending time as Ozzie, I'm able to think clearer and work through them, but as Oscar, it's more difficult."

"You have many people who rely on you, and that can be a lot of weight on your shoulders. I will do everything in my power to help you." He laid his palm against Oscar's nape, and Oscar relaxed into the hold, closing his eyes.

He wasn't sure how long they stayed that way, but then Christian led him into the room and onto the sofa, still safe in his arms. He sat against the arm of the sofa and pulled Oscar between his stretched out legs, letting Oscar curl up against his chest.

"Is this Rexie?" Christian asked, the rumble of his words vibrating through his body.

"Yes." He lifted Rexie to show him Rexie's red head, green body and blue tail. "Wally bought him for me when we first found out I enjoyed being little. He's been with me ever since."

"He's lovely. Such a special little friend for you."

Oscar beamed. "He's my best friend."

Christian smiled and ran a hand through Oscar's hair. "Are you feeling better, little one?"

"Yes, thank you."

"Did you have any other questions about the contract? I think we went through all your concerns."

"I can't think of anything else. Are we signing it now?" Oscar's stomach fluttered, and he sat upright, facing Christian.

Christian chuckled. "If you are sure, we can sign it, yes."

Oscar scrambled from his lap and grabbed the paperwork and pen. He held it out to Christian.

"Are you close to your little side now, Oscar?"

Oscar tilted his head and thought about the question. It was true that he was more playful and excitable than usual, but he wasn't completely in his littlespace either. "Kind of. Not fully there, but it's closer than normal."

"Would you like to be little tonight? You don't have to if you'd like some space to think through everything that's happened."

Oscar ignored the initial instinct to agree and listened to his body. "Can we play like I am for tonight? Not fully little, so no nappies or anything, but my older little. Just playing games with you?"

Christian nodded. "Of course, we can. Do you want me to look after you if I think you need something?"

"Yes, please, Daddy." Oscar grinned when he said it, happiness flowing through him.

"All right, then. What game would you like to play, Ozzie?"

"Mashing Max!" Ozzie stood and put Rexie on the bed, patting him on the head and whispering, "You can watch us, Rexie." He picked the game from the shelf and took it back to his Daddy. Every time he thought about his Daddy, his body felt lighter, but a thought occurred to him, and he faltered as he sat on the floor.

"What's the matter, Ozzie?"

Ozzie bit his lip. "Can I still play with Daddy Wally if he wants to? I don't want him to feel left out."

Christian reached forward, covering his hand. "If you want to, you can, but remember, Daddy Wally will be happy with whatever you choose to do."

"Okay." He smiled and emptied the box onto the floor.

"You'll have to tell me how to play. I've never seen this game before."

Ozzie laughed. "It's lots of fun. Max is always cross and tries to smash the animals who are picking raspberries. We have to keep out of his way, or we'll lose our fruit."

"Wow, grumpy Max indeed."

They played for a while until Ozzie couldn't hide his yawns any longer.

"Okay, Ozzie. It's time to get you ready for bed. You've had a busy day. Would you like a bath?"

Ozzie jumped up, knocking over the game, and bounced up and down. "Yes, Daddy! Bath time!"

"Not yet, little one. Let's tidy these games away, then we can get you ready for your water adventure."

Ozzie pouted, but with a look from Daddy, he sat down and put the pieces back into the box with Daddy's help. Daddy carried them to the shelf, and Ozzie fidgeted in his spot before racing over to grab Rexie.

"I almost forgot you, Rexie! It's bath time!"

Daddy laughed. "It is. Show me the way, Ozzie."

Ozzie grabbed his hand and dragged him towards the stairs. When they reached the bathroom, Ozzie put Rexie on the top of the toilet and dropped to his knees by his toy box.

"You like bubbles, don't you?" Daddy asked as he filled the bath.

"Lots of bubbles. I can be Santa!"

"Santa? Isn't it too early for Santa to visit?"

Ozzie chuckled. "No, silly. I'm not really Santa, but the bubbles give me a white beard."

"Ah, I see. Shall we get you out of those clothes and into the water?"

"Okay." Ozzie stood, holding his chosen toys, and dropped them into the water with a plop. He faced Daddy and held his arms up. Daddy tugged at the hem of his T-shirt and pulled it over his head. Ozzie watched the bubble mountain grow as Daddy undressed him; then, as soon as his briefs were gone, he climbed into the bath.

"Careful, Ozzie. I haven't checked how hot it is. You need to be careful you don't burn yourself," Daddy said.

"Sorry, Daddy."

"It's okay, little one. I just don't want you hurt."

Daddy stopped the water and sat on the closed toilet seat

while Ozzie played. Ozzie complained when Daddy said it was time to get out.

"The towel has been on the radiator, so it'll be toasty warm for you."

Ozzie climbed out, grinning when the towel felt like a little heater against his skin. He snuggled his face into it while Daddy drained the bath.

"Come on, then. Let's get you to bed."

17

CHRISTIAN

Christian loved how easily Oscar slipped into his littlespace. It was seamless. Not everyone could do that, but Oscar must have felt comfortable with him to be able to settle as quickly as he had, which eased something inside of him.

He rested his hand on Oscar's—Ozzie's back and guided him into the bedroom. When they entered, Ozzie wriggled onto the bed and bounced on his knees, a huge smile spreading across his face.

"We need you dry, Ozzie. You don't want to sleep in wet covers now, do you?" Christian said, opening his arms.

Ozzie almost fell into his arms, and Christian pretended to fall backwards, emitting a loud grunt.

"You're stronger than you look, little one." He grinned and rubbed his hands up and down the towel. "Come on, then."

He opened the towel and swiped the fabric over Ozzie's skin, collecting stray droplets, then wrapped the towel around him again.

"Can I have the dinosaur pyjamas today, Daddy?"

"Of course." Christian stepped over to the chest of drawers and opened the top drawer, finding underwear. The second drawer heeded T-shirts, the third trousers and the last drawers found the pyjamas. Ozzie chuckled, and Christian shook his head at him. "You just wanted me to look in all the drawers, didn't you?"

Ozzie giggled and rolled onto his back. "It was funny."

Christian chuckled and pulled out the dinosaur pyjamas. Facing Ozzie once more, he held up the clothing. "Do you want these on, or are you going to sleep in your towel?"

"Dinosaurs!" Ozzie shouted, flinging open the towel and jumping to his feet, naked as the day he was born.

Christian slung the pyjama top over his shoulder, dropped to one knee and held open the trousers. Ozzie stepped into them, wobbling when he was on one foot. "Hold on to my shoulder if you need to, Ozzie. I don't want you to fall." He pulled the trousers up and secured them around Ozzie's waist, then stood. "Arms up." The top went on easily enough, and Ozzie poked his head out with a big grin.

"Thank you, Daddy."

Christian ruffled his hair. "You're welcome. Let's get you into bed."

Ozzie clambered onto the bed, then gasped and jumped off again. "Rexie!" he called as he ran out of the room.

"Walk, Ozzie!"

Ozzie walked back into the room, clutching his T-Rex, and climbed onto the bed again. Christian thought of something they hadn't spoken about, but he didn't bring it up yet because he didn't want to jerk Ozzie out of his little time just yet.

"I'll tuck you in. Then would you like me to read you a story?"

"Yes, please, Daddy." Ozzie yawned as he answered.

"Okay, story, it is." Christian folded the cover back, and Ozzie slid underneath, blinking up at Christian as he tucked the cover around his shoulders. "Snug as a bug in a rug," Christian said with a smile. He smoothed his hand over Ozzie's head, then crouched to pick a book from the bottom shelf of a bookcase closest to the bed. He sat on the edge of the bed, and Oscar tucked the cover under his chin, probably to see the pages.

By the time Christian had finished reading *Dinosaurumpus,* Ozzie's blinking had increased, as had the length of his blinks. Christian replaced the book in its place and knelt beside the bed.

"I'm going to let you sleep, Ozzie."

Ozzie gave a barely perceptible nod, and Christian smiled. Ozzie frowned and blinked again, then the creases on his forehead cleared. Christian pressed a kiss to his temple and left the room. He entered the bathroom and set about cleaning up. Oscar's phone was still in his trouser pocket, and Christian put it in his own until he finished, then switched off the bathroom light and crept across the hallway to Oscar's room.

Plugging the phone into the charger on the bedside table, he stared at the man huddled beneath the covers, snoring lightly. He swallowed a lump in his throat as a shiver went through him at the idea of something happening to him. Was Christian selfish for wanting Oscar for himself? Should he have found someone else for him? Someone who wouldn't bring with him all the issues Christian did?

Every answer was a resounding yes, but he couldn't bring

himself to break what they'd just started. He found a note-book and pen on the shelf and wrote a brief note for Oscar to see when he woke, hopefully, in the morning. He rested it against the phone and slipped out of the room, closing the door behind him.

He descended the stairs and went through the house, checking the doors and windows were locked, tidied up the playroom and grabbed his things, including the signed contract and NDA, leaving copies for Oscar. He locked the door with a key he'd found in a bowl in the hallway—some-thing he'd have to speak to Oscar about another day—and slid it into his pocket for when he saw Oscar the following day.

Sliding behind the wheel, he stared out of the window, thinking about his options. As much as he wanted to stay away from Oscar because of everything Christian was going through, he couldn't. There was something about the man that pulled him in. From the moment he'd entered the cafe, he'd found himself mesmerised by the man who seemed to favour the colour black.

Christian shook his head and started the engine. He hadn't spoken to Oscar about the issues surrounding him, and he felt bad about that because Oscar should've had the information before he signed the contract. When they next met, he would rectify that, and if Oscar wanted him to rip up the contract, he would.

He nodded to Brett as he drove past, slowing to allow him to fall in behind him. Some of the family had the guards in the same car, but Christian liked to drive himself, and as far as he was concerned, if something happened, it was better to have another car available to leave in if one got damaged. Plus, he enjoyed having his car to himself.

He drove with no destination in mind, his mind reeling with images of Oscar and the memory of tasting his lips. He wanted more from Oscar—he could admit that to himself—but he wouldn't push. Oscar had seemed content with his kiss, but Christian refused to push his boundaries. It was another thing they needed to speak about. He was lax in his conversation skills lately, and he needed to do better. Oscar needed him to do better.

When he parked, he came out of his thoughts and found himself at the barracks. Brett parked beside him and climbed out of the car, Christian following suit.

"Sorry, Brett. You can head out if you like. I'll be fine here."

As professional as he was, Brett still made a noise of protest. "I'm fine, Your Highness. Are you working or sleeping?"

Christian rubbed a hand over his face and leaned against his car, crossing his arms over his chest. "I have no idea."

"Might I make a suggestion?" Christian nodded. "Sleep. Things are not going to get any easier. Sleep while you can. You know this better than most."

Christian nodded. "You're right. Sleep it is."

"I'll see you to your room and stay until my relief arrives."

"I'll be fine here."

"With all due respect, Your Highness, you weren't safe when Prince Charles entered your room. It was a failure on my part that I was not close enough to help."

Christian rose from his lean. "It's not your fault, Brett. We all thought I would be safe here, and I still believe that I am. I can take care of myself," He held up his hand when

Brett went to argue, "but at the very least, I can hold my own until the cavalry arrives."

Brett clenched his jaw and looked away before returning his focus to Christian and giving a nod. "You will have a guard posted outside wherever you are from this point forward."

Christian nodded. "I don't like it, but I understand. I wouldn't risk your jobs by being an asshole." He grinned and won a small smile from Brett.

"Glad to hear it."

They strode towards the room Christian used when he stayed at the barracks, and Christian had to stifle more than one yawn. He couldn't remember the last time he'd slept properly. Maybe Oscar was right. He needed to learn to take as well as give, but it wasn't in his nature. He would happily give everything he had before he'd take for himself. He was rapidly burning out, though. A quick recharge would do him good.

At his door, he turned to Brett. "I'll be up at six o'clock tomorrow at the latest. I plan to spend most of the day here, but I will head to Book Drunk afterwards."

Brett smiled at that. "Thank you for letting me know." He opened his mouth as if to say something but kept quiet.

"What?"

"I might be out of order saying this, but you and Oscar are good together. I can tell you both care for each other."

Someone else confirming what Christian felt in his bones had a warm sensation starting in his stomach. "Thank you. I wish I could save him from the potential problems of being associated with me."

"We'll keep him safe."

Christian clapped him on the shoulder, bid goodnight and

closed the door. Christian stripped, showered and fell into bed.

"Kean is having a party this weekend. Are you coming?" George said into his ear, where his headphones sat.

"What day?"

"Sunday."

Would Oscar want to come and meet his family? Christian shook his head at the idea. They hadn't even been together for more than a day, and Christian was already thinking too far into the future he wasn't sure he would have. He sighed, the negative thoughts difficult to ignore that day.

"Yeah, sure. Send me the details, and I'll be there."

"Great. What are your plans today?"

Christian currently sat at his desk in the room they were using for research. They'd been at it for hours already that day. "Working, then I'll be heading to the cafe later."

"No surprise there. You're spending more time there than you are with us. That hurts my feelings, Chris." George ruined his words with a laugh, but Christian wondered if there wasn't some truth to them.

"Sorry. I'll come to visit afterwards."

"You're not visiting. You live with us, bro. You're ours now."

Christian closed his eyes at the love in George's voice, wanting nothing more than to feel it fill every part of him that had been emptied by the treatment of his parents, but it was as if he had a barrier protecting his heart. As much as he loved his cousins, he couldn't let them get too close, afraid he would end up getting them killed.

His father hadn't stopped leaving voicemail messages for him since his escape, and he wasn't sure if the man would escalate further to get Christian in his clutches again. It was yet another reason he needed to speak with Oscar. They were no closer to finding out who or what the next target was, but some of the places had been put on alert. Christian didn't think it was enough, but until they had some sort of key to figuring out which places or people were of higher priority, they were stuck. The key they had made no sense, even filtered through the Army's computer system. Christian had been working on it for hours, trying to remember everything his mother had taught him about code-breaking. It had been something of a shock when he was younger to find out his mother was a computer expert and ex-hacker, but it was something that had interested him, and his mother had been happy to show him. This key screamed her work, but he couldn't crack it. He wasn't as good as his mother.

"Chris?"

"Huh? Oh, sorry, George. I spaced out."

George was quiet for a minute. "Have you been sleeping?"

Christian smiled. "Yes, I had a solid eight hours last night, thank you very much."

"Wow, you're spoilt."

Christian chuckled. "Don't I know it."

"Okay, I'll leave you to your work, but make sure you visit Windsor before you go to the cafe. If you go there first, you'll get distracted, and we'll never see you."

"I don't know what you mean." Christian huffed a laugh. "Okay. I'll see you at about two o'clock."

"Done."

The music turned back on when George hung up the phone, and Christian refocused on the screen. There had to be something he had missed or was forgetting. There had to be a way to figure this out. He dropped his head back, closed his eyes and exhaled towards the ceiling. The headphones were yanked from his ears.

"Christian, take a breather. You've not moved in hours."

"This needs to be cracked."

Neil glared at him. "But you won't do it when your brain is mush. Now, grab some food before your stomach eats your liver."

At the growl of his stomach, he caved and pushed away from the desk. "You want anything?"

"Coffee," Neil replied as he dropped into his chair.

Daniel and Gia had worked through the night, and Neil had sent them packing earlier that morning. If Christian knew Gia at all, she'd be back before lunch, giving her less than five hours' sleep. This code was annoying her as much as it was him.

Gia proved him right, and they worked steadily side by side until one o'clock, when Christian apologised for needing to leave.

"Jesus, Christian. Don't apologise for being with your family. I would be if I had one, as I'm sure Daniel and Gia would, too. You need to update them; therefore, why not make it a social call as well? I don't want to see you back here until zero-nine-hundred tomorrow at the earliest."

It wasn't often Neil pulled rank, but Christian understood an order when he received one, and though it would kill him, he would do it.

"Yes, sir."

Neil clapped his shoulder and pushed him towards the door. "Disappear before I find you some toilets to clean."

Christian left, finding Brett in his usual place outside the door. "You could come inside, you know."

Brett's mouth curved. "And as I've told you before, if I get distracted trying to help you figure out the stuff, I'll not be doing my job properly. Although you only have to ask, and I will help where I can."

"I know. I just hate the thought of you sitting outside." They wandered down the corridor side by side.

"Hazard of the job. I've had worse."

Brett was one of the better bodyguards he'd had over the years. He'd never had one for this long before, but he couldn't have asked for a better choice.

"Where are we heading?"

"Windsor. George has requested my presence." He chuckled to lighten the solemnly spoken words.

"It's too early for tequila, so be thankful."

"Trust me, I am."

They separated at the cars, Christian climbing into his and letting the tension seep from his shoulders. He wanted to drive and keep driving until the thoughts were all gone. Until there was nothing but the road, but he had too many responsibilities to do that. The journey was uneventful but quick, and as Christian pulled into Windsor, he smiled. His cousins made everything better, and he could do with their advice about Oscar, too.

He parked the car, waiting until Brett was by his side before entering the castle. He wasn't sure where the group would be, so he started at Freddie's room and found them causing chaos as usual.

"Christian! Settle this dispute," George said. "Gerard Butler or David Tennant?"

Christian raised his eyebrows. "Both."

"You can't… That doesn't… No! Choose one."

Christian sighed. "James McAvoy."

George growled. "Stop being annoying, little brother. Choose either Gerard or David."

"David." He tried to ignore the warmth he felt from the use of "little brother."

"Dammit!" George flung himself onto Freddie's sofa and put his hands over his eyes. "None of you have any taste."

"There are plenty of Scottish actors who are drool-worthy. Why do we have to pick?" Henry said.

"Because then we can decide what film to pick."

Christian hadn't planned on staying for the length of a film, but it wouldn't hurt. Oscar knew he'd be there. It just might be slightly later than Christian had planned.

"So, we're not choosing based on the film? We're choosing based on who's in it?" Patrick asked.

"Yep," George said, grabbing the remote. "Freddie, Henry and now, Christian have chosen David. I want Gerard. You, Douglas and Mav have to decide."

"What are the films?" Patrick asked.

"We've not decided on which of their films we're watching. We'll decide once we have a winning actor."

Patrick tapped his thumbs together, his forehead creasing, then he said, "Gerard."

"Whoop!" George lifted a fist in the air. "Now, to get Douglas and Mav on our side."

"Your side for what?" Douglas said as he entered, holding the door for Mav.

George jumped up and raced to stop them from going any

further. "Choose a favourite actor out of David Tennant or Gerard Butler."

Douglas glanced at Mav with his eyebrows raised. Mav's cheeks flushed, and he cleared his throat. "Gerard Butler," he said.

Douglas smirked. "A quiet fan, but watching a film of his makes him thrilled to go back to our room." He winked and slid his arm around Mav's shoulder, earning a punch in his ribs for his effort. "What? It's true!" he said as Mav skirted around him and plopped down beside Christian. "Thanks for that," he said to George.

"You're the tie-breaker, Douglas. Who?"

Douglas put his hands on his hips. "Did you not hear my answer?"

George frowned. "You didn't say who."

"Well, put it this way. If you had a partner who enjoyed watching a film with a specific actor, which would *you* choose?"

George grinned. "Yes! Gerard Butler for the win!"

Freddie and Henry groaned, and Christian glanced around the room. "Where's Damon?" It was unusual for him to be somewhere Freddie was not.

"He had a family thing," Freddie said, rising and heading for the drinks table. "Drinks, anyone?"

Christian frowned at Freddie's tension, but he wouldn't bring it up now. He'd corner him later, as Freddie always did with him. If he could help his cousin with anything, he would. After all, they were his family.

18

GEORGE

There was so much tension running rampant around them at the moment that George wanted to do something fun for a change. Other than for their usual working hours, they hadn't been to the club. They hadn't been to The Den. They hadn't even had any royal events to attend, so it had been boring, to say the least. The current issues notwithstanding.

He'd put together this movie afternoon because they all needed some reprieve from the state of their family. Some of them more than others. He glanced at Freddie, who appeared like he'd lost his arm because Damon wasn't there, and Christian, who had been through hell.

"Okay. As we have a winning actor—my hero—we need to choose one of his films. The choices are *Geostorm, Olympus Has Fallen, Law Abiding Citizen* or *The Ugly Truth.* Cast your votes now."

He held up the first and received two hands, the second received six hands, the third received five hands and the final received one.

"I can't believe no one wants to see *The Ugly Truth* but me. You're all idiots." He grinned as he set *Olympus Has Fallen* to play. Once he'd done that, he strode for the table where he'd requested the household staff bring snacks and drinks for them to have during their movie. "Henry, heads up!" He threw a packet of fudge over everyone's heads, straight into Henry's waiting hands. "Douglas, my man." He threw a packet of cheesy crisps and a dip towards him. "Mav, yours will be here soon, as will Robert's and boyfriend number 2." He winked at Timothy—he never gave them the same number each time because one was not more important than the other.

He checked what they had left and grabbed the tray with three slices of chocolate cake on it, passing a plate each to Eddie, Christian and Patrick. Followed by some chocolate spread and breadsticks for Freddie. When he'd finished dealing out snacks, he grabbed two tubes of love heart sweets and wedged himself between Timothy and Eddie.

They were fifteen minutes into the film when someone rapped on the door. Patrick stood and opened it, taking the tray from the household staff member with a smile.

"Pizza, Chinese food and cheesy chips. Are you trying to fatten us up, George?"

"All the better to eat you, my dear," George growled.

Everyone laughed, and the sound lifted George's spirits. Patrick passed around the food, and everyone took what they wanted. Eddie snuggled into his side, and he slid his arm around him, Timothy doing the same around George's back to hold them both.

Despite the problems they were facing, they were together. The Outrageous Eleven were here, all in one room. Then he had a thought.

"Oh, for fuck's sake," he said, glaring at Christian.

"What did I do?"

"I have to think up *another* name for us now."

Christian raised his eyebrows. "Huh?"

"We're adding Oscar into the mix, so we'll now be twelve. Bloody hell."

Christian snickered, and George threw a chip at him. He didn't mind, really. He enjoyed trying to figure out the best names for them. The Outrageous Eleven had worked well while they needed it, but now they needed a new, more powerful name.

"Twirling?" Eddie whispered. "Twiddling?" He giggled.

George laughed. "The Twiddling Twelve? I don't think that sounds quite right coming from us."

"Does it have to start with 'TW?'" Mav asked.

"Not necessarily."

"What about tantalising?"

"The Tantalising Twelve." George nodded. "I like it. Fits in with our niche. It'll work unless someone thinks of a better one."

"I thought that was your job?" Freddie asked.

"Nah, I'm holding out for a replacement," he joked. "Seems like Mav is up for it. We'll need at least two more added to the list when Patrick and Freddie find their partners."

Patrick held up his hand. "I'm happy staying as I am, George. Don't count on me to increase our numbers."

"That's what we all said," Douglas said, kissing Mav on the cheek.

"Everyone falls at some point," Robert said. "There's no disrespecting fate. You'll have no choice in the matter."

George grinned. He couldn't wait to see his brother and

his cousin fall. They might think they were immune, but soon enough, they'd find someone or several someone's to knock their socks off.

19

OSCAR

Oscar couldn't get the words out of his mind. Christian's note had been sweet, and Oscar smiled every time he thought about it.

Little one,

Thank you for an amazing evening. I'm so happy that you are comfortable enough to relax in my presence. I will check the house and lock everything up before I leave. I'm sorry I didn't say goodbye before I left, but you looked so adorably peaceful that I couldn't bring myself to disturb you. I will visit the cafe tomorrow, but I have work, and I won't be able to come until late afternoon. Make sure you have a healthy, filling breakfast before work. Don't wait for the cake or muffins from the bakery. I'll see you very soon.

C x

When he'd woken that morning, a sense of peace had fallen over him. It wasn't often he'd fall asleep as Ozzie and woke as Oscar. If he slept while Wally was looking after him, he woke as Ozzie and played longer, then went to bed as Oscar once he was out of his littlespace. It had been refreshing to his brain, and he'd slept better than he had for a long time.

He leaned on the counter, drinking his coffee, watching the customers chatting, reading and eating. Contentedness spread through him at what he'd achieved, and the reminder was good for him. He spent many hours thinking about what he could do better when, in fact, he had already done something amazing. He was self-employed and making a decent profit. What more could he ask for?

In the late afternoon, he couldn't keep his gaze from straying to the door and windows every few minutes, awaiting his Daddy to arrive. He noticed him walking down the road from the castle with his bodyguard and couldn't help but smile.

"I assume he's here," Hilary snorted.

"Shut up," he replied.

Christian and Brett entered the cafe, and Christian's gaze immediately found his own. A flush started at Oscar's toes and spread higher until he felt breathless with want. He wanted to kiss him but knew he couldn't. When Christian stopped in front of him, Oscar was mesmerised by the spark in his eyes. He inhaled deeply.

"Your usual?" he croaked.

"Please." Christian's voice was rough.

"Brett, would you like a drink?"

"No, thank you," the bodyguard answered.

Oscar tore his gaze from Christian and turned his back, slowly exhaling to stop from going lightheaded. He focused on making the drink, then placed it on the counter and slid it across towards Christian. The prince caught his fingers and squeezed them before letting go. Oscar licked his dry lips and swallowed.

"Anything else?"

"Cake?"

Oscar smiled. "Of course. Chocolate, carrot or red velvet?"

Christian's forehead creased, and he pursed his lips, a picture-perfect rendition of something thinking about a tricky question. "I might try the red velvet today."

Picking up a plate, he slid open the glass case and lifted a slice of cake, placing it on the plate. "Enjoy," he said, sending that across the counter, too.

"I plan to." Christian's gaze didn't leave his.

"Do you want privacy today, or are you sitting in your usual seat?"

"I'll lose myself in a book while you're working." Christian smiled.

"I put a stool in the corner for you, Brett."

Christian and Brett glanced over to the table Christian used and the stool that now stood waiting for the bodyguard.

"You didn't have to, but thank you."

"No point making your legs ache when you might need them for…" He stopped, not wanting to think why he might want to save his energy.

Christian covered his hand, smoothing his fingers over the back of it and along his fingers until he let go again. "Don't worry. He's good. We're good." Christian dropped his head forward, keeping his eyes on Oscar.

Oscar nodded. "Okay."

Christian smiled and grabbed the cup and plate, and headed for his table. Oscar watched as Brett took a perch on the stool, then winked in Oscar's direction. Oscar coughed to hide his grin and turned to the coffee machine.

"You'll break your cheeks if you smile much more," Hilary said, sidling up beside him and nudging his shoulder with hers.

Oscar shoved her back, chuckling. "It's not against the rules to smile."

She rested her arm around his shoulders and pulled him closer. "I'm not complaining. I'm happy to see you happy. You've never really shown it, but you've not been content for a while. I could see it in you, but there was nothing anyone could do about it. You needed to find the one person who could give you what others couldn't." At Oscar's raised eyebrows, Hilary smiled. "His heart."

Oscar shook his head and looked away. "He doesn't love me, Hils. We've barely started. Last night was the first time we'd spent time as Daddy and little. We can't be in love that quickly."

She squeezed him. "Can't you?" she whispered, then went to deal with a customer.

Oscar stared at the coffee machine, thoughts rattling around, but he couldn't understand any of them. There was no way. Not at all. He pushed the idea aside and began cataloguing what stock he needed to fetch from the stockroom. There weren't many people in the cafe, so he told Hilary where he was going and grabbed a rolling trolley to carry everything back. It was monotonous work, but it helped settle him. He updated the stock sheet on the wall as he pulled items from boxes and set them on the tray.

By the time he was done, he felt centred again and entered the front of the store, immediately glancing over at Christian as he did. He raised his eyebrows when he saw a woman sitting across from Christian, gesturing wildly, and Christian staring at her with a blank expression. From what he could see, she looked similar to Christian, and Oscar assumed it was a relative. One Christian wasn't happy to see if Oscar had to guess.

Taking a breath, he left the trolley to the side and ventured closer, wanting to soothe Christian as best as he could during the meeting. Christian glanced at him when he stopped at their table, and he saw the slight widening of his eyes, but nothing else changed in his expression.

"Good afternoon. Can I get you a drink or something to eat?" he asked the woman. Now he was closer, he could see similarities between them, and he wondered if they were siblings. He didn't recognise the woman, but he didn't keep on top of the royal family as much as he probably should when he worked so close to them.

The woman glared at him and huffed. "If I'd wanted a drink, I would've asked for one. Carry on." She waved her hand, dismissing him.

"Lottie, enough. There's no need to be rude," Christian said.

"I don't want a drink, Christian."

Christian sighed and glanced at Oscar. "Thank you, Oscar, but we're fine."

"No problem. Holler if you need anything at all."

"You're barking up the wrong tree if you're after a piece of this fine specimen." Lottie snorted, her mouth curling as she stared at him.

"Lottie!" Christian barked.

"A good day to you both."

Oscar kept his tone jovial, turning away as his chest splintered at her words. Why did he think he had a chance with him? He was a prince, for god's sake. He returned to the counter and filled the stock, ignoring the concerned looks from Hilary.

When it came time for Hilary to leave several minutes later, she stepped close and lowered her voice. "I'm staying until the evil witch has gone. I don't care how long I have to stay, but you're not being left alone with that witch with a 'B.'"

Oscar tried for a smile but didn't succeed if Hilary's expression was anything to go by.

"I'll be fine with Sam, don't worry."

"Nope. Not happening."

Oscar didn't try to dissuade her again, quietly pleased she planned to stay. He concentrated on cleaning the empty tables as far away from Christian and his guest as he could. Unfortunately, whatever they were talking about was getting louder and carried across the cafe. Oscar made a decision and murmured to the two women who were the only other customers in the cafe.

"I apologise for the inconvenience, but I need to ask you to leave. We're closing a little earlier today."

"Of course. We've finished anyway. Thank you for the coffee and cake. It was delicious," one woman said as she picked up her bags.

"Yes, it was. We'll definitely be back again."

"I'm glad to hear it. When you come back next time, remind me I said you could have a free coffee on me." Oscar smiled and ushered them out of the door, closing it behind them and flipping the sign to closed. He glanced at Brett and swiped a hand over his neck to show he'd closed up. Brett nodded and smiled. It was only twenty minutes early, but it would make things easier. The three of them that were left—

Jonas had left at his normal time as he'd needed to collect his kids from the childminder—continued to clean up around Christian and Lottie, staying away from that side of the cafe.

"This is a fucking joke, Christian. You're just playing up because you're not getting the attention otherwise."

The venom was audible in her voice, and it was all Oscar could do to stay away and not react to it. He wanted to hide away.

"This has nothing to do with you, Lottie. Run along back to Father and tell him to do his own dirty work instead of sending his minions."

"I'll have you know he didn't want me to do this. I thought I could get you to see sense."

"I don't need to see sense. I need to be left alone. I need my family to be left alone."

"I'm your family, Christian! I'm your sister, for fuck's sake. You should protect us, not those abominations you call cousins."

Oscar couldn't see their body language because he was purposefully keeping his gaze averted, but he could hear the tone of their voices. Lottie was angry, furious even, but Christian sounded resigned. Like he'd given up on trying to reason with her.

"Stop it! Enough is enough. Leave now. I don't want anything else to do with you and *your* family."

"They're your family—"

A chair scraped, and it took everything in Oscar to stop from looking over.

"No, they're not. When they imprisoned me in the cellar, they lost the right to be called family. When Father beat me, he lost the right to anything other than my hatred. When Mother ignored everything, she lost the right to be called anything but a *monster*. When are you going to see them for what they are?”

“There is nothing wrong with fighting for what you believe in.”

Christian snorted. “No, except when it causes people to lose their lives.”

Silence settled, and Oscar chanced a glance at their table, seeing them both standing, staring at each other.

“I can see you won’t change your mind. Be careful, brother. Changing sides is not an option in this family. You do this, you’ll be looking over your shoulder for years to come.”

“I’ve already been looking over my shoulder, Lottie. Ever since I was a kid. This changes nothing.”

“Not for you, maybe. But what about those you care for?”

The words were quieter than the others had been, but Oscar still heard them.

“Don’t make threats, Lottie. You won’t like my reaction.”

“Goodbye, Christian. I would wish you a good life, but I doubt you’ll get one.”

The woman’s steps headed for the door, and Oscar hurried forward to open the door for her. She sneered at him, despite his courteous goodbye, complete with an honorific he doubted she deserved. He locked the door behind them and pulled the blind down. Sam and Hilary had already closed the other blinds, shielding them from view.

Oscar glanced at Christian. He stood at the side of his table, staring at the window as if he could see outside. His fists clenched beside him, and his expression was closed off, but Oscar could feel the pain threatening to overflow from him.

“Hilary, Sam, you can go now. I’ll finish up,” he mumbled.

He gave them a look to stop any arguments they may have had, and they hurried through the back door before returning with their bags and coats. He let them out the door with a whispered goodbye and locked the door again.

"I'll stay by the door to make sure no one comes in," Brett said from behind him, making him jump.

"Oh, okay, great. Thanks." Oscar hesitated to approach Christian.

"He needs you, Oscar," Brett whispered.

Oscar swallowed and nodded. He took off his apron and left it and the cloth on a table, approaching Christian from the front. He didn't want to surprise him. Christian's gaze met his, and the pain in them was too much for him. He threw his arms around him and held him as tight as he could. The tension in Christian's body was like a bow stretched as far as it could before it broke. Christian's arms came around Oscar, and his head dropped to his neck, hiding his face there and breathing deeply. He shuddered, and Oscar tightened his grip. He felt wet heat seep through the shoulder of his T-shirt. Christian's legs gave out as a sob tore from him. Oscar took them to the floor, letting his legs spread around Christian's body to surround him.

The sobs sounded painful, and Oscar's tears freely streamed down his face as he held him through his pain. He brushed a hand up and down his back, saying, "It's okay. It's okay," even though he knew it probably wasn't. This was Christian's time to take from Oscar, and Oscar wouldn't stop him until he was spent.

There was obviously a lot that they hadn't spoken about the previous evening. Their discussion about Christian's issues had never happened because Oscar had become side-tracked by becoming little. It was an oversight they would need to rectify because Oscar didn't like being kept in the dark. He needed to know exactly what was going on so he could make an informed decision. It was unlikely that whatever Christian had to say would make Oscar not want to continue with their growing relationship, but he would hold his answer until he knew everything.

When Christian loosened his hold a little, Oscar glanced at the clock. Oscar's ass was numb from being sat there for about half an hour, but he would sit there for another ten hours if that was what Christian needed.

Christian pulled back enough to rest their foreheads together. "Sorry." His voice cracked, and he sniffed.

"You don't need to be sorry. I'm glad I was here to help."

"I've always done so well at keeping everything tightly locked away," he whispered, "but meeting you makes me want to be *clean*." Oscar frowned at the word but said nothing. "We need to talk," he whispered.

"We do. Shall we go to my house?"

Christian lifted his head, and Oscar saw the red, swollen eyes of a man on the brink. "Would you mind if we went across the road instead?"

Oscar's heart jumped, but he nodded. He didn't care what obstacles he had to go through as long as Christian had the support he needed to get through the conversation he knew would be difficult, even if he had no idea what it was about.

"I will take you home afterwards, if that's what you want."

"Let's get this conversation done, and we'll discuss our options after, okay?" Oscar said.

Christian cupped Oscar's face. "I'm sorry for everything."

Oscar gripped the back of Christian's head. "I keep telling you, you've nothing to be sorry about."

Christian's eyes roamed his face, and he leaned forward, closing the gap between their mouths. The kiss was quick but meaningful, and Oscar pecked another kiss on his lips when it ended.

"Come on. I need to finish up for tomorrow."

They rose, and he deposited Christian back at his table while he took the till tray into the back and counted it before putting it in the safe. He locked everything up, made sure the ovens were off, then headed back through to the main room. Christian was where he left him, and Oscar strode over.

"I'm ready."

Christian gave him a wan smile and stood. They wandered over to Brett, who still waited by the door. The bodyguard wore a pain-filled expression, and Oscar knew he was hurting like Oscar was. Until Oscar knew what the problem was, there was nothing he could do to help either of them.

Once they were outside, he locked up the cafe and turned to them. He didn't reach for Christian, knowing they were in public and could easily have photos taken of them, but how he wished he could. They wandered across the road, being joined by the guard who had been watching Oscar, and down the path towards the castle, side by side. As they approached, his heart pounded in time with their steps, and he couldn't keep his gaze from bouncing around the entire building, filling his body with awe.

"Wow," he whispered as they climbed the steps and entered through a large ornate doorway.

His words brought out a chuckle from Christian, and Oscar nudged him with a smile. If his wonder at the castle brought Christian back to himself, he'd make a fool of himself to do it.

20

CHRISTIAN

The wide-eyed reverence from beside him reminded Christian what it was like for those who didn't live as he did. He loved being brought down to earth because he didn't want to forget completely. He was scared that if he did, he'd also forget who he was inside.

He wanted to grab hold of Oscar's hand and thread their fingers together, but he couldn't guarantee that one or more of the household staff weren't on his parents' payroll. Until they were behind closed doors, he would keep his hands to himself. That Oscar was on their radar at all worried Christian immensely, but to show how much he cared for the man would be detrimental to Oscar's livelihood. He'd seen what had happened to Robert's flower shop when they were pissed off and what they were capable of with regards to Aunt Louisa's death. Saving Oscar from that fate was worth the excruciating wait of holding him.

They arrived at the rooms he'd been given when he'd moved in at Uncle Andrew's insistence. He opened the door and gestured for Oscar to enter before him. He glanced at Brett and Felix.

"We'll wait out here, Your Highness."

Christian pursed his lips. "You should probably hear all of this, too."

Brett shook his head. "I'll get what information I need from my boss, don't worry."

Christian sighed. "Okay."

He entered the room and closed the door, leaning back against it as he watched Oscar stare around him.

"It's not what I expected from you," Oscar said.

Christian chuckled. "It's not my choice of decoration. I moved in here a couple of weeks ago."

Oscar peered at him, saying nothing for a moment. "And that there is part of the story," he mumbled.

Christian was no longer surprised Oscar could read him, so he just nodded. "Would you like a drink?" he asked, pushing away from the door and wandering over to the drinks table where a kettle sat from when he'd asked for one so he could make his own coffee whenever the urge took him rather than calling for someone to bring him one.

"I think we need coffee for this conversation," Oscar said, settling onto the sofa in the middle of the large room.

Christian made two coffees and carried them over to Oscar, sitting beside him and shuffling to his side to see him easier. He rested his arm on the back of the sofa but let his fingers run through the back of Oscar's hair. Oscar's eyes fluttered shut, then he smiled.

Oscar shifted his knee onto the sofa between them. "Okay. Coffee, check. Comfortable chair, check. Now, tell me what's happening. I hate seeing you upset." Oscar stroked his fingers down Christian's jaw, and Christian closed his eyes for a brief moment.

"There's so much to go through, I'm not sure where to start." He sighed and sipped his coffee. "There are some people with the royal family who do not agree with homosexuality or anything that is deemed...unclean." Oscar's eyebrows rose, but he didn't interrupt. "There have been several incidents over a long period of time where accidents have happened to other members of the family. We now believe they weren't accidents after all. Instinct is telling us that these unhappy members are responsible, but we have no proof." He licked his lips, his eyes focusing on a spot behind Oscar's shoulder. "Recently, a list has come to light of locations where incidents have and haven't occurred. From what we can tell, these locations are places important to certain members of the family."

"My house?"

Christian shook his head. "Book Drunk, but if they think the cafe is important to us, then they'll soon realise you are, too. Hence the bodyguard." Oscar nodded, and Christian continued, "These people are not messing around. We believe they are responsible for the bomb that took Aunt Louisa's life, the fire that took Robert's flower shop, Douglas's arrest, plus so many other things. I don't want this to touch you, but if we stay together, I'm afraid it will." He stared into Oscar's eyes. "I don't want you hurt."

Oscar gave a small smile. "And your sister today?"

Christian huffed a laugh. "Well, my parents are part of *that* group." Oscar gasped, and Christian nodded. "I didn't know anything about it until just before New Year. I just thought they were assholes, not murdering assholes." He placed his drink on the coffee table and dropped his head into his hands. "When I found out, I went undercover. Pretending to be part of that group and doing their bidding, following in my siblings' footsteps. I searched for evidence everywhere I could think of, but nothing ever came of it. Mortified didn't come close when the bomb claimed Aunt Louisa. I knew nothing about it."

Oscar's hand rested on his back. "Are you sure it was them?"

"I don't have evidence, but I'm pretty sure." Christian blew out a breath. "I was supposed to still be undercover, but I couldn't take anymore. I let my guard down and told Father exactly what I thought of him, exactly what I was. He beat me and had me locked in a cell beneath the house."

Oscar pulled him close, and he lay his head on his shoulder. "The bruises."

"Yes."

"How did you get out?"

"A household staff member left the cell door unlocked, and I sneaked out of the house and came here. Uncle Andrew took me in straight away."

"He's a good man."

"Lottie came to try to convince me to come back into the fold and deny my true self for the good of the people. I can't do it, and it doesn't solve the problems we're having. We're still in the dark as to which of the locations or people they are targeting next. The list we have is partially in code. The dates and times are still trying to be unravelled. Anyone could be a target at any time, and there's nothing we can do about it."

"You're doing everything you can. You can't be expected to carry this burden yourself, Christian."

"I'm trying to save my family." Christian lifted his head and cupped Oscar's cheek. "That includes you."

Oscar's eyes filled. "Thank you."

"I should've told you about all of this before we started anything. I'm sorry."

Oscar chuckled. "I don't think it would've mattered. We'd still have ended up here."

"What do you mean?"

Oscar's cheeks flushed, and he bit his lower lip, even though he didn't drop his gaze as he usually did when he was uncomfortable. His eyes were bright as he looked at him.

"You mean a lot to me, Christian. Not just because of the Daddy and little relationship. That is a bonus, but ever since you set foot in the cafe, I've felt a draw to you. I can't stop wanting to be around you, with you. Nothing that happens would take that away."

Christian stared at him, his heart pounding as he tried to wrap his head around Oscar's words. "No one has ever wanted me for *me*," he whispered. "Only what they could get."

"If you were with nothing to your name, I still would've felt this. I know it. Your title, your money, your belongings mean nothing. It's what's in here that I care about." Oscar lay his hand on Christian's chest. "And I know the man in there is perfect for me, and I'm perfect for him."

Christian brought their mouths together even as tears fell. He tasted the saltiness in their kiss and wanted more, but he needed to check one last time. He pulled back, resting their foreheads together. "Are you sure? This is a lot to take on, and you have to be looking over your shoulder every day. I need you to be certain because once I give you my heart, I'm done for."

Oscar clasped his hands on either side of Christian's face and stared him right in the eye as he said, "You're mine, Christian, and everything that comes with you is fine by me."

Christian closed his eyes and let himself feel everything he'd been keeping back. When he glanced back at Oscar, the man gasped, then smiled and kissed him. Their tongues duelled, their lips connected time and again, their air shared between them as the kiss continued. This was the first proper kiss he'd ever had with a man, and it was everything he'd ever hoped it would be.

Oscar pulled on him, and Christian settled over him, the feel of him beneath him exciting Christian in a way the only woman he'd ever been with never had. The firmness of the body, however slight, was perfect. Oscar lifted his leg over Christian's hip, bringing their centres closer and lighting up Christian's nerve endings. He never wanted the kiss to end, but too soon, Oscar pulled away, gasping for air. Christian continued across Oscar's jaw and down the column of his neck.

"God, Christian. You're an amazing kisser."

When he reached the collar of the T-shirt Oscar wore, Christian bit at it and gave a small growl. Oscar chuckled. Christian reached for the hem of it and dragged it up his skin, exposing the pale skin speckled with moles. His mouth landed on each brown spot, however small, and he pulled the T-shirt over the man's head without breaking away from his body. Oscar's fingers threaded through Christian's hair with a whimper. His body bowed beneath him, and Christian smiled, licking across his nipples with a barely-there touch.

His head was all over the place. The sensation of having another body beneath him, the scent and taste of Oscar's skin, the sounds of his mewls and whimpers, and the sight of him writhing. All of it added up to intoxicate him. Even being at the club had never felt as good as this. He couldn't stop tasting, scenting and touching him. He closed his eyes, rubbing his face against Oscar's stomach.

Oscar tugged at Christian's shirt. "Take it off."

Christian opened his eyes and smirked at him. "Say please."

Oscar's eyes widened. "Please. Please take it off."

Christian rose to his knees, unbuttoning his shirt one pop at a time as Oscar squirmed beneath him. A flush heated Oscar's skin, and Christian watched it lower from his cheeks, down his neck and to his chest, spreading across. It fascinated him.

"Please," Oscar murmured.

Christian yanked the shirt over his head, no longer able to go slowly to tease Oscar. "What do you need?"

Oscar reached for him. "You. Just you."

Christian lowered over him, his skin sparking when it met Oscar's. He needed to get him to a bed, wanting to give him the best experience instead of humping on the uncomfortable sofa, but he couldn't resist the temptation to kiss him again. He slipped his tongue into Oscar's mouth, sliding it along the roof of his mouth and tasting the remnants of coffee. Oscar wrapped his other leg around Christian's waist and lifted his hips, bumping their groins together. Christian hissed and arched his neck back, closing his eyes at the pleasure streaming through him.

He widened his eyes at Oscar. It had never been like this. His one act, porn and what he'd heard from his cousins had been his only experience, but it hadn't given justice to what feelings were flowing through him. Oscar grasped his cheeks, staring into his eyes while he rotated his hips against Christian's.

Christian inhaled through his nose and rose to his knees, taking Oscar with him. He wrapped his arms around Oscar's back and stood. Oscar squeaked and slid his arms around Christian's neck.

"You'll put your back out," Oscar said.

Christian chuckled. "I've carried more weight when I've been on a training exercise in the Army. Stop worrying."

He aimed for the bedroom, repositioning Oscar in one arm to open the door, then kicked it shut behind them. He strode for the bed, crawling onto it before lowering Oscar to the soft covers. He came down over him and cradled his head, gaze roaming his face.

"You're perfect for me, too," he whispered, pressing a soft kiss to his lips. "You might have to guide me through this." He felt uncomfortable admitting to it, but he refused to keep secrets from Oscar, especially ones that could hurt him.

Oscar frowned, playing with the hair at the back of Christian's neck. "Guide you?"

Christian nodded. "I've only ever done this once, and that was with a woman."

A variety of expressions floated across Oscar's face and settled on holding back a smile, his eyes sparkling in delight if Christian wasn't mistaken. "You're truly mine?" he asked.

Christian nodded. "All yours for as long as you'll have me."

Oscar lifted his head and fused their lips, his hands skimming across Christian's back and sending goosebumps in his wake. Christian broke away, moving down his body, intent on finding out if what he'd seen in the porn videos was as good as he wanted it to be. He licked a stripe across Oscar's waist, just above the band of his trousers, then made quick work of the button and zip. Oscar's erection strained against the confines of his black briefs, and Christian's mouth watered. He pulled on the trousers, taking them lower, then kneeling to pull them off completely, along with his socks. He removed his own trousers while he was there, then lowered his face to Oscar's groin, inhaling the musky scent deeply into his lungs.

He peered up Oscar's body to meet his eyes, Oscar's eyes blown wide with only a small ring of the hazel colour left. He dragged his chin down Oscar's shaft, following it with his nose as he broke his gaze away. Dipping his fingers inside the waistband of the briefs, he lifted it over the solid rod, exposing him to his view. The deep red head peeked through the foreskin, and Christian licked his lips, darting his gaze up when Oscar groaned.

Christian's lips curled, and he lay on the bed, refocusing on the cock requiring his attention. He'd never done this, but he'd dreamt about it many, many times. He wrapped his hand around the shaft, the heat of it similar to when he gripped his own, and gave an experimental stroke. Oscar's body bowed while his hands clenched in the covers.

Christian pulled the foreskin down and licked at the exposed head, the bitter, salty taste exploding over his tongue. He closed his eyes and lapped at the slit, wanting everything Oscar was willing to give him. Tonguing around the head, he took every drop from his skin, then couldn't wait any longer and took as much of Oscar's cock into his mouth as he could. He'd been practising on a silicone dildo for years—while he'd been at the barracks, not at home—and relaxed his throat, breathing through his nose as Oscar sank deep. Christian's nose met Oscar's pubic hair, and he closed his eyes, keeping him there for as long as he could. When he pulled off, he inhaled while stroking the cock.

"Jesus Christ," Oscar gasped. "How...Why...? Fuck." He panted. "If you do that much more, I'll be coming."

"I don't mind. I'll be happy to make you come again later." Christian winked.

"No. I want you inside me." Oscar grabbed for his shoulders, but Christian only kissed his knuckles.

"If you want me inside you, I have to prepare you."

He jumped off the bed to Oscar's whimper, grabbed what he needed from the bedside table and returned to his previous position after removing both of their briefs. He thrust his hips against the cover, pushing his cock into the fabric, making his eyes roll back. Undoing the lid of the lube, he squirted some onto his fingers and pushed against Oscar's legs. Oscar widened them further, bringing his pucker into view. Christian wanted his mouth on it, but he'd made them wait long enough. Next time.

Resting his fingers against the bud, he massaged in circles, pressing gently against it each time. When the tip of his finger sank inside as Oscar relaxed, Christian pushed the lube inside until his finger easily slipped through. He used more lube and pressed two fingers in, going slowly enough to make sure he didn't hurt Oscar and also drive him crazy. Christian loved the sounds Oscar made, and he wanted to pull more of them out of him, but he needed more.

"Can you take three?" he asked.

"Yes!" Oscar called, his head pushing into the bed as his body reached for more.

Christian rose to his knees and speared three fingers into Oscar. The man pushed against him, taking them deeper, and Christian fisted the base of his own cock to stop him from coming at the sight. He thrust them in and out several times, then removed them. He wiped his fingers on the covers and rolled the condom down his length before slicking it. Bracing one hand beside Oscar's chest, he used his other to position him at Oscar's entrance.

He raised his eyes to Oscar's, and they locked. He watched every expression cross Oscar's face through narrowed eyes as Christian pushed through his ring, the tight heat surrounding him better than he could ever have hoped for. Pulling back a bit, he thrust forward again, gaining inches each time. When he finally sank deep, he blew out a breath and panted through the need to slam into Oscar repeatedly.

Oscar's eyes were closed, a small smile playing across his lips.

"Are you okay?" Christian asked.

Oscar blinked at him. "Perfect." He pulled Christian down on top of him, both hissing at the change of position, then he nibbled Christian's ear and whispered, "Now, fuck me."

2 1

OSCAR

*C*hristian's breath shuddered out of him, bathing Oscar's neck in warmth, just like his heart and body were. He rose to brace on his hands and withdrew slowly, his eyelids fluttering, then he locked gazes with Oscar and slammed home.

Christian was larger than some men Oscar had slept with, and the burn was incredible. Oscar lifted his legs higher up Christian's body, giving him more room to move. And move he did. Sweat dripped off Christian's body and onto Oscar's, their scents mingling in the air. The man thrust forward again and again, and Oscar held onto Christian's forearms.

Then, Christian slid his arms underneath Oscar's knees, almost bending him in half, and continued sliding deep. The change in position had Oscar keening as Christian hit his prostate with each forward motion. Oscar wrapped his hand around his cock and stroked in time with Christian's hips. He bowed his neck back as his release screamed through him, soaking his stomach.

"God damn," Christian growled. "Videos don't do this justice. Fuck!"

Oscar reached for Christian's nipples to see if the extra stimulation would send him over, and after several flicks with the tip of his nail, Christian tensed and held deep, screwing his eyes shut and holding his breath as he filled the condom. Oscar would've liked to feel it inside him. Maybe one day.

Christian's body relaxed, and he panted into Oscar's stomach, narrowly avoiding the mess Oscar had made. Oscar couldn't see Christian's face, but he felt the tentative licks of his tongue as he cleaned Oscar. He hadn't thought Christian would do that, with it being his first time. As usual, the man surprised him. Christian's licks grew stronger until he had cleaned every inch of him, then he held the end of the condom and pulled free.

Oscar hissed and bit his lip. "God, could you do that again?"

Christian laughed and pecked at his lips. "Soon maybe, but not right now."

"No fair."

Oscar closed his eyes and rested, legs akimbo. He had no energy left, and even though he would happily do it all over again, he also could do with some sleep. Undoubtedly, Christian needed some, too.

Christian brought a cloth from the bathroom and wiped Oscar, the cool flannel easing the sting of his ass. "Let's get you into bed." Christian paused. "Are you staying? Will you stay?"

"I am, and I will if that's okay with you."

"Definitely okay." Christian held the covers up, and Oscar scrambled underneath, sliding across to the opposite side so

Christian could climb under with him. As soon as Christian lay on his back, Oscar snuggled into his side. "Do you need Rexie?"

Oscar smiled and rubbed his cheek on Christian's chest. "Not when I have my human hot water bottle right here."

Christian chuckled. "Nice to know I'm good for something."

Oscar paused. "I don't want to sound unsure or like I'm looking for compliments, but how was it for you? I know you said it was your first time with a man…"

Christian pulled him closer and kissed his head. "It was amazing. I never believed it could've felt like that. Orgasming with my hand doesn't come close to what it felt like to be inside you. Thank you."

Oscar smiled and licked at his nipple, making Christian jerk. "Sorry, couldn't resist."

"Is that something that interests you? Suckling?"

Oscar stared at the little round disc, a little fuzzy from how close he was to it, and frowned. "I don't know. It's not been something I've ever thought about, to be honest, but it makes sense, I suppose. I like the occasional bottle with warm milk as you read on my list, and I like dummies if I'm feeling cranky or unsure, but it's never crossed my mind."

"Well, if it's something you decide you want to try, let me know."

"Thank you," Oscar said after a few minutes.

"For what?"

"For being so good at being a Daddy. At being a man. At being a person. It's difficult to find someone to gel with, but with you…it's like we've always been together. It's seamless."

Christian skimmed his hand up and down his arm, and

Oscar shivered. After pulling the cover more firmly around him, Christian said, "It is seamless, and I think that's a good thing. We have other things working against us, but our relationship is perfect. You can spend as much time as a little as you want to, and when you don't, we'll still be together because we have two parts of our lives that blend perfectly with each other."

"You have a way with words, Your Highness," Oscar murmured.

Christian tickled his sides, and Oscar yelped. He was too ticklish, and now Christian knew it. "Less of the 'Your Highness' crap, Mr Hall."

They fell into a comfortable silence, and Oscar drifted away, not sleeping but not fully awake either. A beep sounded, and the bed bounced. Oscar reached for Christian, who pressed a kiss to his hand and tucked him under the covers before disappearing.

Oscar woke with a warm body wrapped around him and felt extremely relaxed. So relaxed that he refused to move, even though he needed the toilet. He dozed for as long as he could before he had no choice and slipped out of bed. After using the toilet, he washed his hands and stared at his reflection. He had a sudden thought he should look different for some reason, but there he was, the same old Oscar. The same old Oscar who was now in a relationship with a prince.

It was stupid that he hadn't thought of the implications of that until now. The media would hound him. He would need to go to events. He would have to attend meetings and have dinner with important people. Could he do that? He wasn't brought up knowing which fork to use, and he had to hope that what Julia Roberts had been told in *Pretty Woman* was correct and he should work from the furthest away from the plate to the nearest.

Hands slid around his waist, jerking him from his thoughts.

"What's wrong?" Christian asked, pressing a kiss to his shoulder.

"What fork do you use first when you have lots of choices around your plate?" he blurted.

Christian raised his eyebrows. "What?"

"That's something I'll need to know, isn't it? Will people mock me if I don't know which one to use?"

Christian spun Oscar around. "What are you talking about?"

Oscar dropped his gaze. "If we're in a relationship—"

Christian growled. "Not *if*."

Oscar cleared his throat. "*As* we're in a relationship, I'm assuming I'll have to attend events and dinners and such like? Will someone teach me? Do you have people who do that? Would they—"

Oscar's words were swept away when Christian took his mouth. He briefly wondered about morning breath, although he had no idea what time it was, but those thoughts floated away as Christian plundered his mouth, robbing him of any kind of reaction except where his mouth ended and Christian's began. He had no idea how long they kissed, but Oscar's body was back to being jelly, and Christian held him steady.

"Shall we get back into bed? It's too early to be up yet," Christian said.

Oscar could barely open his eyes after being so entirely overcome by the kisses. "I bet you're up this early on a normal day." He chuckled. "Yes, bed, please."

Christian bent and picked him up, holding him to his chest while Oscar's head lolled on his shoulder.

"I could get used to this," he murmured. "Don't let me wake up later than seven o'clock. I have to be at the cafe."

"Okay, shh. Don't worry."

Oscar sank into the mattress and curled onto his side, humming when his hot water bottle wrapped around his back.

Soft circles on his stomach woke him, the kind that didn't tickle, thankfully. That would not have been a nice way to wake up.

"Good morning," Christian said from behind.

"Morning," Oscar mumbled.

"Are you a morning person?" Christian asked with a chuckle.

"Once I've pried my eyes open, I'm fine. It's the prying my eyes open thing that's the problem."

Christian's laughter vibrated through Oscar's back, and he smiled. He was surprisingly awake that morning, and he knew it was because of his companion. He shuffled over onto his other side, facing Christian, his short black hair scruffily stylish regardless of bed hair. His eyes appeared more electric blue if that was even possible, and his scruff... Oscar leaned forward, brushing his jaw against Christian's scratchy cheek, then chasing his lips.

The kiss was unhurried. A slow exploration. A reminder of what they were building.

A knock disturbed his contentment, and Christian dropped another kiss on him before sliding out of bed.

"Sorry, sweetheart. I need to check-in." He pulled on some joggers.

Oscar stretched, ignoring his need to pout. "It's okay. Can I use the shower?"

Christian grinned. "You don't have to ask. There should be a new toothbrush under the sink if you want one."

"I *need* one."

"Not as far as I'm concerned." Christian winked and left the room, closing the door firmly behind him.

Oscar flung the covers back and raced into the bathroom. He'd seen the shower earlier that morning, and it was huge. He might not have a clue how to turn the damn thing on, but he would try. Enclosed in glass, it could probably fit four or five people in it—not that he wanted to have that many people in with him—and from what he could see, the showerheads were built into the ceiling. He slid into the shower and over to the dials. He hoped it was as simple as it looked, and he pressed "on."

Warm water drenched him in seconds, and he loved it. It was as if he were standing outside in a torrential downpour. He ducked his head out of the spray and turned the dial. The pressure increased, so he turned it the other way, and it slowed down. No part of his body didn't have constant water dripping over him, unlike his shower at home, where he had to move from side to side and turn around in circles to keep from getting too cold. He could stand in the centre of the spray and it would coat his entire body in water. It was divine.

He spied the shelf holding bottles and chose one that reminded him of Christian. Stepping out of the spray while he soaped himself, he wished Christian would hurry and join him. Although saying that, he probably wouldn't get to work on time if they shared a shower. He rinsed off, then washed his hair. Christian still hadn't arrived when he finished, so he turned the shower off and stepped out, realising he hadn't thought about a towel in his haste to try out the shiny new toy. Luckily for him, a towel waited on the heated radiator. Whether it had been there all the time or if Christian had brought it in for him, he didn't know, but he was grateful all the same.

He dried off and tucked the towel around his waist, brushing his teeth and trying to do something with his hair. It didn't work, so he ignored it as he usually did and strode for the bedroom. He'd have to wear the clothes he'd arrived in yesterday, at least until he got to the cafe because he had another set of clothes there he could change into.

Once he was ready, there was still no sign of Christian, so he wandered into the main room and froze. There, sitting on the sofa, was the king.

"Sorry. I'll…" He pointed behind him and retraced his steps until Christian called for him.

"It's okay. Come say hi."

"Hi?" Oscar stared at Christian as if he was mad. How could he just say "hi" to the king?

Christian stood and held out his hand, pulling Oscar into his arms as soon as he was close enough. He turned them to face the leader of the country. "Uncle Andrew, this is Oscar. Oscar, I'd like you to meet my uncle."

"Your Majesty," Oscar croaked.

Andrew chuckled. "Now, now. No need for the titles. I prefer to go by Andrew—or Uncle Andrew—with family."

Oscar squeaked, then rolled his lips inwards to stop any other embarrassing noises from escaping. Christian laughed. "He's shy. Sometimes, at least."

"I won't bite. I promise," he said to Oscar before turning his gaze on Christian." I just wanted to check in with you and make sure you're doing all right. Brett told me about Lottie's visit."

Christian guided him onto the sofa, and Oscar surreptitiously checked the time. He had a few minutes before he needed to go.

"Yeah, she was trying to get me to reconsider. As if it was my choice about leaving the family." Christian shook his head, but Oscar could feel the tension in him.

"They will try anything to get you back, but I don't think it will be because they want you back. No offence intended." Andrew grinned, then sobered. "They'll want to rub it into our faces and potentially use you against us."

"I know. It's a case of if they can't have me, they don't want anyone else to, either."

"Exactly. What are your plans for today?" He glanced at Oscar.

"Oh, um, I have to work at the cafe. As usual. Nothing special."

"If my family has anything to say about it, your coffee is divine. I will make sure to drop by one day soon."

"Oh, I can get one sent over for you. You don't have to go out of your way—"

"That would be great, Uncle Andrew. I'll take you over one day."

Oscar's mouth opened and closed, but he couldn't think of anything remotely interesting to say, so he snapped his mouth shut.

"As for me, I'll be heading back to the barracks and seeing what Neil has uncovered, if anything."

Andrew rose to his feet. "Don't work too hard. You hear me? Either of you."

Christian stood, and Oscar followed suit. Andrew pulled

Christian in for a hug, whispering something in his ear that caused Christian to tighten his hold, then pulled back. Andrew faced Oscar. "It was nice to meet you, Oscar." He wrapped his arms around Oscar. "Thank you for making him smile again. A proper smile. Not the one he usually gives us. This one reaches his eyes," he whispered, and Oscar scrunched his eyes closed to stop the tears.

"I will do anything for him," he murmured back.

"I can see that."

Andrew pulled back and smiled at them both. "Have a good day, boys."

Oscar stared after him, dumbfounded. "I expected him to be…"

"Haughty? High-handed?"

"No, just…less down to earth, I suppose. I've seen him on TV loads of times, but never that relaxed. Understandable, really." He checked the clock. "Oh, I have to go!" He patted his pockets. "Where's my phone?"

Christian whirled around and grabbed it from a table. "I put it on charge last night for you."

Oscar smiled. "Thank you."

Christian stepped closer, sliding his arms around his waist. "I wish I could spend today with you." He kissed his cheek. "I would insist on spending it in bed." He kissed the other cheek. "I would worship your body." He kissed his nose. "I would give you hundreds of orgasms." He kissed his chin. "And devour every inch of your body." He kissed his lips. "But, alas, off to work we must go." He stepped back.

Oscar swayed and blinked. "That was mean." He adjusted himself, narrowing his eyes.

Christian smiled. "But you'll be thinking about me all day now, won't you?"

"I would've been, anyway."

"I'll walk you to the cafe, then head back here for the car."

"You don't have to if you need to get moving."

Christian shrugged. "A few more minutes won't make any difference.

They grabbed everything they needed and opened the door to the corridor. Brett and Felix stood there as if they'd been on sentry duty all night. They hadn't, had they? Brett grinned when Oscar asked.

"No, we swapped out with some other guards for the night shift, but we made sure to be back for morning. Thank you for thinking of us."

"I'll make sure you all get coffee when we get to the cafe." He glanced at Christian. "If you have time for me to switch the machines on?"

"I always have time for coffee." Christian grinned and led the way, threading their fingers together. Oscar tried to pull away, but Christian wouldn't let him. "If someone was watching us, they would've seen that you arrived last night and didn't leave until this morning. There's no hiding that. Besides..." He leaned closer and lowered his voice. "You're mine."

Oscar bit his lip to contain his smile, but it was too big. "And you're mine."

"And I'll never forget it."

Oscar practically floated to the cafe. He unlocked the door, let everyone in, and locked it behind them again. He still had twenty minutes before he needed to open. Flicking the switch on the coffee machines, he let them warm up and locked himself in the office while he did a quick outfit change. Within minutes, he was back out again and set about making coffees for everyone. He even made an extra for the king and told Christian to get it to him.

"You're going to spoil us all," he said with a grin.

"You deserve it."

Christian exhaled and smiled, and Oscar knew he was beginning to believe it. Not quite there yet, but soon. He kissed Christian goodbye, then settled Felix at the end of the counter instead of outside in his car and went about getting the place ready. He felt like he was walking on clouds, and every problem seemed tiny compared to his feelings for Christian.

Was this the start of the rest of his life?

22

CHRISTIAN

Christian entered the office and saluted Neil before relaxing. "Anything?"

Neil shook his head. "Gia hasn't been able to crack the code. Some of the symbols don't match anything we've seen before or can find on the internet. There could be a lost language or something that hasn't been uploaded to the internet yet, but that's next to impossible to find unless we want to send the details out to other people, which wouldn't be advisable."

"Are we looking into this too deep? Is it something a lot simpler than we think it is?" he asked.

Gia shook her head. "I've had it run through simplified programmes as well, but there's nothing. It's as if they created the code from scratch with no rhyme or reason," she murmured.

Christian stared at the screen, his thoughts running over what Gia had just said. He'd been creating codes with his mother for years as a child. She taught him how to use random aspects of languages to create a new code that could be almost indecipherable. He rubbed a hand over his mouth. If this *was* her work, that's what she would've done, but there was no way of telling which languages or sets of rules she used.

There was something just out of reach that he couldn't grasp, and it was driving him crazy. His phone rang, and he pulled it from his pocket, his heart pounding when he saw who it was.

"Felix? What's wrong?"

"He's fine. Everyone is fine. There was a gas leak at the cafe, and we've had to evacuate so the fire brigade can check it out, but everyone is fine. I promise."

Christian blew out a breath as his heart calmed. "Take the staff over to Windsor. I'll call ahead and let them know, and I'll call Douglas because he's most likely there already. Let them relax for a bit, and I'll get over there as soon as I can."

"They won't let anyone leave yet, but as soon as they do, I'll take them."

"Thanks, Felix. How's Oscar?"

"Shaken. The alarms scared him, I think."

"I can imagine. Tell him to call me when he can. I want to check in with him."

"Will do."

He ended the call and dropped his head back. When were they going to get a break?

"Everything okay?" Neil asked.

Christian nodded. "There's been a gas leak at a cafe near home. Friends of mine were involved."

"Oscar?"

Christian smiled. "My boyfriend. He owns the cafe."

"Ah, Book Drunk." Neil grinned. "And everything slots into place," he said, linking his fingers.

Christian frowned. "Gia, you've probably already done this, but have you cross-referenced the code with the dates we already know?"

Gia nodded. "Yes. Even the numbers we know are identical don't match within the code. The code almost...evolves each time it's used."

Christian froze. "Evolves," he whispered.

"Yeah, it changes once it's been used..."

He didn't hear any more of what she said because his mind went back to his childhood when he and his mother were working on the code, sitting cross-legged at the coffee table with paper spread out before them.

"So, you see here, where you've already used the number one? You can't use this symbol again for the number 1 because it becomes useless information once someone knows what the symbol means. If you keep it the same, every time you use that symbol, they'll know it means one. You have to evolve the symbol in some form each time it's used," his mother explained.

"Evolve it?"

"Change it but make it so that you can understand what the changes are, but someone reading it wouldn't. Here, let me show you." She reached for a pen and paper, drawing a vertical line. "This is the symbol for one when it's used the first time." She drew a vertical line with a small dash at the top of it. "This is the symbol when you use one the second time." She drew a vertical line with a dash at the top and the bottom. "The third time." A vertical line with a dash at the top, bottom and middle. "The fourth time, and so on. You can't make it easy for them; otherwise, they'll break your code in no time."

"Can we create our own code?" he asked.

She smiled and smoothed his hair. "Of course, we can. Any symbols, in particular, you'd like to use?"

"Can we draw our own versions?"

"You can do whatever you want. It's your code."

Christian blanched. It couldn't be. There was no way she would use *his* code to do this. Would she?

"Gia, bring up every symbol in the code that has a vertical line in it."

He stepped closer to the screen, squinting as she did what he asked.

"What are you thinking?" Neil asked, he and Daniel stopping beside him.

"I'm not sure."

A table of symbols appeared. He dismissed the first few, concentrating on the ones they had chosen for the number 1 when he was a child. There, amongst others, were the vertical lines with dashes in all the places he had created them.

"Holy shit," he whispered.

The implications of this were immense. As far as he knew, no one had been told about the code he had created when he was nine. It had stayed between him and his mother. Was she trying to point the finger at him?

"Christian!" He blinked and faced Neil. "What's going on?"

He inhaled and debated making up a lie but knew they needed the information as fast as they could. "That's my code."

Neil frowned. "What do you mean, *your* code?"

Christian rubbed both hands over his face and stepped

away, giving him room to pace. He explained what he and his mother had done when he was younger. "We never used the code again. It was just something I'd created because I could."

"Is she trying to frame you?"

He swallowed. "It's likely."

"Do you remember the code?"

He shook his head. "I have it, though."

"Where?" Christian lifted his head and stared at Neil, who shook his head. "It's too dangerous, Christian. You don't even know if it's still there."

"We need it, Neil. I can't remember the symbols from that long ago. I need the cheat sheet."

Neil exhaled and wandered to the window, crossing his arms over his chest. "This is a bad idea."

Daniel cleared his throat. "Can you enlighten us?"

Christian sighed. "The cheat sheet is at home. My parents' home."

"The same parents who imprisoned you? The same parents who beat you? Are you crazy?" Daniel said.

Gia piped up, "Give me what you can remember. I can work from there. You don't need to go back."

"I don't remember enough, Gia. I remember the number 1—some of it, anyhow—and I remember the letters 'C' and 'M'. That's not enough."

"Give me those to start with. I might be able to work out the other evolutions with those to work with," Gia said.

"I'll give you the information, but it's still the only choice we have." He looked at Neil, who still had his back to them. "Sir?"

Neil whirled around and leaned against the wall. "You need to have a tracker on you. Several, in fact. I want to know where you are at all times. If I thought it wouldn't be suspicious, you'd be in full tactical uniform. I'm going on the record here saying this is a bad idea."

"We need that paper."

Christian didn't want to go back to that house any more than they wanted him to go, but he had no choice. He knew he'd kept the cheat sheet because he had a box of things he'd kept as memories from when his life hadn't turned to shit. It was one of the better memories he'd had, but then memories of what he'd seen his parents do edged in, and he hoped he could get in and out before being found. He didn't want to be on the receiving end of his family's wrath.

His phone rang, and Oscar's name flashed up. He had a momentary pause, thinking the idea was nuts and he was crazy to ruin the chance he had with Oscar, but he knew there was no other option.

"Hey, how are you doing?" he said, wandering out of the room and into the corridor, where Brett waited.

"I'm okay. We're closing the cafe today because the fire brigade said we need to air the place out and get the gas checked before we can open again. I think I can get the gas engineer out this afternoon."

"That's good. Hopefully, you'll only lose today. Do you know what caused it?"

Oscar sighed. "From what the firefighter said, it was a loose connection at the back of one of the ovens. It could've been there for ages, but I've never smelt gas before, and Jonas has been using the ovens every day. I hate to think what could've happened."

Christian didn't want to think about the chances, but maybe this was not such an accident after all. Even more reason to get the cheat sheet. He needed to know when Oscar would be in danger.

"You're all fine, though. Try not to think about what-ifs. Are you at Windsor now?"

"Yes. Mav and Randall have set us up in one of the receiving rooms. It's bigger than my house, Christian!"

Christian chuckled. "Yeah, they certainly didn't scrimp on building materials for that place."

"Felix said you were coming over soon. Do you know when?"

Christian closed his eyes. "I don't think I'm going to make it. Let me know when you get home, and I'll pop over tonight. Things are busy here."

"Of course." Oscar sounded upbeat but sad all the same. Christian had to hope he made good on his promise.

"Sorry, sweetheart. I will be there as soon as I can."

"I know. I'm sorry. I'll get Hilary and Wally together tonight, then you don't have to worry about me moping around. If you can't get to me tonight, I'll see you tomorrow."

"Without a doubt," he agreed, though he couldn't be sure. It all depended on what happened at his parents' house.

"Anyway, go. Get your work done." Oscar tried to sound stern, but it didn't work.

"Yes, sir." He chuckled.

"Christian, I…"

Christian waited, but Oscar didn't say anything else. He took a breath and laid it all on the line. "I love you, too."

He heard Oscar sniffling and wished he could be there reassuring him, but he needed to focus on his plan. If he worried about him, Christian would be no good to anyone.

"I'll see you soon."

"Bye, Daddy."

"Bye, little one."

He immediately dialled Felix, staring at Brett, who stepped closer. "Felix, keep a close eye on Oscar. Bring someone else in if you need to. I'm not convinced that the gas leak was accidental, and I'm about to go on a…training exercise. I need someone in the house with him in case things go wrong."

"Understood. I won't leave his side."

Christian sighed, still keeping his gaze locked with Brett. "If something goes wrong, Felix…"

"He will remain unharmed. I promise."

He knew Felix couldn't give that promise, but his wavering confidence settled Christian. "Thank you."

He hung up. "Questions?"

"Hundreds," Brett said. "Where, when, how?"

"Come on in," Christian said, opening the door to the office. "Sir, I'm bringing Brett in."

Neil nodded, and Christian held the door open for his bodyguard. "Nice to see you again, Brett." Neil held out his hand, and they shook.

"What's going on?" Brett glanced around the room, settling on Neil.

"Boy hero here is going back into the lion's den." He huffed a laugh.

Brett raised his eyebrows. "Is that wise?"

"No!" Neil said, throwing his hand up in the air.

Christian sighed. "There is no other choice. No one will know where I've put the box holding that paper, and even if I tried to explain it, it would be next to impossible. I have to go in myself."

"How are you going to do that?" Brett asked.

"There is an underground tunnel going from the road to the cellars. It's the best option. It doesn't have cameras because they don't want anything recording their actions. It's where they bring their..." Christian swallowed.

Neil nodded. "As long as no one else is using the tunnel at the time, that would work. What if you come across someone? Surely everyone knows you're not in with them anymore."

"Probably, but I could play it that I'm changing sides after my conversation with Lottie." He quickly filled them in on the meeting with his sister.

"Wouldn't it be better if you brought someone else with you, pretending that you've brought them as an offering?" Brett asked.

Neil nodded. "That would work."

"No," Christian said. "I don't want anyone else near them unless there is no other option."

"Two are better odds than one, Christian. I'll send Daniel in with you."

"No, I'll do it," Brett said. "You need someone they know is gay; otherwise, it will prove futile if they decide to research them. They will, undoubtedly, know I'm your bodyguard and will have already checked me out."

Christian raised his eyebrows. "I didn't know you were gay."

Brett smiled. "It doesn't matter to you, so you didn't need to know. I only tell those who might have problems with my choices in life."

Christian chuckled and shook his head. "You're full of surprises." He sobered. "I don't want you in danger. I know what they're capable of if this goes wrong."

"With all due respect, Your Highness, I have the least to lose."

"What do you mean?"

Brett swallowed hard. "I have no one left. My family is dead, and I only have work. If something goes wrong, I'm not leaving anyone behind."

Christian sank into a chair and dropped his head into his hands. "That doesn't help me come on board with you being with me. It makes me want to show you the world."

Brett chuckled. "When we get out of this, you can do that, too."

Christian stared at him. "Deal."

"Okay. Now that's sorted. Do you have any idea of the best time to do this?" Neil said.

For the next two hours, they went through every potential outcome, every escape route, every contingency they could think of. They chose dinner time to be the best choice of entry because Christian knew his family would congregate in the dining room together as they did every day.

He and Brett suited up in black clothes, complete with trackers in each item of clothing and their shoes. They drove towards the property, parked several streets away and left their phones in the car. Trekking down the streets to the hidden entrance to the tunnel was easier than he expected, and they saw no one. Christian's stomach churned the closer they came.

"Last chance to turn around," he whispered.

Brett smiled. "No way."

"Brett, I don't want you to go through what I've seen them do. Please reconsider?"

Brett shook his head. "No matter what they do, they'll

never hurt me as much as losing my family hurt. My body can heal; my heart can't."

Christian cupped his cheek. "After this is done, you and I are having a talk."

Brett nodded. Christian let him go and inhaled. "Let's do this."

They slipped into the quiet alleyway that gave access to the back gardens of the surrounding houses, and he slid through a gate at the end. Just beyond that was a door. He pulled his lock pick from his pocket and set about opening it—a handy trick one of his colleagues had taught him a few years ago.

When the door clicked open, he paused, waiting to see if anyone would come and check out the noise. After a couple of minutes, he entered, followed by Brett.

"Ready?" he said when they closed the door behind them.

"Ready."

Christian led the way down the long, claustrophobic tunnel, ready to grab Brett's arm if he needed to prove the man was a prisoner. No one stopped them. They reached the door leading to the cellars, and Christian picked the lock again. Yet again, no one was on the other side, and Christian's instinct prickled.

"This is too easy," he whispered.

"Do you think they've cleared out?" Brett also kept his voice low.

Christian shook his head. "No way. There's too much here for them to easily move. They would've added more defences to it before leaving."

They crept out into the hallway, listening for any noise. Christian could hear talking, which sounded like it came from the dining room, but usually, there were more guards around. They might've reduced their indoor guards since Christian was no longer living there and no longer a risk to them.

Christian led the way to the stairs. This would be the only part where they were completely exposed. He raised his fingers to Brett, counting down, and they sped across the expanse and up the stairs without encountering anyone. Within seconds, he enclosed them in Christian's old room. He wasn't surprised to find it ransacked. Chairs and tables overturned, drawers and boxes emptied and strewn around. His heart raced as he aimed for the bathroom.

He stepped into the shower and reached for the back of it. He picked at the white tack he'd used to hide the box, then pulled the tile free. Behind it lay a small box, maybe four inches by four inches, and replaced the tile and tack.

He nodded at Brett and pulled out a pen. Across the top, he wrote a message, then aimed for the bedroom. As he entered, he froze. Sliding the box behind his back, he felt Brett take it from his hands.

"To what do we owe the pleasure, Christian?" Aunt Charlotte said, a sickly smile on her face. "If I'd realised John was going to have guests, we would've prepared better."

"We're not staying. I just wanted to grab a few items I'd left, but I see most of that has been removed. I won't stain your evening any longer."

"Oh, hogwash. Come. Join us. Bring your…*friend.*"

She turned and exited the room, and guards grabbed hold of them both. This was what he'd been afraid of.

23

OSCAR

Oscar knew something was wrong because Felix hovered more than usual, but he didn't call him out on it. He pretended everything was fine during the day and didn't cancel the movie night with Hilary and Wally like he wanted to. They didn't seem to feel any tension, but Oscar sure could.

Felix paced from one room to another, disturbing Oscar's peace with every entry and exit. He took the empty bowl of popcorn to the kitchen and opened another packet, emptying the contents into the bowl. He didn't take it back, though. He waited until Felix made another pass through the kitchen and pounced.

"What's going on?"

"Nothing. Are you enjoying your movie night?" Felix asked, bypassing Oscar's position and glancing out of the window into the rapidly darkening night.

"Not really. What's happened?"

"Stop worrying, Oscar. Everything is fine."

Oscar bit his bottom lip. "Now I know there's something

wrong. When people say everything's fine, it means there's something to worry about."

Felix stopped beside him and set his hand on Oscar's shoulder. "Christian had to go on a training exercise, so he asked me to take care of you. That's all it is."

Oscar worried his lip further. "I don't believe you."

Felix stared at him, then looked away. "That is what he told me."

"But you don't believe him." It wasn't a question.

Felix cleared his throat. "There is a lot we don't know about the situation. Even as bodyguards, we're not given all the information we should be, especially when it comes to royalty. I can honestly tell you, I don't know what's happening, but my gut is telling me..."

"There's something wrong."

"Not wrong as such, but something's coming. I shouldn't be telling you this because you'll worry." Felix shook his head.

"Don't. I prefer to know everything. Please. How can I help protect myself when I don't know?"

Felix seemed to consider his words and nodded. "As soon as I have more information, I will share it with you."

"Thank you." He held out the bowl. "Popcorn?"

Felix smiled and grabbed a handful. Oscar wandered back into the living room, and Hilary caught his eye. He smiled and settled beside her, mechanically eating popcorn while his mind was anywhere but on the film.

What was Christian doing? Was it really a training exercise, or was he doing something dangerous that he deemed Oscar too fragile to know about? If it was the latter, the man would be hearing about it from him when he got back. *If* he got back. No, he couldn't think like that. *When* he got back.

Did it have something to do with the code he was trying to break? Had they found a clue? All the secrecy annoyed him, but he could understand why the royal family needed it. If information got into the wrong hands, who knew what could happen?

He refocused on the film, trying to ignore the thoughts tumbling through his head and the passing figure of Felix.

When the film finished, both Hilary and Wally passed on another one. Even though Oscar was tired, he wished they'd stayed to keep him from whittling about what danger Christian might be in. Instead, he flicked a disaster movie on and cuddled under the blanket with Rexie. He got lost in the story, then the next thing he knew, he was being shaken awake. Blinking blearily at Felix, he registered Felix had his finger over his mouth. Shivers swept through him, and he kept his teeth apart to stop the noise from them clattering together.

Felix pulled the blanket from him and dragged him to his feet. He pointed to the window and held up two fingers. Oscar assumed that meant there were two people there.

"Who?" he mouthed.

Felix shrugged. Oscar pointed to himself, then his eye, then the window, asking if he wanted him to look. Felix frowned but nodded. Oscar peered out into the dark night, noticing the streetlight wasn't on, which meant it was either after midnight or something was wrong with it. He saw two figures huddled in the driveway, neither wearing a coat. They appeared muscular, and one held a cigarette that he kept taking an inhale from because the tip glowed brighter at regular intervals. The glow didn't make their features any easier to discern. At least until they turned around. Oscar's shoulders lowered, and he faced Felix.

"They're my neighbours. Both of them live next door, but they've been away for a couple of weeks on holiday. His wife doesn't let them smoke in the house because they have a child, so they always come outside," he whispered.

"But why are they on your driveway?" Felix murmured.

Oscar opened his mouth to answer, but a scream rent the air. He froze, but Felix peered out of the window, then tugged him through the hallway to the kitchen door, pulling his gun from the back of his waistband. He pressed Oscar against the wall.

"Do not move from this position until I say you can."

"But—"

"I need to know where you are so that if I have to shoot anyone, I will know where to avoid. Don't make me shoot you by accident," Felix warned.

"Okay."

Felix crept into the kitchen, his gun held in front of him, and Oscar wished he could be more of a help than a hindrance, but he did what Felix had told him. He, too, didn't want to end up shot. Felix disappeared from view, and Oscar tried to quiet his breathing. One, he didn't want to hyperventilate, and two, he didn't want someone to find him because they could hear his harsh panting.

Felix appeared before him again, making him jump, but he bit off the sound of his surprise. "I can't see anything. That scream sounded too close—"

A shattering of glass sounded, and Felix grabbed his arm, running them for the front door. He threw it open, dragged Oscar down the path and into Felix's car before Oscar could process anything that was happening. Felix slammed the door shut, racing around to the driver's side and climbing in. The engine roared in the otherwise quiet night, and they took off. A couple of pings hit the car, but they continued as fast as Felix could take them.

"That's not good," Felix murmured. "Call Brett Cage," he said.

"Sorry?"

"I'm talking to the car," Felix said as ringing sounded through the speakers. It continued to ring before going to voicemail. Felix cancelled the call. "Call Christian Sutcliffe." The same thing happened. Felix cursed and rubbed his head. "Call Randall Hopkins." The phone rang and rang until a husky voice filled the car.

"Hello?"

"Randall, it's Felix Jamison. I'm here with Oscar Hall. I'm watching him as per Christian's orders, but we've just had to leave his house because non-nice people came in and shot at us. Where is the best place to head for?"

Oscar was sure Randall would be too sleep-disturbed to understand what Felix had just said, but he replied instantly, "Come here. It's the best place for him. Is the house a loss?"

"Unconfirmed. They entered through the back, and we took off through the front. I didn't stay around to check out."

"Understood. Make your way to King Andrew's rooms when you arrive. Both of you, please. We need to get more information."

"Okay. We're a few minutes out."

With how Felix was driving, Oscar was sure they would be there in less than a minute, but he didn't feel the slightest bit unsafe.

"I'll see you when you get here."

The call ended, and Oscar asked, "What the hell is going on?"

Felix glanced at him before returning his gaze to the road. "I'm not entirely sure."

"But you have an idea?"

Felix paused, then nodded. "Yes."

"Which is?"

"Why don't we wait until we get to Windsor? Then we can all have a discussion."

Oscar opened his mouth to argue but decided against it. His stomach churned, and he knew, he just knew, that Christian was in danger.

They pulled into Windsor two minutes later, and guards surrounded them as they strode from the car to the front door. Felix led the way to the king's rooms and knocked.

Randall opened the door a short distance, then further when he saw who it was. "Come on in." He closed the door behind them. "His Majesty will be with us shortly, as will some others. Would you like a drink?" Randall looked at Oscar with his eyebrows raised.

"Oh, um, coffee, if it wouldn't be too much trouble. I'm a little cold," he admitted.

"Of course." Randall wandered over to the drinks table while Oscar sat on a chair Felix pointed to. Felix stayed standing behind him.

Before Randall had even finished making the drink, King Andrew had entered the room, carrying something over his arm. He strode right up to Oscar and stood before him, flapping open a blanket and tucking it around Oscar's shoulders.

"I heard you were cold. I thought this might help a little. I've also asked Mav to bring a change of clothes for you."

"Thank you, Your Majesty," Oscar said.

"Andrew, please. Haven't we had this discussion?" He winked.

"Sorry. Thank you, Andrew."

"Now, I know you have a lot of questions, as do I, but let's get some warm drinks inside us and wait for the rest of the party to arrive. Then we can get to the bottom of this situation."

Oscar glanced at Felix. "I don't have my phone. Is there some way of letting Hilary and Wally know I'm okay?"

Randall held out a mug to him. "I will see to that immediately. You don't need to worry. I will also arrange for Book Drunk to be closed tomorrow. I know it's not the best option for you, but until we know what's happening, it's the best choice."

Oscar nodded. "Thank you."

His mind was whirling with hundreds of thoughts, but he couldn't properly catch onto any of them. All he could think about was Christian and if he was in danger. All he could think was that he hadn't said "I love you" to him on their last call. He hoped that wouldn't be the last chance he got.

A hand covered his and urged the mug to his mouth. "Drink. It will help," Andrew said from his crouch beside him. Oscar hadn't even seen him move.

So, he drank. By the time he'd finished his mug, everyone had arrived, settling around the array of chairs and sofas and a couple of them on the floor.

Andrew crossed his legs. "Okay, does anyone know what's going on before we get down to trying to figure this out?"

Felix spoke up. "The only thing I know is that Christian called me and asked me to keep a close eye on Oscar. He said he was going on a training exercise, and he wanted as much security as I deemed necessary to keep him safe." He glanced at Oscar. "I didn't do a great job."

"Oscar is alive and in one piece. In my books, that counts as a win," Andrew said.

"I've not heard from Christian in a day or two," George said.

"Me neither," Frederick said.

Andrew sighed. "Randall, could you get Neil on the phone, please?"

"Of course, sir." Randall disappeared.

"Felix, explain what happened tonight."

Everyone listened as Felix recounted their actions and the things he'd seen and heard. Oscar explained who the two men were that they'd seen in his driveway.

"Who screamed?"

Felix shrugged. "It sounded close enough to be a neighbour, but I couldn't tell for definite. I was planning to search the back garden to see what I could find until they smashed through the door."

"Did you see who they were?" Frederick asked.

"No."

Randall entered, carrying a phone. "Neil for you, sir."

Andrew put the phone to his ear. "Evening, Neil. I hope I didn't disturb your—" He listened, and his expression darkened. "I see. Why didn't you clear this with me first?" He frowned. "That wasn't your call to make." He stared at Frederick. "I want to know everything. Start from the beginning. I'm going to put you on speakerphone, but be warned, Christian's boyfriend is here, too." His mouth pursed. "I don't care, Neil. Explain. Now." Andrew's voice brooked no argument, and he pressed a button and placed the phone on the arm of his chair. "Go ahead."

Neil's sigh was audible through the line. "Christian figured out what the code was, but he needed the key, which was located in his parents' house. He and Brett headed over there to retrieve it quietly. They were both wearing trackers in all their clothes—"

"Were?" Frederick interrupted to ask.

Neil's silence explained a lot. "They were wearing trackers in every item of clothing. Those trackers are now disabled. All of them."

"So you have no idea where they are?" Douglas said, his tone sharp.

"No. We have a last known position as of two hours ago, which is in his parents' house. That's where they went dark. We've had no communication since."

"What was the backup plan?" Frederick asked.

"If Christian was able to get to the box holding the key, he would ensure it got to a household staff member with a note attached. If they were able, they would get that key here somehow."

"That's a lot of ifs, Neil," Andrew said. "Give us something more to work with."

Neil sighed. "I don't have anything else, sir. I didn't want Christian to do this, but none of us could see an alternative."

"What was the code?" Oscar asked. Neil didn't reply. "Sorry, did you hear me?"

"Is that Oscar?" Neil asked.

"Yes, sir."

"The code was something Christian and his mother had worked on when he was a child. We're not sure if she's trying to implicate him in their deeds, but it's a possibility."

"They have him, don't they?"

"We have reason to believe they have them both," Neil said, his voice grave.

Oscar froze. What was Christian going through while they chatted on the phone? What would they do to him?

George's boyfriend Eddie came over and perched on the arm of the chair, wrapping his arm around his shoulders. They spoke between them for a few minutes, but Oscar didn't hear any of it. In the end, he stood and wandered over to the window, tugging the blanket tighter around his shoulders. He leaned against the frame, resting his forehead against the cold glass and closed his eyes.

Christian hadn't told him everything that had happened during his time with his parents, but his body had told some of the story. He'd seen some scarring when they'd made love but hadn't brought attention to it. His story had led him to Oscar, and for that, he was grateful, but if it was also the reason Oscar lost him, he would never forgive them.

"Oscar?" He opened his eyes and glanced over his shoulder at George. "We'll find him."

He returned his gaze to the window, not replying. They couldn't promise that, but he appreciated the sentiment.

However long later, Felix took him to Christian's rooms. Oscar was too tired to be nosy and climbed into bed, still wrapped in the blanket from Andrew, and closed his eyes. Then, and only then, did he let his tears fall. A physical ache shot through his chest as he keened and cried for Christian. For Brett. He could scent Christian on the pillows, and he pulled them closer, though it was a poor substitute for the man.

Would he ever see Christian again? He had never seen so many grave-looking faces in one room as he had that evening, and it worried him. He knew there was a high possibility that Christian and Brett wouldn't come out of the situation whole. Would they even survive?

Someone climbed onto the bed behind him, and he lifted his head. Henry stood at the end of the bed, and Robert gave him a sad smile from behind him, wrapping his arms around him.

"Go to sleep, little one. Your Daddy will be home soon, but in the meantime, I'm here. Let me help you."

The words, however nice the meaning, made Oscar cry harder. He curled into a ball, sobbed until his entire body hurt and let Robert hold him.

Nothing would ever be the same again.

2 4

HENRY

*H*enry's heart hurt as he heard Oscar's sobs through the closed bedroom door. He dropped onto the sofa and rested his head on the back of it, staring at the ceiling. He hoped Christian was okay. For all their sakes. If they lost another of their own, he didn't know how they'd cope. Losing Aunt Louisa had been shattering, but to lose more than one to those deceitful, disgusting assholes was nothing short of devastating.

He could hear Robert's low murmurs, the soothing tones helping Henry as well as Oscar, whose crying had subdued into sniffles. Undoubtedly, Oscar would sleep, but it was unlikely that he would stay that way. Dreams and nightmares would plague his sleep, disturbing his rest, and wouldn't leave until Christian was back with him.

Henry knew what it was like to have nightmares chasing after him. He'd been dealing with them for years, and even though they were better now he had Robert, they still showed their ugly faces now and then. He doubted anything would ever remove them completely. In some ways, he was glad of them because they made him remember what he'd been through and what others were still going through. He was scared he'd forget now that he was living a good life with Robert. Those people he'd witnessed being tortured didn't deserve to be forgotten.

The bedroom door opened, and he stood, holding his arms open for his boyfriend.

"How is he?"

"He's asleep for the moment, but it won't last long. I won't leave him alone for more than a minute or two." Robert sighed. "I know I have experience as a Daddy, but I'm not what he needs."

Henry rubbed his back. "I know, but you're what he has at the minute. We can't lose him. When Christian comes back, Oscar needs to be here. In mind and body."

"He will. He's stronger than he thinks."

Oscar's cries increased, and Robert pecked Henry on the lips and raced back into the room. It would be a long night, so Henry called down for some food and drinks. Hopefully, Robert could get something into Oscar at some point, even if it was just water.

While he waited, he wandered around the room, being nosey. The books Christian had in there amazed him. He'd only been at the castle for a short time, but he'd amassed a sizeable collection. He chose one to look at and sank onto a chair close to the bedroom door in case he was needed.

The food and drink arrived after a couple of pages, then his phone rang, and he found himself annoyed at the interruption. The thought made him chuckle. Pulling out his phone, he answered, smiling, though the other person couldn't see him.

"It's nearly happy birthday, Kean," he said as a greeting.

Laughter floated across the line. "Yes, it is. Are you still coming tomorrow for dinner?"

"Yes. Robert and I will be there."

"Good. How are things?"

Henry sighed. "Not great, in all honesty. Christian's gone into…an undercover operation, and we're worried for him. His boyfriend isn't taking it too well, so Robert's helping him."

"Oh, wow. Do you know how long he'll be gone?"

"No idea. We're hoping it will just be a few hours, but we won't know until it happens."

He wished he could tell Kean more, but they had to be so careful about the information they were giving out until they knew who was involved. As much as he trusted Kean, he couldn't go against what Uncle Andrew had requested of them, and that was to keep things between them unless they had no other option.

"Is there anything I can do?"

"No. I think we're good. If something happens, I'll let you know."

"Let me know either way, okay? I'll keep everything crossed for a quick return."

"Thanks."

They ended the call, and Henry stared at the book, no longer interested in reading it. He replaced it and paced around the room, Oscar's cries intermittently breaking the silence. When it went quiet once more, he cracked open the bedroom door, and Robert came over to him.

"Do you want something to eat or drink?"

Robert tilted his head back and forth, and Henry heard the click of his bones. "Water would be good. Can I have one for Oscar, too?"

Henry grabbed two bottles and passed them over. "How's he doing?"

"Same. You should try to get some sleep. I can manage here."

He shook his head. "I might try on the sofa, but I'm not leaving."

"Okay." Robert kissed him, resting their foreheads together afterwards for a long minute. "He has to come back."

"He will."

Henry gave him no other choice.

25

CHRISTIAN

To Christian's surprise, they hadn't taken them to the cells. They were sitting on comfortable chairs in the living room, albeit *handcuffed*, but he'd take a win where he could. No one had laid a hand on them. He frowned at Charlotte, who was sitting on a chaise lounge sipping her tea. She had the audacity to roll her eyes at him.

"What? Did you think we'd lock you in the cellar? You're my nephew, Christian. I'd never do that to you."

The smirk she ended with belied her words.

"What do you want?" he gritted out.

"What everyone else wants. Peace on earth." She smiled.

"Bullshit."

"Language!" Her voice whipped across the distance, but he no longer felt the need to cower inside. "I want things to be how they have always been. If...*people*," She grimaced at the word, "want to hide things behind their doors, that's perfectly okay with me. But it should stay behind those closed doors. No one wants to see it on the street. Or in their family." She glowered at him. "While you were hiding, Christian, you were the perfect soldier. The perfect spy. If you had just continued like that, we wouldn't have had any problems, would we?"

"I wouldn't have been happy."

"Now, now. Yes, you would. We could've done so much. Your vision is so narrowed. I told your father years ago that we should've tried conversion with you. As you hadn't experienced *it*, it probably would've worked."

"You didn't know I was bisexual. No one did."

Charlotte laughed, her deceptively delicate hand covering her mouth as her eyes sparkled. "Oh, my dear boy. Of course, I knew. I'm not stupid, young man. I've been doing this for longer than any of you have been alive. I can spot an unclean person in a crowd of hundreds."

"Why didn't you do anything?"

"I told you. You were the perfect spy."

Christian smiled. "So perfect you didn't know I was helping the other side."

Charlotte's façade broke for a second, her mouth pinching at the corners. "That was an unfortunate lapse in judgement on your mother's side that has now been rectified."

He held no love for his mother, except for what they'd had before he'd grown older, which made him ask, "What did you do to her?"

She waved him away. "She's been punished. She won't make the same mistake again."

The door opened, and Charles wandered in, smirking.

"Good evening, Mother. I see we have guests," he said, kissing her cheek.

"Yes, quite unexpected. Christian has so much potential, don't you think, Charles?"

Christian didn't miss the anger in Charles's expression

when he looked at him. It seemed Charlotte was quite taken with Christian, and Charles didn't like the idea. Could he use that to their advantage? He had no idea how to get them out of their current situation.

"Of course, Mother." He turned to her. "Aunt Miranda would like to speak with you."

"Send her in. She should've learnt her lesson by now."

Charles strode to the door, opened it, and there was Christian's mother. She looked the same as she had when teaching him code-breaking at age nine, time having passed in her favour, except for the new bruises on her cheek and jaw. She didn't look at him as she entered, focusing on his aunt.

"Charlotte, thank you for seeing me. I wondered if you would allow me to honour you by breaking in our new guest?" Miranda glanced at Brett, then wandered over behind him, running her hands over his shoulders and down his chest and back up again. "He has muscles we could use. You know I'm good at helping people swap allegiances." She crouched beside Brett, sliding her hands down his arm to his hand. "Hmm, firm hands. He could do wonders, Charlotte." She looked over at his aunt. "Please? I really am sorry about my lapse with him." She nodded at Christian.

Charlotte tapped a finger on her lips. "I believe you, Miranda, but not right now, okay? We're going to have a nice dinner and decide what to do with them while we eat. You'll most likely be able to *persuade* afterwards." Charlotte chuckled. "Maybe we should let Christian watch exactly *how* you persuade those we need."

"Of course. That sounds perfect."

Miranda's smile didn't reach her eyes, from what Christian could tell. There was no surprise who was the mastermind behind this whole thing. Miranda rose and settled into a chair near Charlotte.

"Charles, I need you to arrange to visit someone. We might need some leverage, if you understand me?" Charlotte stared at Christian as she spoke to her son.

Charles grinned. "Perfectly. I'll send someone over now. It's late enough."

"Good boy."

Charles preened, and Christian barely held in his laughter. It seemed Charles was a dog in more ways than one. Then Charlotte's words sank in. Who were they going after for leverage? If what Brett had told him before was true, he had no family. There would be no leverage from his side, which meant it would be someone Christian knew. He could only hope someone protected Oscar as securely as he'd asked him to be.

"I'm supposed to be at the club, Aunt Charlotte. Would you like me to call in sick?" Christian asked.

"No need, dear boy. It's already been reassigned. Your brother has taken your place tonight."

He didn't think she would let him, but he'd thought it was worth a try. He glanced at Brett.

"Are you okay?" he murmured.

Brett smiled at him. "Great, thanks."

Christian raised his eyebrows at the upbeat tone. He assumed Brett was trying to show the situation didn't bother him. He was good at it, too. His thoughts moved to Oscar again. Did they have enough people to protect him? Was he safe? Had Rodriguez found his note, or had someone who was on Charlotte's side found it instead? It had been a shot in the dark, but he'd had to try. If luck was in their favour, Rodriguez had the box and had kept hold of it or passed it onto someone to get to Neil. Christian wished he'd had his phone to take a photo of it and send it directly to Gia, but they hadn't wanted the chance of having their phones taken off them. He'd been surprised when the only thing Charlotte had done was to insist they strip and change into different clothes. Somehow, she knew they had trackers. Either that or she was suspicious of everyone and everything, which wouldn't surprise him. As she'd mentioned earlier, she'd been doing this a long time.

A knock sounded, and Charlotte called for them to enter. A household staff member entered and bowed. "Your Highnesses, dinner is ready."

Charlotte clapped her hands. "Wonderful." She stood, smoothing down her skirt. "It's a lot later than planned, but never mind. Come, Miranda, Charles. Let's eat. John will join us shortly."

Christian watched as they headed for the door under his aunt's orders. He couldn't remember her treating that house as her own when she'd visited before. Had that been a show for his sake? Charlotte wasn't scared to show how much power she had now. And where was his father?

She stopped by a guard and tapped his cheek. "Peter, be a dear and monitor these two, please. We'll be back after dinner."

"Yes, Your Highness."

Christian noticed his mother had stayed back a little and stared at Brett. He barely restrained the urge to gag at the way she looked at him.

Charlotte clicked her fingers, and Miranda jumped. "Come, Miranda. You can most likely play after dinner." She chuckled, the sound lingering after the door was closed, leaving them with two guards stationed in front of the only exit.

Christian repositioned himself on the seat, hiding the fact that he was trying to loosen the handcuffs. It was no use, though. They were too tight. He'd probably have to dislocate his thumb to get them off, and he'd prefer not to do that.

Brett faced him and smirked. "Want to see a magic trick?" He raised his eyebrows when Christian frowned. He held up his hands, free of the cuffs. Before Christian could say a word in response, Brett had disarmed and knocked out the two guards, making Christian very glad the man was on his side.

"How the hell…?"

Brett crouched behind him, unlocking the cuffs. Christian rubbed his wrists. "Your mother."

Christian stared at him. "What?"

"When she was touching me. Remember, she said about my hands. She slipped the key into my hand."

"Why you?"

Brett shook his head. "I can only think because she wouldn't act that way with you. She had to make it believable, and unless she was into family liaisons…"

Christian blanched at the thought. "Okay, I'm tucking that away to never think of again. Why? Do you know what? I don't care. We need to get out of here, preferably checking in with Rodriguez first."

"What about your mother?"

Christian paused, his heart warring with his head. "We should leave her, but when they find us gone, she'll be the first they turn on."

"Are we able to get to her without the others seeing?"

"Let's find Rodriguez. Then we might be able to do something."

Christian opened the door and peered into the hallway. They crept out, keeping to the wall, and neared the dining room. Luckily, the door was closed, and they raced past to get to the kitchen, where Christian had last seen Rodriguez when he'd escaped the last time. It seemed to be a recurring thing for him in this house, escaping. The kitchen sounded busy, as was to be expected at dinnertime. Christian peered through the slightly open door, noticing several staff members at the centre island chopping fruit. Rodriguez was there, too.

Christian made a small noise, then when no one heard, he made it louder. A couple of staff glanced over their shoulders, and Rodriguez looked up. Rodriguez's eyes widened, and he refocused on the fruit before making an excuse and wiping his hands. He headed for the door and walked straight past their hiding spot, disappearing into the staff bathroom. Christian wasn't sure if they should follow, but they waited, then Rodriguez returned. He met Christian's gaze, tilted his head towards the bathroom, then went to walk past them again.

Christian grabbed his arm and yanked him closer. "We need to get Mother to us, too."

Rodriguez pulled away, nodded and returned to his station. Christian glanced at him once more before heading for the bathroom. Brett searched the stalls while Christian looked around the sinks. Brett called him from the last stall. When Christian joined him, Brett was holding the box and a note.

I couldn't get it out. I don't trust anyone here any longer. When I leave tonight, I won't be coming back. I'm sorry.

Christian blew out a breath. "It could be worse, I suppose. At least we have the box."

Brett nodded. "Are we going out the way we came in?"

"That's our best option. They will most likely not guard the door because they think us locked in the living room."

"How are we going to get your mother?"

Christian sighed. "I don't know. We might have to come back for her."

He met Brett's gaze, both understanding what that could mean. A noise sounded outside the door, and they scrambled into the stall, closing it behind them.

"I'm so sorry, Your Highness. I'm so clumsy. Can I help clean it?" Rodriguez's voice came through loud and clear.

"No need, Rodriguez. It was an accident. I'll mop it up here, then change," Miranda said, her voice different from when Christian usually heard it.

"You don't have time to change," Christian said, exiting the stall. "We need to leave. Now."

Miranda gasped and whirled towards them. "I thought you would've left already! You need to go! Please! Go before they find you!" Tears threatened to leak from her eyes, and Christian warred again with his heart and mind, not knowing which Mother was the real one.

"Not without you. The minute they see us gone, you're going to shoot to number one suspect. You need to come with us. Help us."

Miranda shook her head. "I'm already dead, Christian. It's just a matter of time." She stepped closer, cupping his cheek. "I'm so sorry for everything. I've tried to shelter you from it as much as I could, but the older you grew, the less control I had."

He pulled her in for a hug, then held her at arm's length

again. "You're coming with us." He grabbed her hand, checked Brett still had the box, then headed for the door. "Are you coming with us, Rodriguez?"

"If you don't mind?"

"Come on, then. We're heading for the cellars."

Rodriguez checked outside the door first, then they all followed in his wake until they neared the cellar door, and Christian took over. He'd been right. There were no guards in sight, so he opened the door, and they all squeezed through. When the door closed, they jogged through the tunnel, picking up the pace when they heard the door behind them open again.

"Faster," Christian said, glancing back.

Two guards, Charlotte, Charles and John stood watching. Then, John raised a gun and fired several times. Miranda stumbled, and he caught her, helping her walk. Rodriguez fell, and Brett picked him up.

"Leave me. Go," she said.

"No," Christian growled.

"It's...too late...for me," she panted. "I love you, Christian." She stumbled again and fell to the ground, taking Christian with her. "Go. Take these...fuckers down...for me." She pushed him away, reached beneath her dress and retrieved a gun. "Go!" She began firing towards the opposite end of the tunnel, and Brett pulled him away, still carrying Rodriguez over his shoulder.

"No!"

"Christian, we *have* to go!" Brett shouted.

Christian stared at his mother as he ran away from her, watching several more bullets hit her before she slumped to the ground. Brett shoved him through the door to the street and slammed the door shut behind them.

"Run, Christian!"

Brett pushed against his back, and they broke into a run, down the alleyway towards where they'd left the inconspicuous car. Brett opened the back door and laid Rodriguez on the seat, checking the pulse in his neck before closing the door again. He opened the passenger side door, shoved Christian in and ran around to the driver's side. Brett tore down the street and away from the chaos they'd left behind. He resumed a normal speed as they exited the estate, obviously not wanting to draw attention to them.

Christian couldn't do anything but close his eyes and see his mother falling over and over. In the end, she hadn't seemed as evil as the rest of them. How much had she sheltered him? How much had she taken on for him? Had she done it all for *him*? It seemed unlikely, but he'd never know now.

"We can't go directly home, even if we wanted to. We can't draw their attention there," Brett said. "I'll take you to the barracks. I'll get the medics to help with Rodriguez while you crack that code."

Christian nodded absently. He reached for his phone, locked away in the glove compartment. He'd missed calls from Felix, Freddie, Douglas and George. Even one from Uncle Andrew.

"Shit." He dialled Felix, wanting to know what the problem was with Oscar. "Felix? What happened?"

"They hit the house. Oscar's fine. We're at Windsor."

Christian bowed his head. "Thank you."

"Hold on." There were mumbles on the other end, and Uncle Andrew's voice came on. "Where are you? We haven't been able to get hold of you. Neil told us what you were doing. You and I are going to have words when you get home."

Christian smiled at the fatherly words and instantly felt bad for his mother. "Lots has happened. We're heading to the barracks because we have the key to the code, and we didn't want to bring any problems to your door."

"What happened?"

Christian sighed. "Long story short, we got caught, then found an unexpected ally and escaped."

"An unexpected ally?"

"A long story."

Silence. "Okay. Get that code to Neil, then get home. Oscar is waiting in your rooms. Bring Brett with you."

"Yes, sir."

"See you soon, son."

Christian's throat closed, and he couldn't reply. Brett took the phone from him, but Christian didn't hear what he said. He closed his eyes and linked his fingers over the back of his neck, leaning his head down so his elbows rested on his knees. He tried his hardest to shove everything back inside him so he could do his job. He'd be able to see Oscar when he got home.

"Oscar's fine, Christian. They didn't get him."

"What was their end game, though?"

"What?"

Christian sat back, ignoring everything but the thought that kept circling. "If we ignore everything Mother did for us, we'd still be there. What were their plans? She'd already said that I was valuable to her. In what way?"

"Maybe Charlotte thought having you on a leash would keep your mother closer to her. She seemed aware of your mother's love for you."

They arrived at the barracks long minutes later. Brett gave Rodriguez to another guard, who carried him in the direction of the doctor, and followed Christian towards the office. Both looked worse for wear, but Christian carried the box with both hands. The contents were now even more valuable than they had been before, especially knowing what he knew now.

The office held Neil, Daniel and Gia despite the late hour.

"Christian!" Neil said, coming closer. "What the hell is going on?"

Christian put the box on a table, opening it and ignoring anything but the piece of paper he'd folded at the bottom. He held it up. "The key." He handed it to Gia. "Please be careful with it." She raised her eyebrows, then nodded. He closed the box again, facing Neil, but keeping his hand on it. "It's been a long night."

Neil stared at him. "Give us the important stuff, then go home. We'll debrief tomorrow."

Christian and Brett filled them in, then they both showered and changed before heading back to the car. Brett drove again, taking liberties with the speed limit, and they were at Windsor before either of them could power nap. Christian ran up the steps, holding the box he vowed to keep close to him. He aimed for Andrew's rooms, but Brett stilled him with a hand on his arm.

"I'll speak to them. You find Oscar."

Christian opened his mouth to argue, then nodded. He changed direction and raced down the hallways until he reached his rooms. Felix stood outside, and Christian dragged him into a hug.

"Thank you."

Felix smiled and nodded. Christian entered as quietly as

he could, making Henry jump from his seat on the sofa. Henry smiled and relaxed.

"He's sleeping. Robert's been keeping him as calm as he could."

"Thank you." He entered his room, placing the box on the table just by the door, then focused on the bed. Robert glanced up at him and smiled. He gently extracted himself from Oscar, who whimpered.

"He's been sleeping fitfully, waking now and then. I'm glad you're back." Robert squeezed his arm, then left, closing the door.

Christian climbed onto the bed and wrapped himself carefully around Oscar. Oscar's hands gripped his shirt, and Christian tucked Oscar's head under his chin. He was going nowhere until he had no choice. He was right where he belonged, and he had to hope that Oscar would allow him to stay after giving him so much trouble.

26

OSCAR

Oscar felt uncomfortably warm, and he tried to push the blanket away from his shoulders, but the blanket tightened its hold. Everything came rushing back, and he opened his eyes, jerking his head back to find Christian watching him with a sad smile. He burst into tears.

"It's okay, little one. I'm here. You're safe." Christian's words washed over him, and Oscar buried his face in his chest, holding tighter than he'd ever held anyone before. If Christian never went anywhere without him again, it would be too soon.

His chest and face hurt by the time he calmed enough to think coherently again. "Rexie?" he whispered.

Christian moved, and Oscar whimpered, gripping his shirt tighter. "It's okay. I'm not going anywhere. I just need to reach the bedside table." He continued moving, Oscar moving with him, then they returned to their original position, and Rexie was in his arms.

Oscar held Rexie to his face, using the cuddly dinosaur to dry his tears. "What happened?"

Christian sighed. "A lot of things. Do you want me to tell you about it, or would you like to be little so you can relax first?"

Oscar considered his answer. "Will you tell me everything first? Then I might need to be little to process it all?"

"Of course, sweetheart. Anything you want."

Christian tucked Oscar into him again and rubbed a hand up and down his back as he started talking. Oscar got angrier and angrier as he spoke—not at Christian but at his so-called family. As for his mother, she had a lot to answer for. Well, she did until Christian explained what she'd done for them.

When he finished talking, Christian said, "I don't know what to think about my mother now. I want to believe she had been protecting me all along, but I don't know. How could you allow your children to go through what we've been through and not do something?"

"Maybe she didn't have as much leeway as it appeared she did?" Oscar didn't want to defend her actions, but at the same time, he was grateful she had helped them escape, though not that it was at the loss of her life.

"Maybe." Christian pressed a kiss to Oscar's forehead. "I'm so sorry I wasn't there for you. You must hate me after what you've been through these past couple of days."

"Never," Oscar said vehemently. "It's a bit of a shock to the system, but I love you." He cupped Christian's jaw. "Whatever we need to go through, we'll go through together and come out the other side stronger for it."

"I love you. I'm so sorry for everything."

"Stop apologising. The only people who should be sorry are the ones doing this to your family. Those people are *not* your family, no matter the blood binding you. Your family is here in this castle—and I can't believe I can say you live in a castle." Oscar chuckled, though a little watery.

Christian smiled and sniffed. "Everything is so messed up. I thought my parents were so in love, despite their life choices, and to see him shoot her… I can't understand it."

Oscar slid an arm around his waist, nestling his head beneath his chin once more. "That must've been awful. Charlotte could've been testing his loyalty."

Christian tensed. "That's possible, but I have a feeling he would've done it, anyway. He is as firm in his belief that he's doing the right thing as Charlotte is. Though I would've said that about Mother, too, and look where that got me."

They stayed silent, locked together as close as they could get until a soft knock disturbed their contentment.

"Come in," Christian called, not moving from their position.

Robert popped his head in. "Andrew would like to know if you're up for a visit? He would like everyone to attend but has said we can fill you in later if you're not feeling up to it."

Christian glanced at Oscar and raised his eyebrows. "Your choice. I know you want to be little. I don't want you to feel overloaded."

Surprisingly, Oscar felt okay. He didn't sense the same foreboding he usually did when he *needed* to be little. It was in the background, so he knew he'd need to soon, but it was a necessity at that moment. "I'm okay. We can visit."

Christian rolled them until Oscar was resting on his chest. "Ask them to give us half an hour to clean up, please, Robert."

"Of course." Robert left and closed the door.

"I think we need a shower—together—and then we can have breakfast while we're visiting with everyone."

"What time is it?"

"A little after five in the morning."

Oscar blew out his breath. He'd slept for hours. He left Rexie resting on his pillow and followed Christian into the bathroom. He gripped the hem of the T-shirt he'd worn, but Christian stayed his hands.

"Can I?" he whispered.

Oscar nodded. Christian smoothed his hands up his stomach, bunching the T-shirt as he went, then tugged it over his head. Oscar returned the favour, throwing it somewhere behind him. Christian dragged his trousers down his legs, taking his briefs with them. He didn't wait for Oscar to do his, instead rushing to pull them off and sliding his arms around Oscar.

"I want to make love to you," Christian murmured in his ear.

"Yes, please. But do it here. I've always wanted to try shower sex."

Christian snorted, burying his head in Oscar's neck. "I can help with that."

He pulled away, dug into the cupboard beneath the sink and returned with two foil wrappers.

"You're prepared."

"I asked George to get me some."

Oscar blinked at him. "Seriously?" Christian nodded. "You don't mind talking to them about our sex life?"

Christian shook his head, frowning, then it cleared as if he understood. "There is still one part of my life I haven't explained." Oscar shivered. "Nothing bad. At least, I don't think it is. Let's get in the shower so you don't get cold." Christin started the shower, and they climbed in, huddling under the water. Christian pressed his mouth to Oscar's ear, making it easier for him to hear over the sound of the shower. "You've signed an NDA, so I can tell you. Have you heard of Club Royal?" Oscar nodded. "It's our not-so-secret secret. We own the club, and we all work there as Monitors, making sure the place is running smoothly and helping those who need it."

By the time Christian had finished explaining his role in the club, Oscar was gaping at him. "How do you get away with that?"

Christian grinned, making him look his age rather than much older. "*The first rule of Fight Club…*"

Oscar chuckled at the film reference. "If no one corroborates a story, they don't have a story, only rumours."

"Exactly." Christian shrugged. "We choose our members wisely."

"Understandably." Oscar reached for the foil packet Christian had placed on a shelf out of the reach of the spray. He waggled it in front of Christian. "Am I preparing myself, or do you want to do the honours?"

Christian's eyes darkened. "You prepare yourself. If I do it, I won't be able to hold myself back."

"Did I say you had to?"

Christian chuckled and tapped his ass. "Minx. Get on with it."

"Sir, yes, sir!"

Christian went to slap his ass again, but Oscar danced out of reach, tearing the foil and squeezing the lube onto his fingers. He'd never believed sex could be fun. It had always been a means to an end for him, completely focused on the end goal rather than playful banter that he'd realised was as sexy as physical foreplay. He held onto the tiles with one hand while he reached behind him and pressed his fingers into his hole. His eyelids fluttered closed at the sensation, but he didn't mess around. He quickly stretched himself, eyeing Christian's cock as he did, his mouth watering at the idea that it would be inside him soon.

"Ready," he gasped. "Now." He spun around, giving Christian his back, and stuck his ass out.

He squealed when Christian spun him around again, spread Oscar's legs, then reached his arms under them and picked him up. He hissed when the cold tiles met his back, but his attention was on the bulging muscles of his man holding him up and open while his cock pressed against his entrance.

"Oh, fuck, yes. I love that you're so strong," he mumbled.

"I love looking into your eyes when we make love." Christian slid through the ring of muscles. "I love watching your eyes darken the closer you get to orgasm." He pushed further. "I love feeling your tight heat wrap around me." He pressed Oscar into the wall as he thrust a few inches more. "I love the sensation of your nails digging into my skin as I bring you closer to the edge." He bottomed out, and Oscar's breath caught. "I love the sounds you make when I move," Christian whispered, and he withdrew before slamming back in. "I love you."

Oscar lasted a few strokes, then he came with a shout and held on to Christian as the man increased his thrusts until he shivered and released. They stood slumped against the wall while Christian recovered enough to pull free and help Oscar down onto shaky legs. Christian disposed of the condom and then held Oscar tightly under the warm water. After a few minutes, he pulled back and washed Oscar with shower gel, then shampooed his hair. Oscar brushed Christian's hands away when he went to wash and took over for him.

When they were clean, they shared a soft kiss and switched off the shower. Towels were waiting for them, and Oscar wondered again if they had already been there or if someone had put them in while they were showering. He needed to pay more attention. Christian dried him off and wrapped the towel around him, then dried himself. Clothes were waiting on the bed when they came out, and Oscar stopped short, a hand covering his mouth.

Christian rushed over. "What's wrong?"

Oscar pointed at the clothes. "Did someone come in while we were showering?" Christian nodded. "They would've heard us!"

Christian smiled. "Possibly, but it doesn't matter. No one will say anything."

Oscar covered his face. "This is mortifying."

Christian wrapped an arm around his shoulders. "I can ask them not to do it again if you don't like it. I'm so used to having someone come in and clean the place when I'm not here that I don't acknowledge it anymore. Maybe I should, though. Sorry. I should've thought."

Oscar took a deep breath. "It's okay. It's just a lot to take in. We live such different lives. I don't even..."

"Is it too much?" Christian asked.

Oscar shook his head. "No! Just different. I need to get used to it."

"I'll ask them not to come in while we're here from now on. It never occurred to me because I've never had anyone here before."

Oscar cupped his face. "It's okay. Just an adjustment, that's all. Not a deal-breaker. I promise."

Christian kissed him, exploring his mouth with his tongue before pulling back. "We have to get ready."

Oscar smiled. "Rain check."

"Definitely."

They dressed in comfortable silence, and Oscar wished for more mornings like this. "Oh! What about the cafe? Does it have to stay closed for longer than a day?"

"Let's see what's happening when we get to the meeting. I don't know how Felix left things."

They exited the room, finding Felix and another guard Oscar didn't know the name of. Christian shook hands with Felix.

"Have you slept at all?" Christian asked him.

"A little."

"You need to find someone to cover for you," Christian said.

The other guard chuckled. "We tried, Your Highness. He won't leave."

Christian stared at Felix and nodded as if making a decision. "Felix, can you walk with Oscar for a minute? I need to speak with…"

"Matt," the guard supplied.

"Of course."

Oscar frowned but didn't argue when Christian disentangled their hands and stepped closer to Matt, who pulled out his phone. Felix guided him down a corridor.

"How are you?" Felix asked.

"I'm fine. How are you? You look tired."

Felix shrugged. "I've had worse."

When they reached Andrew's rooms, they paused, waiting for Christian to catch up. As they did, Brett came barrelling down the corridor at a run. Oscar's heart leapt. What had happened?

Brett clapped hands with Christian, then focused on Felix,

gripping the back of his neck and resting their foreheads together. Oscar could just hear what he said.

"You've done your duty for today, Felix. They're safe. You can relax. You did good." Oscar's eyes filled as Felix slumped against Brett. Brett smiled and nodded at them. "I'll take care of him. He'll be good as new in no time." Brett led Felix away, and Christian wrapped his arm around Oscar's shoulders.

"Thank you, Matt."

"You're welcome, sir. Another guard will be here to replace Felix in a few minutes."

Christian nodded and knocked on Andrew's door, entering when he was told.

"Ah, just the people we were waiting to see." Andrew stood, crossing over to them. He hugged Oscar and then dragged Christian into his arms. They held onto each other for a long time, and Oscar sat on the sofa beside Robert and Henry.

"Thank you for before. I appreciate you helping me."

Robert squeezed his leg. "You're welcome. We all care for each other around here. Even when you don't want it." He winked.

Henry chuckled. "Especially when you don't want it."

Robert pulled Henry into his arms but glanced at Oscar. "When you're feeling up to it, I think we should have a play-date. I'm sure Ozzie would love to meet Dusty." Henry lifted his head.

"That would be awesome!"

Robert chuckled. "You've been listening to George too much. 'Awesome' sounds strange coming out of your mouth."

Henry pouted, and Oscar laughed. The sofa dipped beside

him, and he faced Christian. It was a squeeze, but they managed to fit in. As far as Oscar could tell, everyone was there, but he didn't know everyone's relationships or who was allowed to be there.

Andrew cleared his throat. "Brett caught us up on everything that happened while you were at John's house," he said to Christian. "Gia has made progress with the code and thinks it will be fully translated within the hour. She's been working on it all night." He stared at his hands. "Miranda's death has not yet been made public knowledge or even told to me. I don't know what they plan to do about it. I will make some enquiries, though."

"Do you know how Rodriguez is?" Christian asked.

"He's in a stable condition. One bullet hit him in the upper thigh but missed any arteries. The other bullet grazed his head, knocking him out. He'll be fine."

A knock sounded, and Andrew called out for them to enter. Damon, Frederick's best friend from what Christian had told him, wandered in. "Sorry, I'm late." He glanced at Frederick, who hadn't lifted his head, and settled into the chair closest to the heir.

Andrew smiled. "Nice to see you, Damon. Did you find anything out?"

At that, Frederick's head shot up. "What?" He flicked his gaze between the two men.

Andrew sighed and grimaced. "I sent Damon on a mission with strict instructions not to tell anyone. Including you, Freddie."

Frederick glared at Damon, who held up his hands. "What did you want me to do? Ignore a direct order from the king? You're my best friend, Freddie, but not even I can do that."

Frederick clenched his jaw and stared at the floor.

"Damon?" Andrew said.

Damon cast a pained look at Frederick, then focused on Andrew. "From what I could gather from the staff at Sandringham, it had no visitors that they were aware of. I checked the rooms Henry had mentioned before, and nothing seemed to have been used recently. I did the same at Gatcombe Park, Balmoral and Holyrood. All with the same results. However, when I tried to gain entry to Highgrove House and Clarence House, I was denied. I couldn't even get in the door."

"That's what I was afraid of." Andrew rubbed a finger over his mouth.

"You mean to tell me you've been gallivanting all over the country, trying to find where they're working from? Alone!" Frederick stood, towering over Damon. He spun to Andrew. "And you *let* him! You could've at least sent a guard with him."

Damon rested a hand on Frederick's arm, but Frederick ripped his arm away. Hurt flashed across Damon's face, but he sat taller, his mouth flattening in a line.

"I'm more than capable, Freddie."

"No! I won't let anyone get close enough to hurt you! You're mine to protect!" Frederick stormed out of the room, and Damon glanced at Andrew, who waved for him to leave, and raced after him.

Andrew sighed. "I thought Freddie would see clearer than that," he murmured.

Oscar glanced around the room, seeing similar expressions. He cleared his throat. "Why? Neither would want the other hurt, especially if they could avoid it. It's obvious they're in love with each other."

Everyone looked at him, shock, surprise and confusion on their faces, even Christian.

"They're best friends, not boyfriends. Freddie is straight," Christian said.

Oscar raised his eyebrows. "Oh, okay. My bad." He bit his lip. They could deny it as much as they wanted, but he knew what he saw.

27

DOUGLAS

Douglas frowned as Freddie stormed from the room. What had come over Freddie in the last few days or even weeks? He'd not been his usual jovial self, and even though they were going through some tough times at the minute, Freddie's moods seemed excessive. He understood why Freddie might be feeling a little miffed at not being told what Damon had been doing, but there had been no need for his behaviour. Damon could no more deny an order from the king than any of them could.

He tried to refocus on the conversation.

"—possible that it's Highgrove or Clarence House where these people are being held. If the household staff aren't letting other royal members into the building, then it's safe to assume that it's where these...tortures are happening," Patrick said.

"I agree." Andrew sighed. "I'm not sure where to go from here, though. If we try to investigate, they might move their operation, but if we don't..."

"People could lose their lives," Douglas finished for him.

"Exactly."

"I wonder if this is what they wanted?" Mav leaned forward, resting his tablet on his knees. "At the moment, we're divided. We're not sure where to focus our efforts."

"What do you mean?" Andrew asked.

"Well, we have the code we're trying to translate. We have the people potentially being tortured. We have the attacks on the royal family." He tilted his head. "Our focus is being split, meaning they're more likely to get away with things that slip through the cracks."

Andrew nodded. "But I don't see a way around it. Until we know who we can trust, we are limited to the number of people we can call on."

"Can we get a faster turnaround on some security checks?" Timothy asked. "It might help us narrow down who we *can* trust. Maybe those we want to trust but need to double-check first."

"Like who?" Mav asked, pressing on his tablet.

"Our closest security guards, close friends, people who might be able to help us?"

"Good idea. I'll collate a list and get approval from you," Mav nodded at Andrew, "and then ask them to speed up the checks. We need more people on our side."

Douglas rubbed a hand up and down Mav's back. He wished they had more to go on. Damon's investigation had helped some, but their hands were still tied. They were going around in circles. What they needed was a break. He lifted his head to the ceiling and closed his eyes, sending a hope and a prayer to whoever might be listening. Someone had to root for them.

He peered across at Christian, who had a frown on his face and was staring at the carpet. It seemed like he'd checked out of the conversation, which was understandable. With everything he'd been through, it had to be hitting him the hardest of all, especially with his parents being central to it. It had just about killed Douglas when he found out what Christian had been through at the hands of his father. Douglas had wanted to barrel through the house until he had Uncle John's neck in his hands, but he couldn't. It didn't stop him from thinking about it, though. It was a very nice daydream if he said so himself.

"Neil should call soon. I'm hoping he'll be able to give us a breakthrough," Andrew said.

Douglas stood. "Would anyone like a drink while we're waiting?"

Several rounds of yeses sounded, and Douglas set about making the drinks. It kept his mind and hands busy. He felt frozen, unable to do anything, and he hated it. It reminded him too much of when he'd received the call to help Kendal. The submissive had been brutally attacked by a dominant outside of the club, and Douglas was the reason for it. Feeling helpless was not something he enjoyed.

He passed out the drinks and returned to his seat. Mav leaned into him, pressing a kiss to the underside of his jaw and resting his head against his shoulder. His man always knew when things were pressing in on him and never failed to show he cared. He still often thought it was more than he deserved, but he was selfish. If Mav wanted to spend his time with Douglas, then Douglas wasn't going to push him away. He loved Mav with everything in him and always would.

He glanced at Christian and Oscar, loving how in tune

they were with each other. Even though Christian was lost in his thoughts, Oscar had given Douglas his drink order and placed it in front of him. All the while holding his hand, keeping him grounded without Christian even realising it.

That's what a relationship was. That's what they all strived for.

28

CHRISTIAN

Conversation started up around them, but Christian focused on Oscar's observation of Freddie and Damon. He knew his cousin and best friend were close, but *that* close? He wasn't sure, but he could see why Oscar thought it. He thought back through all the times they'd been together, seeing things in a different light.

He pushed it aside to think about another time when Andrew's phone rang.

"Neil, you're on speaker. What have you got?"

"Craziness is what I have. Where am I sending this list?"

Andrew gave him the details, and Mav reached for a tablet, tapping away at it before nodding.

"Okay, we have it. Bear with us."

"Is Christian there?"

"I'm here," he said, leaning forward.

"There's part of the code that didn't translate. None of the symbols match what you brought us. I've sent that over, too. It doesn't follow the same pattern as the others. Gia says it looks more like a paragraph of writing rather than a list of times or dates like the others are. It could be a message from whoever gave this to us. Can you have a look at it?"

"Of course."

"Okay, I'm ringing off. I need to get onto the first of these. I'll call back later, sir."

Christian assumed Neil was talking to Andrew and didn't reply. Mav passed the tablet to Andrew, who studied it intently.

"Father?" Douglas said.

Andrew glanced at him, and Christian could see the tremor in his hands as he handed it to Douglas.

"Not a minute too soon," Andrew murmured. He stared at Christian. "Apparently, we have a mole inside the castle."

"A mole. I thought they were just dates, times and locations."

Douglas cleared his throat. "They are, but to be able to hit Father in his rooms, they'd need to be close."

"What?" Christian accepted the tablet when Douglas passed it over. He read the information Gia had decoded and put into date order. The earliest one was that day, eleven o'clock in the evening, in Andrew Sutcliffe's bedroom. He met Andrew's gaze. "Who?"

"There are only a few possibilities unless someone else gains access."

"Right. We need that list, and we need to get hold of those people as soon as possible. I want guards on the king today and tomorrow, at all times, until we find more information about this hit," Christian barked orders at everyone, uncaring of whether or not it was his place. He had been a team leader in the Army, and he wouldn't stop now.

"I was supposed to visit Kean for his birthday today,"

Andrew murmured. He glanced at Henry. "Could you send my apologies to him?"

"Of course, Uncle. We'll all stay here—"

"No," Andrew said. "Keep everything normal. We don't want to tip them off that we have this list. I have no idea where it came from, although I have an idea," he glanced at Christian, "but we can assume they don't know we have this information. I would've thought they would've mentioned it to Christian yesterday if they knew."

The door opened, and Andrew opened his mouth but stopped when he saw Freddie and Damon. "I'm sorry for walking out, Father."

Andrew nodded. "It's fine. We have another problem on our hands." He explained the situation, and Freddie agreed with Christian's orders and called for the people Andrew had told them about. Freddie would take point and interview them as if it were an employee meeting. They were hoping to catch all of them before anyone else became suspicious and tried to communicate with someone outside of the walls. That would mess up their chances of keeping the list a secret.

They turned the discussion to other dates on the list, but Oscar discreetly nudged him.

"Are you okay?"

Oscar nodded. "I need to open the cafe," he whispered.

Christian held up a finger. "Does anyone have any information about the cafe? We know it was closed because of a gas leak, and then everything else happened, and I didn't get the chance to ask Felix."

Patrick spoke up, "Randall arranged for it to be closed today and for Hilary and Sam to open it for you tomorrow. They've brought in Chloe as extra help. Kieren will arrange a bodyguard for them. I hope that's okay?"

Oscar nodded. "I remember now, sorry. Thank you. Um, who's Kieren?"

Patrick smiled. "My bodyguard. I think everyone has a bodyguard about now." Patrick frowned and focused on Christian. "That could be another issue. Are any of the bodyguards in on it?"

Christian wanted to say no, but he couldn't be sure. He would stake his life on Brett and Felix not being part of it, but they could just as easily be "saving" them from the situations to curry favour. Then when their guard was down… It didn't bear thinking about, but he had to.

"We need to check them out. All of them."

"I can do that," Mav said. "It will be easier if I do it rather than going through an outsider."

"The first thing we need to do is go through this list and determine who was due to visit each of the locations on the dates listed here," Freddie said, "and then work out who knows about who is visiting."

"We need to speak with Arthur, too," Douglas said. "He might have more insight."

Arthur was Charlotte's oldest son and the one who had recently defected from her side, much to her annoyance. His wife, Evanna, was a transwoman, and he'd chosen to side with Andrew, hoping to keep her safe. If he believed, even a little, the same as Charlotte, there was no way he would've taken Evanna as his wife.

"Christian, focus on that paragraph Neil mentioned. See if you can't figure out what it's all about," Andrew said. "We'll work on the list for now."

"Yes, sir."

Andrew's expression softened. "No 'sir' required." He tilted his head towards the door. "Go on with you."

Christian smiled, grabbed Oscar's hand and stood. "Mav, could you send the details over to my email, please?" Mav nodded. "I'll be back soon."

They exited, and Christian aimed for his rooms, one guard in front of them and Matt behind. Both guards stopped by the door when they entered the rooms.

Oscar chuckled. "What's the rush?"

"I wanted to be able to give you some little time."

Oscar shook his head. "Let's check over this email. If you can't decode it straight away, we can, but you won't be happy if you don't check it first."

Christian cupped his face. "How have you figured me out so easily when everyone else hasn't?"

"It's a gift." Oscar smirked.

Christian pressed his lips to Oscar's, sipping from the top, then the bottom before deepening it and tasting the coffee they'd drank in his uncle's room. He slid his hands into Oscar's hair, tugging at the scruffy strands and eliciting soft moans from his mouth. Too soon, he pulled back and exhaled.

"You're too addictive," he murmured.

"Not addictive enough if you stopped." Oscar chuckled and walked backwards, holding Christian's hands and taking him to the sofa. "Let's get this done."

Oscar dropped into the seat, and Christian grabbed his laptop from the desk and sat beside him. He logged in and brought up his emails. Mav had sent the document, and he opened it. The jumble of symbols was about ten lines long, and he could see what Neil meant about it not following the same patterns as the dates and times. He focused on the first part of it, zooming in to make it large enough to see the intricacies of the symbols. It wasn't anything he could remember seeing before, but there were some similarities between his code and this one.

He grabbed his phone and dialled. "Gia, can you send me a copy of the key I gave you, please?"

"Sure thing." The sound of clicking came over the line. "Done. Are you looking at the paragraph?"

"Yeah. It's definitely not my code, but there's something similar about it."

"I tried to search for similarities, but it didn't bring anything up."

"Can you also send me a list of these symbols individually?"

"Sure. Done."

"Okay. I'll have a look and let you know what I find. Thanks, Gia."

He closed the phone and refocused on the screen, squinting at it. He pulled a pad of paper towards him and scribbled notes on it. This code was a lot more angular than the one he'd created. There was something about it, but he couldn't figure it out.

A head resting against his shoulder jerked him from his musings, and he realised Oscar had fallen asleep on him. He checked the time. Three hours had passed. He pressed a kiss on Oscar's hair and closed his laptop, pushing it aside. He'd ignored his boyfriend for too long. He slid his arms around Oscar and cuddled him closer, skimming his hands over his body. The man must be tired, but Christian had a feeling that he was more in need of being little than sleeping.

"Hmm?" Oscar's sleepy sigh made Christian smile.

"Would Ozzie like to come and play, or would Oscar like to sleep?" He hadn't told Oscar, but he arranged for what had been his office to be transformed into a playroom for them. Everything he could think of was in that space. And if Oscar didn't like it, they would find another place, but they couldn't take the chance of going back to Oscar's house yet.

"Yes, please, Daddy." Oscar smacked his mouth as he woke.

Christian chuckled. "Which one, little one? Sleep or play?"

"Play, please." Oscar blinked open his eyes. "But where?"

Christian kissed him, then stood, pulling the sleepy little with him. "I have a surprise for you. Do you want to get Rexie first?"

Oscar widened his eyes at the word "surprise" and raced into the bedroom to grab his dinosaur. He skidded to a stop beside Christian several seconds later.

"I'm ready!"

"I can see that, Ozzie." That quickly, Oscar had moved into littlespace. Christian loved it. He pressed a hand to Ozzie's back and led him to the door of the room Oscar had never been in. "Close your eyes."

Ozzie did, and Christian took hold of his arm, opening the door and leading him forward. He stopped just inside and closed the door again. "Okay, open them."

Ozzie opened his eyes and stared around him, mouth wide. Dinosaur pictures were pinned to the walls. There were shelves of books, paper, pens and every craft item imaginable. There was a small desk and chair for drawing and painting. A changing table. A single bed with a dinosaur cover. A chest of drawers with clothes inside. A fridge full of snacks and drinks. Christian couldn't think of anything they'd missed, but Ozzie might.

"What do you think, little one?"

Ozzie sniffed, and Christian pulled him close. "Is something wrong?"

Ozzie shook his head. "It's like a wonderland," he whispered.

"What would you like to do first? Get changed? Draw? Read? So many choices!"

"Can I be *little* little, Daddy?"

Christian knew what he was asking. "You can be whatever you want to be, sweetheart. I'll look after you either way."

Ozzie beamed up at him. "Nappy, Daddy!"

"Okay, sweet boy. Let's choose some clothes first, then we can get you changed."

Ozzie danced over to the drawers and placed Rexie on top. He opened the top drawer. "Look, Rexie! Dinosaurs!" He pulled out a T-shirt with a T-Rex on the front, then another with a stegosaurus on it. Each one he pulled out had another dinosaur on it.

"Ozzie, let's not get them all out. We need room for you to play."

"But how will I know which one to choose if I don't know what there is?"

Christian could see his dilemma. Too many choices for little ones could cause anxiety. He should've remembered that. "Would you like me to choose for you?"

"Yeah!" He grabbed Rexie and raced over to the changing table.

"Be careful, Ozzie." Christian chose the T-Rex T-shirt and a pair of dark blue, knee-length shorts. It was warm in the room because it had the sun on it throughout the day. He folded the other T-shirts, then closed the drawers, turning to Ozzie, who was lying on the changing table with his legs dangling off the end.

Christian knelt beside him and began untying Ozzie's shoes. "We need to make you comfortable, don't we?" He removed the shoes and socks, watching Ozzie flex his toes. Then he pulled off the T-shirt with Ozzie's help. The trousers came next, then he checked in before removing his briefs. "How are you doing, Ozzie?"

Ozzie bounced Rexie on his stomach, lifting him high into the air, then back down again. Ozzie smiled at him, unadulterated joy on his face, and it sent a flood of calm through Christian. It had been a long time since he'd cared for someone who was so carefree, and he loved it.

Without thinking twice, he brought his Daddy forward and removed Ozzie's briefs. Using the wipes to clean him, he lifted his legs to put the nappy underneath, then lowered them again. He taped it shut, grabbed the shorts and pulled them up his legs, covering the nappy, then had Ozzie sit up so he could pull his T-shirt on. As soon as he was dressed, Ozzie jumped and raced over to the toy box in the corner. While Ozzie explored, Christian washed his hands and put the clothes in a pile by the changing table for when Ozzie wanted to change back.

When he was done, he faced Ozzie and watched him set out the train track.

"Daddy! Help!"

"Okay, little one. I'm here." He sat beside Ozzie, and they worked together to make the track into a figure of eight. Once it was completed, they had a "race" with their trains, and for some reason, Ozzie always won—until Christian clicked his train to the back of it, then they both won.

"Do you want to add some shops to the track? The passengers might get hungry and need a cafe."

Ozzie looked in the box. "No shops." He pouted.

Christian smiled. "What about in that box?"

Ozzie scrambled over, lifting the lid and giggled. "Bricks!"

"We can make shops."

They put some bricks together and stood them next to the track. While Ozzie worked, Christian stood. "I'll get a drink, Ozzie." He ran his hand through Ozzie's hair.

Ozzie didn't reply, but he didn't expect him to. He was everything Christian could've asked for, and if it hadn't been for Freddie, they probably wouldn't be in this situation now. He'd have to speak with him and see what was going on with him. If there was any truth to what Oscar had noticed, Freddie might need some support. He made some juice for him and Ozzie, grabbed two biscuits and before going back, checked his phone, which he'd put on silent. Think of the devil, as they say. There was a message from Freddie.

FREDDIE: We've spoken to the staff but are no closer to figuring it out. Don't worry, though. We have it under control. You concentrate on Oscar right now. CU.

CHRISTIAN: I'll be there in a bit. Oscar needs his littlespace for a bit to work through everything that's happened. As soon as he's settled, we'll be over.

He put the phone back in his pocket and refocused on Ozzie. "Wow, Ozzie. Those shops look great. Here's a snack and some juice. Come for a break, and then we can build some more if you want."

Ozzie jumped up and wandered over. Christian sat in a rocking chair, and Ozzie climbed onto his lap, which Christian had expected. Christian held the sippy cup up to Ozzie's mouth, and he grabbed it, sucking hard on it. After a few mouthfuls, he let go, and Christian held up a biscuit.

"Ta, Daddy."

"You're welcome, sweetheart."

Christian pulled Ozzie close, uncaring of the crumbs that were probably covering his clothes. He needed his boy close. He inhaled and exhaled several times, breathing him in. If anyone hurt a hair on his head, they better run. The same goes for everyone else. They needed to figure out a way to get Charlotte's hold on people removed. He pushed it aside for the moment, needing more time to think about the code.

After their brief snack, they played for a little longer, then he changed Ozzie again, and they did some drawing. Christian showed Ozzie how to draw swirls and squiggles, then colour in the middle of them, making a multi-coloured picture. Christian began doodling until the shapes came into focus. Eyes wide, he stared at them. He knew how to decode the message.

29

OSCAR

Ozzie had fun colouring, but he struggled to concentrate. He bounded from the drawing to the toy box again, and then when he didn't want to play with that, he went to the books.

"Ozzie, what's the matter?" Daddy asked.

He stopped in the middle of the room and stamped his foot. "Don't know!" He burst into tears.

Daddy swept him into his arms, and they snuggled onto the bed, which made Ozzie laugh because Daddy was hanging off the end of it. He sniffled and wiped his nose with the back of his hand. Daddy tutted, reached for a tissue and wiped the back of his hand and his nose.

"Okay. Now, we're comfortable, tell me how you're feeling, little one."

Ozzie tucked his head beneath Daddy's chin, and Daddy squeezed Rexie between them. "Don't know, Daddy. Tummy feels bubbly."

"Okay, sweetheart. I think you have a lot of things running around in your head that we need big boy Oscar to talk through. How about we get things tidied up in here, and then we can have a shower and relax for a little bit?"

"Okay." Ozzie sniffed again. "Daddy?"

"Yes, little one?"

Ozzie picked at the edge of Rexie's ear. "Will you stay with me?"

Daddy kissed his head. "Always."

They stayed snuggled together for a while longer, then Daddy said they needed to tidy up. Although Ozzie hated tidying, he did it because he wanted to have a shower in the enormous bathroom.

"Can we leave the train track, Daddy?" he asked as he stood over it.

"I don't see why not. Everything else has to go away, though; otherwise, we won't have room to play."

Ozzie grinned. "We could run races in this room! It's so big!"

Daddy laughed. "We could, but it's probably not very safe. We can race in the gardens one day. There are lots of bushes to run around."

Ozzie picked up Rexie once the toys were tidy and sat in the middle of the room, looking around. Daddy sat beside him.

"Why are you sad, Ozzie?"

"How often can we do this?"

Christian wrapped his arms around Oscar's shoulders. "As often as you want to, sweetheart. And..." Christian inhaled, "if you want to stay here with me, you can. Again, as often as you want."

Oscar stared at him. "I'd love that," he whispered.

"Are you back with me, baby?"

Oscar nodded. "Everything seems so seamless with you.

The tidying up helped take me from Ozzie to Oscar. It's hard to explain."

"However it works is fine. There is no right or wrong in our relationship. We find our own way. If you're happy, then everything is great." He kissed Oscar's head. "Are you happy?"

"Extremely."

Oscar smiled and lifted his head for a kiss. Christian hesitated. "Is this okay? You're still partially in littlespace."

"It's good. My head is back. It's only my body that's still straddling the line."

Christian lowered his head and pressed a chaste kiss on his lips. "Let's get you changed. Then your body can catch up with your head."

Christian stood and reached down for Oscar, sweeping him into his arms and onto the changing table. Oscar stared at the ceiling as Christian removed his shorts and nappy, cleaned him, then pulled on the briefs and trousers he'd been wearing when they first entered the room. Christian held out his hands, and Oscar took them, allowing Christian to pull him to his feet.

"Do you want a shower, or do you want to talk?"

"We have a lot to get through, don't we? Let's get the talk out of the way. We can relax later."

Christian slid his arms around him, dropping his face into Oscar's neck. "I've figured out the key for the code," he murmured so quietly Oscar could barely hear.

Oscar pulled back, cupping his face. "You did? Why didn't you say so? Let's go!" He went to move towards the door, but Christian stopped him.

"What if it's something I don't want to know?"

"Oh, my love." Oscar gripped him. "We won't know until we read it, but if you want me to read it first, I will."

"Thank you," he rasped.

The man before him was so strong, but he held so much back from everyone, including his family. He needed to know that they loved him, no matter what. They weren't like his immediate family, who deserved everything that was coming their way. He was under no illusion that it would be easy, but he knew karma would bite them in the ass, and everyone under this roof would do the same.

"Come on," Christian said. "May as well get this over with."

They wandered to the door, meeting Matt and the other guard when they exited. Christian held his hand out to the other guard. "I'm sorry. I didn't get your name earlier."

"Van."

"Nice to meet you, Van. Do you know where everyone is?"

"Prince Frederick is in his rooms with Damon, Prince Douglas and Maverick," Matt answered. "King Andrew, Prince George, Prince Patrick, Timothy and Eddie are in King Andrew's rooms."

"Thank you. We'll head for Uncle Andrew's."

Christian reclaimed Oscar's hand and strode through the hallways. Oscar's head spun again. He didn't think he would ever manage to find his way around a place that big. He hoped he always had someone with him who knew the way to his destination.

He could feel the tension rising in Christian, and he knew they must be getting closer. He wrapped his other arm around Christian's biceps, resting his cheek against him, trying to convey as much comfort as he could. He had an idea who the note was from, taking into consideration the information they already had and the story Christian had told about his mother. If he wasn't mistaken, the list and the note were from her, and he hoped she explained enough to stop Christian from blaming himself for her death. She had written the note before she died, but he hoped it was something that helped Christian not hurt him.

They entered Andrew's rooms and were met with hugs all around.

"How are you both doing?" Andrew asked.

Christian glanced at Oscar, who smiled. "I've had some time to let everything sink in, so I'm good."

"I'm glad. And you?" He stared at Christian.

"I'm okay." He cleared his throat, and Oscar gripped his hand. "I've figured out the key."

Andrew's eyebrows raised. "Do you want to decode it?"

Christian blew out a breath. "I'm not entirely sure, but I know we need to."

"I've offered to do it for him," Oscar said.

Andrew rested his hand on his shoulder. "Any of us will do it for you. You know that."

"I think I need to do it myself."

"Understood." Andrew turned to the table they'd been working at. "Let's get this done."

Christian and Oscar sat beside each other on one side of the table, with Andrew and Douglas at the head and foot and the other men on the opposite side. Christian placed the papers on the table and sorted through them. Oscar could see it was a delaying tactic, but no one called him on it. When he settled his hands on top, Oscar leaned his head on his shoulder.

"One step at a time," he whispered.

Christian kissed his head. "Okay." He retrieved a blank piece of paper and wrote the alphabet down one side, then paused. "They're not that different from the actual letters of the alphabet, but they're more angular and include shapes and lines rather than definitive letters. It was a code Mother had shown me as an example of something she had created herself." He began drawing shapes and lines next to the words. "I might not be able to remember them all, but even if I get some, we should be able to work out the others."

"Do what you can, sweetheart."

He watched as Christian filled in about half of the letters, then paused and shook his head. "I'm not sure about the others."

"Do you want me to translate it?" Oscar asked.

Christian shook his head, then nodded, and Oscar brought the key closer to him. He grabbed another blank paper and began at the top. He worked silently. It was slow going because he had to do each letter individually. When he reached the end, he glanced at the words with missing letters.

"Okay, so some of the words I can't understand, but let me go through it and add in the letters I can guess at." He spent a few more minutes adding in the letters that were easy to guess, then sighed. His heart broke at the emotion pouring from the letter, but he knew it would hurt Christian more when he heard the words.

He glanced at him. "Shall I read it out?"

Christian swallowed hard and nodded.

Oscar peered at George and tilted his head slightly towards Christian, receiving a small nod in return. George would support Christian while Oscar was reading if he needed him to.

"Christian,

I hope it's you that has this because if not, then something's happened. No, I can't think like that. The first thing I need to say is that I'm so sorry. I've put you through so much, but it was to protect you. You might not believe it, but it's true." Christian scoffed. *"I didn't know what your father was like when I first married him, and by that point, it was too late. Lottie was already on the way, and John made sure more children arrived after. I love all of you, but you, Christian, were my pride and joy. You had such an innocence about you as a child that the other children never had. John was more concerned about Arthur being his heir, and he left you alone. I took the opportunity to spend as much time as possible with you, teaching you my work, hoping it would help you when you were older. But then Charlotte got her claws into you, and I knew my time was up. I have given you all the tools you need to take them down, but I know it won't be easy. This was the only other way I knew how to help. I'm so very sorry for everything, and I hope one day you can forgive me. Everything listed here has been finalised and is just a waiting game as far as Charlotte and John are concerned. It's unlikely any of these will change, but I can't promise that. I'm sorry I can't do more. I hope it helps.*

I love you, son, and I will until my final breath.

Love, Mum."

By the time he finished, George was holding on to Christian. Andrew held his hands, and tears streamed down Christian's face. Oscar put down the letter and rested his hands on Christian's thigh.

"I'm sorry, sweetheart," he whispered.

They comforted him as best they could until he sat upright and wiped at his face. "Thank you. At least I know she wasn't as bad as I thought she was. It's still not right what she did, but she has helped us."

Andrew nodded. "She has. Immensely. We won't forget that, either."

Christian cleared his throat. "Any news on what's happening with you?"

Oscar could see he wanted the attention away from himself and onto something else, so Oscar pushed the paper into a pile and moved them to one side, out of Christian's view.

"None of the staff members appear to know about it. At least from the roundabout way Freddie had to ask them. They don't know of any new household staff that has come on board recently, so if it is someone, we know them and have worked with them for a while."

Andrew's voice was grim, understandably. To have that confidence breached was horrible. He didn't know how he'd react if his friends had done that to him. Which reminded him, he needed to get in touch with Hilary and check that everything was going okay.

"What's the plan?" Christian asked.

Douglas leaned forward. "We're going to station one guard in the en-suite bathroom, one in the wardrobe area, and then his usual two outside his room. Everything will appear normal, but he'll be heavily guarded. He'll also have a panic button underneath his pillow." Douglas sighed. "We have no way of knowing what form this attack will come in. We just don't know."

"I'll be fine," Andrew said. "There is nothing more that can be done. And if...the worst happens, there are protocols in place. No matter what, no one will take the crown who isn't the rightful heir."

Douglas stood. "I don't care about the rightful heir, Father! I care about you!"

Andrew rose and gathered his son in his arms, grabbing George as well. "I know, and I don't mean to be blasé about it, but we must think of all contingencies. I know it's not nice, but we *need* to."

Douglas pulled back and wiped his face. Oscar had always thought the royal family could keep their emotions at bay regardless of the situation, but it seemed that wasn't the same as when they were around family and out of the public eye. It reminded him of his own family. He'd explained the bare bones of things when he'd had to close the cafe and couldn't pick Gemma and Tina up from school, but his parents would want more of an explanation soon. It surprised him they hadn't blown his phone up with messages, calls and voicemails already.

He tuned back into the conversation, and they spoke about the staff members Andrew had most contact with. As it was, it wasn't a large number, but there were still more than any of them were comfortable with. Freddie and Damon joined them, and they ended up nowhere closer to finding out who could be responsible for the intended hit.

Christian rubbed his face. "I don't think there is anything else we can do. If we spend too much time together, they will know something is different."

Andrew nodded. "Go! Freddie, you need to attend Kean's dinner as planned. I know I sent apologies with Henry, but please mention it to them. Tell them I've come down with a bug or something."

Freddie appeared like he wanted to argue, but he didn't. "Okay." He stood, and Damon followed suit, barely having said a word. Freddie ignored him but appeared to wait for him near the door, holding it for him.

"As for you lot, go away!" Andrew chuckled, though it

seemed strained, as was to be expected when his life was in danger. "Leave me in peace."

As they were leaving, Andrew pulled Christian aside, whispering something to him, and Oscar waited by the door, giving them their privacy. He smiled and nodded as George, Douglas and everyone else left. He held the code and key in his arms, not wanting to let them out of his sight until Christian had chosen what he was going to do with them. The box Christian had told him about was still at the barracks as far as Oscar knew, but Christian would get it back, eventually; it had all the man's memories in it.

Christian hugged Andrew, then strode towards him. "Let's go." He held open the door for Oscar, nodded at the guards and slid his arm around Oscar's shoulders before heading down the hallway. "You can give Hilary a call and see whether the cafe is still standing." He chuckled.

Oscar gasped. "Don't tempt fate! Oh, god. She's going to have burnt the place down now," he joked, trying to keep the levity going.

"Well, if you promise to keep making coffee as you do, I can guarantee there will be plenty of people willing to throw some money towards you to rebuild."

Oscar play-punched Christian in the ribs. "You just love me for my coffee, don't you?"

"Oh, dear. You have found out my plan." Christian grinned and popped a kiss on Oscar's temple.

They reached Christian's rooms and entered, leaving the guards chuckling in the hallway. Christian pressed Oscar against the door, caging him in and nuzzling his face into his neck. Oscar wrapped his arms around Christian's back.

"Are you okay?"

Christian shook his head against his shoulder. Oscar

tightened his hold, wishing there was more he could do. Unfortunately, Christian had to work through it himself, but Oscar would be there every step of the way.

"Come on. Let's see what Hilary says," Christian said, dragging Oscar towards the sofa and pushing him into it.

Oscar put the papers on the coffee table, then pulled out his phone. "Fingers crossed." He dialled, but she didn't answer. He frowned, staring at his phone.

"What's wrong?"

"She didn't answer."

"Why not try the cafe phone number?" Christian sank into the seat beside him, bringing coffee with him.

Oscar rolled his eyes. "Why didn't I think of that?" He dialled, his heart calming when Hilary's voice came on.

"Book Drunk. What can I get you?"

"Hilary! It's Oscar. How are things going?"

"Oscar! You're alive! It's a miracle! Oh, my lord. Let's celebra—"

"All right. All right. Enough." He sighed. "Honestly. How are things?"

"This place is working like clockwork, as always. You were always so anal about being here that you didn't think we knew what our jobs were unless you were here to tell us. We're doing fine, Oscar. How about you and your yummy boyfriend?"

Oscar chuckled, staring at Christian. "We're good. Or at least, we will be. A few chinks in the armour that needs repairing, but we're good."

"Glad to hear it. You might want to call Wally. He's distraught. He went around to your place this morning and just about had a heart attack when he saw the broken door and everything. Despite being told by some guys—who he assumed were security protecting the place—that you were fine, you know what he's like. Unless he sees first hand, he won't be happy."

"I know. He's next on my list."

"Oh, I rate higher than your best friend. I'm honoured."

"You're my best friend, too, idiot. And besides," he grinned towards Christian, who raised his eyebrows, "I wasn't calling to check on you. I was calling to check on the cafe."

Hilary spluttered, and Oscar and Christian laughed. "I'll get you back for that," she said.

"Are you okay to open up again tomorrow?" he asked.

"Of course."

"Hopefully, I'll be back, but we'll see how things are here." Christian pressed his hand to Oscar's nape, and he closed his eyes, enjoying the sensation.

"Regardless, we'll be fine. Don't sweat it."

He ended the call after saying goodbye, then called Wally. "Hey."

"Jesus, Oscar. You scared the stuffing out of me."

Wally had the kids with him because otherwise, he would've used a different word to stuffing.

"I'm fine. I'm sorry I didn't message or anything. Things have been crazy."

Wally sighed. "It's okay. The guard, or whoever he was, told me you were okay. I'm reserving judgement until I've seen you in person, though, okay?"

"Understood."

They spoke for a few more minutes, then he dialled one final number. "Hi, Mum."

"Sweetheart. What's been going on? We dropped by the cafe this morning, and Hilary told us you were busy. You've never taken a day off unless you've been sick, Oscar. What's happening?"

Oscar chuckled. "A lot is happening at the minute, and when I can explain, I will, but at the moment, I'm fine. Everything is going great. I…" He glanced at Christian, who was busy on his phone. "I have a new boyfriend."

His mother squealed in his ear, and Christian winced, obviously hearing it himself. "Oh, my god! How wonderful! When can we meet him?"

"Maybe in a couple of days."

"As soon as you know, tell me so I can arrange to get everyone here. Might as well get the introductions over and done with altogether."

"I don't know if that's a good—"

"That sounds wonderful, Mrs Hall. Thank you," Christian said, loud enough for his mother to hear.

"Is that him?"

"Yes, Mum." Oscar dropped his head into his hands and groaned. "I'm going now. I'll call you again tomorrow."

"Okay, honey. Make sure you keep in touch. Gemma and Tina are missing their afternoon snacks."

The censure in her voice was mild, so he knew he wasn't in trouble for giving them cake and milkshakes despite having never told her what he fed them. She wasn't stupid. He hung up and fell back against the sofa, groaning.

30

CHRISTIAN

"She sounds lovely," Christian said. His heart wished for the same camaraderie with his own, though it was too late now.

"She is, but you're in for a treat if you're meeting the whole family."

"Can't be worse than mine." Christian raised his eyebrows. "I mean this lot," he waved around them, "not the other."

Oscar snuggled into his side, and his body relaxed. "I could fall asleep, but it's not even dinnertime yet."

"Why not have a nap? In fact, I'll join you." Christian typed into his phone and nodded. "I've told Matt that we're heading for a sleep and to wake us if something happens. I've also told George and Douglas."

"Do you think you'll be able to sleep?"

Christian shrugged. "It's worth a try. I'm hoping my body will just shut down and let me rest, then I can get up and concentrate enough to get through tonight. I hate Uncle Andrew putting himself in danger, but there's no way of knowing who it is. I'm praying to any and every deity that might ever have existed that the guards are enough to keep him safe."

Christian stood and held out his hands. As much as Christian wanted to stay awake, he knew he'd be no use to anyone if he didn't get some sleep. His energy levels were always depleted from lack of sleep. Even though he'd been used to it in the Army, he was out of the habit.

They undressed each other, taking the time to go slow but knowing there was nothing sexual about it. It was almost an assurance that they were both there and doing fine. Everything else was up in the air, but their relationship was one of the solid things that wouldn't change no matter what happened.

Oscar snuggled against Christian's chest with Christian's arm around his back. Their legs twined, and their hands linked over his stomach. Christian sighed and closed his eyes, loving the feeling of having Oscar so close. His eyes opened again when a thought floated through his head.

"Do you regret meeting me?" Christian whispered.

Oscar lifted to his forearm. "What? Of course not." He cupped Christian's jaw. "You are one of the best things to have happened to me in my life. I've been blessed with an amazing family, amazing friends and now you. I couldn't ask for more. If anything, you should regret me and my small-time worries."

Christian's heart melted. "Nothing about you is small-time, Oscar."

Oscar smiled. "Dream big but live bigger. That's my motto."

"Maybe I need to take a leaf out of your book."

"If you weren't in the Army, what would you like to do?" Oscar asked, settling against Christian's chest again.

"Well, I'm not technically in the Army."

"What?" Oscar peered up at him.

Christian grinned, and he felt his cheeks heat. "I used that as an excuse to use their resources. Neil agreed to make it look like I'd rejoined so the higher-ups wouldn't wonder what was happening. But I'm still a civilian."

"And what do you want to do once this is all wrapped up?"

Christian was silent, thinking about what he wanted to do. He felt Oscar relax more as he succumbed to sleep and whispered, "I want to write."

Saying it out loud made it real, but he felt the deep-seated relief that being a soldier was not all he could be. If he hadn't met Oscar, he might not have had the courage to admit what he truly wanted to do. He had no idea if he'd be any good at it, but he'd give it a try—under a pen name, of course.

He didn't think he'd be able to sleep after such a revelation, but he must have because a knock at his bedroom door woke them both.

"Hold on!" Christian called. He dragged on some joggers and opened the door a bit, keeping Oscar from view. He was surprised to see Brett. "Everything okay?"

Brett wore an expression of grim satisfaction. "We have them."

Christian raised his eyebrows. "Already? What time is it?"

"Nine o'clock, sir."

"Bloody hell. I didn't expect to sleep so long. Okay, we'll be there shortly."

"Yes, sir."

Christian closed the door and faced Oscar. "It's done."

Oscar sat upright. "I wasn't expecting them to try for hours yet."

"Me neither." He rested back against the door. "I don't know if I want to know who it is."

"It's going to be a shock no matter who it is," Oscar said. "Andrew must be feeling so upset that his trust has been misplaced."

Christian crossed the space between them, dragging Oscar into his lap and kissing him. "We can help him. I don't know how, but we will."

They showered and dressed, then strode to Andrew's rooms, where Brett told them everyone had congregated. Freddie opened the door and let them in. Christian's gaze went to Andrew, who was sitting in an armchair, looking extremely pale and sweaty. The royal doctor was beside him, taking his blood pressure.

"Is he okay?" Christian asked Freddie quietly.

Freddie nodded. "Luckily."

"Who was it?"

"Mother's assistant."

Christian blanched. "Portia?"

Freddie shook his head quickly. "Her other assistant, Ivy. The one who helped her when Portia couldn't. They had reassigned Ivy when Mother passed. She had recently requested to be moved back to the inner circle because she felt she knew everyone better. They denied her request."

"Revenge?" It didn't make sense to Christian. Just because she wasn't allowed to work with the king or the princes anymore didn't seem enough to kill the king.

"Not according to her. She'd got it into her head that Father wanted to be with Mother again. She thought she was doing him a favour by helping him hurry along the process."

Christian raised his eyebrows. "How?"

"She requested a meeting with him tonight, which he agreed to, even knowing the potential outcome." Freddie gritted his teeth. "She poisoned his tea. Luckily, he'd only taken a sip before he realised it didn't taste right."

"He doesn't look good, though."

Oscar squeezed his hand and strode over to Andrew, sitting on the opposite side to the doctor and chatting with him.

"The doctor said he'll be feeling a little weak for a few hours, but it'll clear from his system quickly enough, especially with how little he drank."

"And we thought the attack would come in the form of knives or guns when he was sleeping." Christian blew out a breath. "Nothing about our situation is simple, is it?"

"They're certainly keeping us on our toes."

"Have we any more information about the next event on the list?"

The hit on Andrew was the closest in time, but the next one was a few months out, and one of them was due to make a speech at a charity gala. As far as they were aware, none of them had been confirmed as attending, so the target was a general "whoever was there" situation.

"Not much. We're trying not to set off any warning bells, but we'll figure something out before the night. We have time."

"They're going to be pissed that this didn't work." Christian rubbed his chin.

Freddie stared at his father. "I don't understand it."

"Understand what?"

Freddie sighed. "What did they have to gain from poisoning him? Even with Father out of the picture," he swallowed hard, "I would be the next king. What are they winning with this?"

"Maybe they want us in upheaval. Losing both parents in such a short time would devastate many people. It would make the foundations shaky."

"I guess. I don't know. I still feel like we're missing a piece of the puzzle." He shook his head. "Never mind."

Christian rested his hand on Freddie's shoulder and steered him to the window. "What's going on, Freddie? You're never like this. What's happened?"

Freddie crossed his arms and leaned against the window frame, staring out into the dark sky. "It's never-ending, Chris. We've suffered so much over the months—years, even. I can't see an end to it."

Christian mirrored Freddie's position, keeping his gaze on his cousin. "That's not all of it."

Freddie met Christian's gaze. "I have a few home truths to sort through, that's all."

Christian tilted his head. "Is this about Damon?"

Freddie flinched, trying to hide it by repositioning himself and taking his focus to the window again. "That's one part."

He leaned closer. "Are you in love with him?" he whispered. Freddie closed his eyes but said nothing. "Because if you are, you know it's not a problem for us. We'd welcome you to the club."

"But would the country?" Freddie's bleak gaze met his own, and he finally showed Christian the confusion he carried.

Christian dragged Freddie into his arms. "As much as it pains me to say, I truly don't know."

Freddie tightened his hold, then stepped back. "Exactly.

It's not as easy as answering a question and it all falling into place. It's not just me I have to think about, Chris."

Christian rested his forefinger beneath Freddie's chin and lifted slightly. "We're all here for you, no matter what happens. We'll have your back."

Freddie inhaled. "Thanks."

"Your Highnesses," the doctor said. "I'm sorry to interrupt." He glanced at Freddie. "Your father is doing much better. I've taken the IV from his hand now, but if you can, ensure he drinks plenty. We need to flush out any remaining toxins. I don't see why he should have any lingering effects, despite the potency of the poison. He'll be tired for a few days, though."

"Thank you, Doctor."

"I'm only a phone call away if you need me."

The doctor left, and Christian watched Oscar chat with Andrew. They appeared to be getting on well. He wandered over, Freddie on his heels.

"Christian, Oscar tells me his mother has arranged for you to meet all his family. Do you think we should make it a complete family affair and invite them for dinner here?"

Christian shrugged. "I'll let Oscar field that question. I'm happy either way."

Oscar grimaced. "I don't know if you'll want my entire family here. They're a bit..."

Andrew chuckled. "No matter what, they're your family, and I can tell you're planning to become part of *our* family, so it would only be a matter of time."

"How about we make that decision another day?" Freddie said. "Let's get you some rest, Father."

"I won't say no to that." Andrew stood, reaching for

Freddie when his legs threatened to sit him down again. Christian could see them tremble from where he stood.

"Goodnight, Uncle Andrew," Christian said.

"Goodnight, kids."

Christian and Oscar left Freddie, Douglas and George to take care of their father and strolled back to his rooms, Brett and Matt on their tail.

"How is Felix?" Oscar asked Brett.

"He's doing well. He was sleeping the last time I checked." Brett rubbed his cheek. "I spiked his drink, which sounds terrible after what has just happened with your uncle." Brett grimaced.

"Spiked it? With what?" Oscar asked.

"A sedative the doctor gave me. It should knock him out long enough to get some rest."

"When he's feeling better, can you get him to visit me, please?"

"Of course."

They left the men at the door and wandered into the living room. Christian dropped onto the sofa, taking Oscar with him and sprawling them across it.

"I'm glad that's over," Christian said. "Though I wish I knew what they planned to do about Mother's funeral."

"It's not over, though, is it?" Oscar shuffled around until he straddled Christian. "This is your life now. Finding those who are trying to take you down."

Christian shook his head. "It's not my job. I've done what I can, and I will help wherever they need me to, but it's the security team's job now. We know when and where, but not who. They can figure it out. We'll have to be careful, no doubt about it, but we need to live our lives, Oscar. If my mother made me realise anything, it was that life is too fleeting to not live it to the fullest extent we can. I want you by my side, Oscar. Every step of the way. Do you want that?"

"I truly do." Oscar kissed him, sliding his hands into his hair and gripping the strands. "I need you, my prince."

Heat bloomed in Christian's groin, and he rose, lifting Oscar with him, and aimed for the bedroom. He closed and locked the door behind them, making sure no one could come in and upset Oscar again. Carrying him to the bed, he laid him down, covering him with his body and peppering kisses over his face until Oscar was laughing.

"I love you, Oscar. Every part of you."

"And I love you. Every princely inch." Oscar's grin turned into a squeal when Christian's tickled his sides. "Okay! Sorry!" Christian subsided. "I do love every inch of you, though."

"I'm sure you do." Christian punctuated his words with a thrust of his hips, making them both groan when their cocks rubbed together. "I know exactly how I want you." He pulled back, rising to his feet. "I want you naked and on your stomach."

Oscar jumped up and undressed in record time, Christian joining him in the race. Their clothes littered the floor, but he didn't care. He needed to be inside his man. Oscar crawled onto the bed and laid down on his stomach as Christian had asked, then Christian grabbed a condom and some lube from the drawer. He dropped them near Oscar's hip and stood behind him, kissing his way up the back of his legs, his ass, his spine, all the way to his nape, skin to skin with his dick resting against Oscar's taint and balls. He nudged his hips a few times, drawing moans from Oscar.

Christian lifted off him, threading his legs between Oscar's so he was spread wide. He licked a stripe over his pucker, and Oscar pushed closer. He spent plenty of time stretching his hole with his tongue. He had seen many men do this to others at the club, and it had always been something he'd wanted to try. After tasting Oscar like that, he would do it as often as he could.

He rolled a condom on, knowing he wouldn't last too much longer without needing to be inside him. Slicking his cock and sliding some inside and around Oscar's entrance, Christian braced himself on one hand.

"Are you ready?"

"Always," Oscar panted.

Christian pressed his cock against Oscar's bud and thrust forward in one long, slow entry. Both groaned when Christian bottomed out. He laid himself over Oscar's back, using his knees and hips to begin a rhythm that would hopefully have Oscar's cock pushing against the covers beneath him with enough friction to help him over the edge.

"Oh, god. This is…the perfect…position," Oscar gasped as Christian's tempo increased. He kissed and nipped at Oscar's skin, wanting Oscar to come first because Christian was already so close.

"Fuck," Christian moaned. "Please tell me you're close already."

"I'm close. I'm close. Yeah."

Christian thrust faster, swivelling his hips as he drilled forward. He raked his teeth across Oscar's shoulder blades, and Oscar's ass tightened.

"Oh, fuck!"

Christian breathed through Oscar's orgasm, wanting to experience every moment; then, when he sank into the covers, Christian rose to his hands and thrust several times before his body spasmed in pleasure. He didn't drop onto

Oscar after, not wanting to smother him, but he barely kept himself on his hands.

"Sorry that was so quick," Christian said when his breathing had returned to normal.

"Don't be sorry. That was…mind-blowing."

Christian chuckled. "Glad to hear it." He pulled free and disposed of the condom, grabbing a flannel from the bathroom and cleaning Oscar's ass, then rolled him onto his back to clean his front. "We need to change the covers." Oscar mumbled something, and Christian shook his head. "All right. *I'll* change the covers."

Once they were set to rights, they snuggled under the clean covers.

"Thank you," Oscar murmured.

"For what?"

"For being you."

Christian smiled and kissed Oscar's head. Who would've thought that by stopping lying to himself and others, he would gain something so precious? His other half.

OSCAR

Four month later

"Don't you think it's too soon?" Oscar asked, wringing his hands together and staring around the large room where Christian's birthday party was being held. He'd taken point in organising it with a lot of help from Christian's cousins, and they would be there any moment. There were plenty of guests who'd arrived so far, and it was heaving.

"Not at all. If this is what you want, then why not? No one has a rule book on when things like this should happen," Wally said, sipping his coffee.

Spying someone coming towards them he'd invited on a whim, he said, "If that's the case, then you need to listen to my advice about Donovan." Oscar chuckled when he received an evil look from his best friend.

"Yeah, I'll get right on that, telling my employer that I'm

in love with him and have been for two years and want to adopt his kids. I'm sure that would go down brilliantly."

Oscar rolled his lips inwards and pointed behind Wally. Wally turned and blanched, going ghostly white. Oscar caught the cup Wally almost dropped, and Donovan caught Wally when his legs didn't want to keep him upright.

"Sorry, Wally. Surprise?"

Wally glared at him, then closed his eyes, his cheeks turning red as he struggled to regain his footing. "I'm sorry, Donovan. I...I shouldn't—"

His words were cut off when Donovan closed the distance between their mouths, and Oscar fist-bumped the air. He'd known Donovan had feelings for Wally. It had been clear every time the man had come into the cafe and they spoke about his two kids and Wally. Oscar had invited the man, hoping they would be able to talk through things without the kids being between them. He hadn't thought Donovan would take the initiative, but he was glad he had. Maybe now, Wally would stop complaining about his lack of sex life.

Oscar disappeared, searching out Mav. The man had been a lifesaver when it had come to all the royal aspects of the party. Oscar was still learning the ropes, and getting used to the media attention was something he struggled with. They had banned cameras from being used within the cafe now because of it, although Oscar allowed photos at the beginning or end of the day, so they'd usually leave him alone.

The cafe was being managed by Hilary while Oscar was adjusting to his new role as Christian's boyfriend, which would come with several royal engagements in the not-too-distant future. Oscar was terrified.

"Hey," Mav said, grasping Oscar's elbow. "How's it going?"

Oscar blew out a breath. "It's going." He smiled, then dropped his head. "I think everything's in place, but my brain is about fried now, so I don't know."

"It looks amazing, Oscar. Don't worry so much."

He glanced around, pleased with the result, despite worrying if he'd forgotten anything. The room had been decorated with the usual birthday accessories, like balloons and streamers, but along the walls were blown up covers of Christian's favourite books. The pictures were about three feet by a foot and a half, and Oscar had managed to get them signed by the authors themselves—well, those who were still alive. He would've struggled to get Gene Wolfe to sign any of his sci-fi books. He hoped Christian liked them.

"Stop worrying. Everything is ready."

Oscar bit his lip. "Not quite everything."

Mav raised his eyebrows, and Oscar explained what he'd done. Mav grinned. "Leave it with me." He patted Oscar on the shoulder and left.

There was nothing else he could do but wait for Christian to arrive, which should be any minute. He glanced over at Wally and smiled, seeing him and Donovan wrapped around each other, talking quietly. He was ecstatic for his best friend. He deserved all the happiness he could find. Felix and Brett were working the event and had become their full-time body-guards. Some days, it worked; other days, it didn't.

Oscar jumped when a hand landed on his shoulder. He spun around and threw his arms around his mother. "I'm so scared!"

His mother, Sally, knew exactly what he was worried about. They'd had a big, long discussion about it, and although she was hesitant in the beginning, she had come around to the idea.

"Don't be. Everything is going perfectly." She squeezed his shoulders and pulled back. "This looks amazing, Oscar. You've done a wonderful job."

"I had plenty of help." He chuckled.

"Despite that, Christian will love it." She glanced at him. "All of it."

Oscar exhaled, trying to relax, then tensed up again when Douglas came through the door calling, "The birthday boy has arrived!"

A cheer sounded as Christian entered, looking delicious in black jeans, a navy-blue shirt and an open black waistcoat. Oscar's mouth watered just looking at him.

"Put your tongue back in your mouth, dear. It's quite unbecoming," Sally said.

Oscar snapped his jaw shut but stared without an ounce of shame at his boyfriend. Christian greeted many of the people who came up to him, but he was searching the room, and Oscar hoped it was for him. He stayed where he was, letting everyone get a piece of the birthday boy before Christian finally saw him. The smile that spread across Christian's face sent butterflies swarming in his stomach. He'd never tire of that look.

Oscar bit his lip to restrain his smile, but he couldn't help it when Christian raced up to him and spun him around.

After putting him back down, Christian said, "Did you do all this?"

"Some of it."

Christian cupped his cheeks. "It's amazing, baby. Thank you so much."

"You're welcome," he said, accepting a kiss.

Now that Christian was here, Oscar wouldn't have much else to do. At least until the moment he did what he feared doing in case it was a refusal. They hadn't really talked about it, as in it happening in their life, but they had spoken about it in general terms. Oscar hoped he wasn't stepping over a line he didn't know was there.

They wandered around the party, speaking with lots of people Oscar knew and didn't know. He introduced him to so many people that he wouldn't remember their names when they next met. No one asked after Christian's other family, only those he lived with now. Christian's mother's death had been announced, but her funeral had been private. Christian hadn't gone because her burial place had been kept a secret by his father. It had taken a long time for Christian to get over that, and in the end, they'd had a memorial bench made and left in a scenic spot on Windsor lands. It was all they could do to honour her sacrifice.

He didn't know how much time had passed when Mav caught his eye and indicated for him to go to him.

"I have to check on something. I'll be back." Oscar pecked Christian's cheek, then drifted towards Mav. "What's up?"

Mav dragged him through a door and closed it behind them. "Are you ready for this?"

"What? Now?"

"Why not? We can't keep it quiet for much longer."

Oscar put his hands together and exhaled. "Okay," he said in a shaky voice. "Might as well get it over with."

He opened the door and stepped back into the room, skirting the perimeter to the DJ's table. "Give me five minutes, then we'll be stopping for speeches."

The DJ nodded, and Oscar weaved through the people to find the men he needed. When they were all positioned, the DJ made the announcement.

"Good evening! Please, could you give a cheer for the

birthday boy, Christian?" A loud cheer went up. "We will need your attention on the stage at the front of the room for the next few minutes as we have a wonderful lineup of comedians—oh, I mean, men who'd like to dish the dirt—um, talk about how amazing Christian is." Laughter abounded. "Over to the stage."

Andrew climbed onto the stage and took the microphone. "Good evening. Thank you so much for being part of this event. Most of you know how trying the past few months have been for us all, including Christian. But I don't think I need to tell you how wonderful this man truly is. You've all experienced it. His kindness and generosity of both his time and skills. The man is a true saint in the flesh. I have said this before to his face, but I will say it now in front of you all as witnesses. Christian, I would consider it a great honour if you would consider yourself one of my sons, not my nephew."

Christian's hand gripped Oscar's as Andrew spoke, and when Christian nodded, tears fell. He let go when Andrew pulled Christian in for a hug, and it took everything in him to stop his own tears from falling.

Douglas took the microphone. "While they're hugging their feelings, I want to tell you a little story about my newest brother." He went on in intricate details about something that had happened when they were younger and had everyone laughing, lifting the mood. George butted Douglas off the stage at one point, continuing in a similar vein. Freddie took over afterwards with a more solemn speech but no less emotional. Each of them highlighted the same fact as their father—that Christian was now their brother.

When Freddie finished, Oscar let go of Christian and stepped up, hands shaking as he took the microphone.

"Hi." He cleared his throat. "I hate being the centre of attention, so being in a relationship with a prince was probably not my best idea." Guests laughed. "Despite that oversight, the man I've come to love deserves all the praises. All the love. All the support." He inhaled. "But there is one last gift I need to give him."

Mav and Douglas carried the box to the stage, placing it beside Oscar. He glanced at Christian. "Can you come up here, please?"

Christian joined him on the stage, and Oscar faced him, needing to speak directly to him and not the crowd of people watching.

"I love you. I want to experience everything with you, and I thought we could start with this." He pointed at the box and nodded for Christian to open it.

Christian chuckled and knelt, lifting the lid. The moment he did, a head poked out and barked. Christian jumped, then grinned and fussed the chocolate brown Labrador puppy, picking it up and holding it close to his chest. The sheer joy on Christian's face set all Oscar's fears to bed. The man looked at him and mouthed, "Thank you."

Oscar joined them and stroked the soft fur of the gorgeous little puppy. "I know we hadn't talked about this properly, but you seemed so sad when you mentioned your family wouldn't allow you to have a dog when you were younger. I thought we could start with this and work our way up to something else if we decide we want to."

Christian's eyes widened. "Kids?" Oscar nodded, and Christian buried his head in the puppy's fur, sniffling. "I'd love kids. Lots of them. And you'll be damn sure I'll treat them right."

"I know you will, sweetheart. You'll be the best dad in the world, but let's start with this." Oscar chuckled.

"What's its name?"

"Whatever you want to call her."

"It's a girl?" Oscar nodded. "Hmm, Oreo."

Oscar laughed. "You're seriously calling it after a cookie?"

"Why not? She's so cute, and she's the same colour." Christian pouted.

Oscar raised his hands. "Oreo, it is."

"Thank you. For everything you've given. Not just today, but ever since I met you. You changed my life. And when we get married, Oreo can be our ring bearer."

Oscar's mouth opened and closed several times before he squeaked, "Married?"

Christian grinned. "Paddy, could you take Oreo for a moment, please?"

"Sure. Come on, beautiful," Patrick crooned, cradling the puppy in his arms.

Christin faced Oscar and dropped to one knee, taking Oscar's breath. "I truly thought you were going to steal my thunder when you brought me up here, but I'm glad I still get to do this." He held out his hand and glanced to the side where Freddie stood. Freddie put a box in his hand, and Christian nodded and stared at Oscar again. "You mean everything to me. Everything. I refuse to live my life without you in it, and I want to ask you a very important question. Oscar Hall, will you do me the honour of marrying me in front of the entire world?"

"Yes," he breathed. "Although please don't mention that last bit again. I'd prefer to be ignorant."

Christian laughed, slid the ring on his finger and sealed their promise with a kiss to the chorus of cheering and whistling. Oscar pulled back and looked at the ring, seeing the patterns etched on the outside—Christian's code. He hadn't learnt all the letters yet, but he thought he understood. "I love you, too."

"And if you want me to wear a ring, too, there is a second one in the box," Christian said. "But if you want to choose a different one, you can."

Oscar opened the box again, taking out the second ring and seeing similar patterns on it. He grabbed Christian's hand and slid the ring on, pressing a kiss to his hand. He grinned at him, then his face fell.

"What's wrong?"

"Holy shit. I'm going to get married in front of the entire world."

Christian pulled him into his chest, his laughter a rumble through their bodies. "Yes, you are. And you're going to love every minute."

Oscar closed his eyes. He didn't care what he had to go through as long as Christian was there with him.

Did you enjoy this book? Order Trained Royal to see how Patrick deals with the emerging feelings he has for his bodyguard. How can he manage the balance between what he wants and what his life allows?

Would you like to see what happens when Ozzie and Dusty get together on a puppy/little playdate? Check out Ozzie Meets Dusty in a short bonus story.

Sign up to my newsletter to get two free short stories, including a prequel from Club Royal called Royal Firsts.

ABOUT ELOUISE EAST

I am Elouise East but feel free to call me Elli. I write sweet and steamy connections in gay romance. I also touch on taboo stories under the name Elouise R East.

Books that tell the stories where friendship and family are the focal point - be it blood family or chosen - is very important to me. That's why I include a variety of personalities, talents, ages, situations and abilities as I believe a story or a character needs. I want my characters to be real, to be relatable, to be free to have whatever views they tell me they have. And trust me, most of the time, I do not have *any* say in the matter!

My characters come to life on the page for me as well as my readers. Their stories unfold in front of me, and I have very little input into how they want to be shown. Just like real life, the lives of my characters change with every choice, every interaction and every conversation. And I wouldn't have it any other way.

I write books that are emotionally realistic, even if liberties are taken with other aspects of my stories. I don't know any other way to write. It comes from deep inside.

Who am I? A single parent to two children who make life worth living. An avid reader who still devours every book she can get her hands on. A student of learning about any subject that takes her fancy. An author of books she would read herself. And a romantic at heart who loves anything cheesy.

Who's in?

<u>Stalk me here... ;-)</u>
Website
https://elouiseeast.com

Newsletter
https://readerlinks.com/l/2368814

All links
https://linktr.ee/elouiseeastauthor

BOOKS BY ELOUISE EAST

<u>CLUB ROYAL</u>

Rogue Royal

Secretive Royal

Grieving Royal

Disowned Royal

Trained Royal

Awakened Royal

Commanding Royal

<u>LOVE IN FLAMES</u>

Out of the Frying Pan

Smokescreen

Breathing Fire

<u>CRUSH</u>

Love Conquers

Crush Series Page

Crush Box Set Series Page

<u>JUST A LITTLE CRUSH</u>

He's Behind You

A Special Love

Three Thirds

<u>DADDY</u>

Love Me, Daddy

Soothe Me, Daddy

Spoil Me, Daddy

The Complete Daddy Series

<u>DARK & DIVERGENT (Elouise R East)</u>

Forbidden Temptation

Too Many Secrets

When Fantasies Collide

When Dreams Collide

<u>STANDALONE</u>

Treehouse Whispers

Star-Crossed

Protecting the Thief